Diary
of a Stressed Out
Mother

Bedlam

(Part One)

NICOLA KELSALL

Little Studio
Publishing Company

Diary of a Stressed Out Mother: Bedlam

First published as an eBook 2015

This first paperback edition published 2017

ISBN: 978-0-9956685-0-8

Many thanks to all my friends and family who have inadvertently inspired the content of this book, and a special 'thank you' to Fiona at Fiona McIntyre Designs, for her work on the cover design.

DEDICATION

This book is dedicated to my own wonderful parents;
Ronald and Ann Kelsall, who have been long-suffering and
endlessly patient in their quest to bring up four children
without killing, maiming, or accidentally losing any.
Although there was that one time...

PROLOGUE

According to my 17-year-old daughter, I have no right to complain - I chose this life, didn't I? Well, yes, it's true - I did. But I didn't know then, what I know now. That one-eyed Romani fortune teller Andrew and I visited on our honeymoon in Istanbul, way back in the summer of '92, obviously got it completely wrong. Her crystal ball was plainly faulty, or else she couldn't see it properly. I mean, according to her, we were destined for a charmed existence full of peace and harmony. So, since things have turned out to be neither peaceful nor harmonious, I could be forgiven for having the odd moment of regret, couldn't I? And even if I do fantasise about living in a parallel universe sometimes, I wouldn't really want to swap it for my own life, although plenty of other people do. Just look at Derek from next door – when his wife Mona got a new nocturnal hobby, he decided he'd had enough, got a train to Woking and went to live with his faithful old Mum. And when my friend Jean decided she couldn't stand her neighbours any more, she sold her house to some gypsies and went on an extended holiday to Cape Cod. I don't think I would ever consider doing anything quite so drastic, but sometimes it's nice to imagine a different world; a place where children are polite and cooperative and tidy up after themselves and never need any money, a husband who comes home from work beaming with happiness, saying he's had a great day and how blessed he feels with his fabulous family and beautiful wife, pets that are self-sufficient, laundry that cleans and irons itself, meals that magically appear on demand, a dust-free, clutter-free house that is always gleaming and fresh, a job that doesn't involve flogging useless and over-priced kitchen utensils to people who probably can't even make a piece of toast … , which brings me to my first diary entry for this year, and as my daughter would say: 'Chillax Mum, it was only a small fire...

JANUARY

New Year's Day (Tuesday 1st January)

I woke up this morning to an acrid burning smell, which mixed with a throbbing hangover and the noise of a loud snoring husband by my side, was not a hopeful start to the New Year. On further investigation, I discovered that the burning was the toaster which was actually on fire. Now that the dogs were barking and everyone was shouting a lot, Andrew was forced to stop snoring and wake up. He descended the stairs pretty quickly for a man who is at least two stones heavier than when we met, and had a purple fit when he saw the toaster.

'Fuck!' He screamed. 'Open the window!' He yanked the plug out of its socket and chucked the burning lump of melting plastic out of the window and into the garden where it landed face down in the pond with a very loud crack. By this time the smoke detectors had gone off, the dogs were barking even louder and the kids were shouting and blaming each other. Frankly, I didn't care whose fault it was – I just wanted all the noise to stop. My head was pounding. Andrew went round the house flapping a magazine frantically at the smoke alarms until they stopped.

'Who the hell thought it was a good idea to put bacon in the toaster!' yelled Andrew, looking alternately at the two children still young enough to be out of bed this early in the morning.

'It was him,' they both said, pointing at each other. Andrew rolled his eyes. 'You swore Daddy!' Billy said, wide-eyed.

'Yes, I bloody well did! I'm going back to bed,' he said, grumbling loudly and holding his head.

'Daddy doesn't feel well,' I told them.

'Is he going to die soon?' Billy asked.

'No, I don't think so – not yet anyway.' *Not unless there's another domestic appliance calamity in the near future, I thought.* In the last six months, we have waved goodbye to the vacuum cleaner, the car radio, two mobile phones, a computer screen, and the downstairs toilet flushing system, not to mention the umpteen small breakages which seem to be an every-day occurrence in our house. I eyeballed them both through the smoke. Billy aged 6 is my youngest and definitely last child, and his brother Luke is 11 and should know better. *It's really quite alarming, I reflected (on my way back to bed with a cup of tea), that my two eldest children could easily have burned to death, as neither of them thought to wake up during all that pandemonium! Honestly! Teenagers!*

The rest of the day was relatively calm thank goodness. We took the dogs out (Cocopuff and Fudgecake). *'Don't let the children choose names for them'*, my mother warned me when we first got them both. They were such sweet little balls of fluffy joy, and we were so disarmed by their big baby eyes that we foolishly indulged Tom and Flora who were 12 and 14 at the time, by letting them do exactly that. Now the dogs are three years older and have lost their fluffy charm, we are stuck with having to call out their names in the public park. Of course, the children have long since lost interest in taking them out for walks. Still, that's what you get for being too soft. We have shortened their names to Cocoa and Fudge these days.

We finished the day off with a roast dinner, cooked by Andrew which is a rare thing and therefore much appreciated as it gave me a rest for once. Just occasionally, we manage to sit round the table in a harmonious atmosphere and it's really wonderful. I bathed in the glory of it for at least ten minutes, before Flora announced that she had 'stuff to do' and that she was *really* tired after staying up all night watching back-to-back episodes of some ghastly thing called *Death Note*.

'But you haven't finished,' complained Andrew.

'I'm not that hungry…' Flora said, slouching out of the kitchen and towards the stairs.

'Probably all those bloody Pringles she's got stashed in her room,' Andrew said under his breath.

'I'm not hungry either!' said Billy.

'Yes, you are! You a very *very* hungry and you *will* eat

your dinner!' Andrew's voice rose to the occasion.

'But the gravy's all cold and lumpy,' moaned Billy.

'Dad, did you mean to burn the sprouts?' said Luke.

We ate in frosty silence.

'I thought it was very nice,' said Tom. 'Can I have some more?'

I smiled at Andrew – just sometimes there's a glimmer of hope – a sign of burgeoning maturity and understanding, with a bit of sympathy thrown in for good measure.

It's funny though, how you can start the day with the worst hangover for months, and say to yourself that you couldn't face another alcoholic drink …ever.

'Mine's a large one,' I said, as Andrew opened the fridge and rummaged for the last bottle of dubious party wine from the night before.

Wednesday 2nd January

Andrew's brother John and his wife Octavia came for lunch today. They brought with them their three precocious children: Atlas, and the 10-year-old twins - Athena, and Aphrodite. It has become a family tradition that we see them the day after New Year's Day every year since Atlas was born just a few days after Luke. I have mixed feelings about it, because although I like Andrew's brother, Octavia is a bit intense, and frankly I think she has a touch of Asperger's. I don't know whether being a Fellow Research Lecturer in Ancient Greek at Cambridge precludes one from joining the rest of humanity, but she seems to view us with a great deal of scepticism and I'm convinced she thinks we are all imbeciles. Andrew says it's not without due cause, but even so, you'd think she could try a little harder. She has no sense of humour and finding any common ground with her is mission impossible. Andrew can't understand what John saw in her. Her preference for 1970's clothing may account for it – Andrew thinks that maybe John saw his mother in her and felt safe. Anyway, she barely speaks when she visits us, and looks miserable most of the time – I don't think I've ever seen her smile come to think of it.

John seems oblivious to her strangeness and dotes on her. Andrew says it's because he's in awe of her super-intelligent brain. 'So why doesn't she know how to use a tin opener then?' I asked him once. He said something about 'concrete thinking' versus 'abstract thinking', and that my brain was more on the concrete side. Well, if having an abstract type of brain means that you and your family could starve to death any minute, I know which one I'd rather have, thank you very much. Anyway, they visited and stayed for four interminable hours. John and Andrew always get on well when they get together – they revert to their pre-married selves, telling rude jokes and laughing very loudly. Octavia tolerates it but you can feel the negative vibes. When she speaks to her children, it's in a sharp whisper that you can't quite make out. I decided to try and engage her in a conversation about school which I thought would sustain us for a while.

'How is Atlas getting on?' I asked her.

'Oh,' she said, vaguely - 'very well.'

'Does he like school?' I asked.

'Of course!' she said, frowning.

'That's good,' I said. 'Luke isn't very keen – we have to threaten him with forced labour to make him go!' She looked at me blankly.

'How do you get Atlas to take school seriously and work hard?' I asked her, genuinely interested in what her methods might entail and whether I could apply them to my lazy lot. She didn't seem to have any tips to share though.

John butted in. 'Atlas is *very* focussed - we've never had to put any pressure on him,' he said smugly.

'So, he doesn't take after you then!' said Andrew, joshing him.

'I don't remember you being particularly industrious at school either!' said John. They congratulated each other on their past fecklessness, high-fived and clanked their beer glasses together.

Octavia looked out of the window and sighed.

'What about the girls Octavia?' I said, persevering. 'Are they getting along well?'

'Athena and Aphrodite are both excelling,' she said. 'They were joint winners of the JNMA in December.'

'What's that?' I asked.

Octavia looked at me as if I should know. 'It's the Junior National Mathematicians Award of course.'

At this point, I decided to go and get lunch ready. I

must say, I can't help feeling like a complete dunce in Octavia's presence.

While I was making the potato salad, Billy came bursting into the kitchen waving a broken Action Man in the air.

'Athena snapped his head right off!' he wailed.

'Oh, dear!' I said, - 'I'm sure she didn't mean to.'

'Yes, she did – she said he was a symbol of man's domination of women and a… a…' He couldn't remember the rest. 'What's a stereopipe Mum?'

'Stereotype,' I said correcting him. 'It's …' I floundered, realising he probably wouldn't grasp the meaning. 'We'll glue it back on later,' I said. 'Tell her she is not to break anything else, or I'll be exercising some domination over *her*.'

When we all sat down for lunch later on, Athena and Aphrodite looked a bit too pleased with themselves, and I wondered what they'd been up to. Later, I discovered that G.I. Joe had been stripped of his army fatigues and was floating naked in the pond keeping the toaster company.

'Those girls are going to be a handful later on,' I said to Andrew when they'd all gone home.

'Yes – poor old John,' said Andrew, - 'he's completely out-classed by all three kids, and his wife to boot!'

'I don't know about 'out-classed',' I said, - 'totally eclipsed more like! What do they find to talk about do you think – he and Octavia?'

'I've no idea. The kids I suppose – same as us.'

I started to think then, about what Andrew and I had in common and realised that it didn't amount to very much either.

'What do you think they saw in each other?' I said.

'How should I know! Love is blind Dora.'

'Is it?'

'Yes – how do you think we ended up together!'

Later on, lying in bed, I was still mulling over the arbitrary nature of life-partnership.

'If you knew then, what you know now, do you think you would you have made a different choice?' I asked him. Luckily, he'd gone to sleep, because I'm not sure I wanted to know the answer.

Thursday 3rd January

It was a lovely crisp winter's day today. Andrew and I took the dogs and the boys over to the common to give the dogs a run and get some fresh air. The boys took their bikes and tore off ahead, racing each other down the road. They've all done the Cycling Proficiency test at school, but you'd never know it. I don't know how many times I've told them to stay off the pavement, wear their helmets *at all times*, and watch out for pensioners, prams and any other objects – moving or otherwise. Mrs Finch from No.21 always peers out from behind her net curtains when my boys go past, as if waiting to see if the bad things that she thinks will happen, actually do. I waved at her today and she just scowled and let go of the curtain.

'Funny woman,' said Andrew.

'She's probably lonely,' I said.

'No wonder,' said Andrew.

My husband is not the most sympathetic person you'll ever meet. I sometimes think he could do with being a little more empathic. I mean, when I'm old and decrepit, I'm not sure I'd want him looking after me – I don't think he'd be very good at it.

'What if I die first and you are on your own?' I said. 'You might become a curtain-twitcher yourself.'

'Never.' he said. 'I'd have much better things to do with my time.'

'Like what?' I said.

'Well …. I might take up swimming, or bowling, or gardening ….'

'Gardening!' I said, laughing.

'Why not?' he said, somewhat indignantly.

'Because you've never shown any interest at all – not even enough to mow that scruffy patch of grass you call our lawn. In fact, the only time I've ever seen you wielding a pair of shears was when the ivy interfered with the TV signal because it was growing over the satellite dish.'

'Well, when I'm an old man I might decide to grow alpines, or marrows, or something.' I gave him a look which left him in no doubt that I thought he was talking complete rubbish.

'It does make you think though,' I said to him – 'don't you wonder what will happen to us when we are both retired?'

'No, I don't want to 'wonder' about that part of my life yet – I haven't finished being a middle-aged stressed-out father of four yet. I can't imagine surviving into old age.'

'Well, you'd better start considering it because I don't want to be on my own – in fact,' I said, getting the bit between my teeth, - 'maybe you should start thinking about getting a bit fitter – you know, losing some of that excess weight.'

Andrew patted his tummy affectionately, as if it were his best friend. 'I need this extra layer of fat to keep me warm in winter,' he said.

'That winter-warmer is not your friend,' I said. 'It is actually your enemy, cleverly disguised as a scatter cushion. It will sneak up on you, take you by surprise and strike when you least expect it – it is in fact a ticking time bomb.'

'Don't be daft Dora!'

'I'm not being daft Andrew. I'm deadly serious – you are heading for trouble if you don't do something about it.' I didn't say anything else – Andrew had a hunted look on his face and I thought I'd better lay off him – at least for a day or two anyway. Of course, truth be told, I am not as slim and fit as I used to be either. As we walked along towards the gates of the park, a couple of joggers ran past in matching running gear. They looked young and vigorous and slim.

'I know what you're thinking,' said Andrew - 'and the

answer is *no*.'

As we closed the gate behind us and let the dogs off their leads, we suddenly heard a plaintive cry, followed by a lot of bellowing from beyond a cluster of birch trees. The dogs took off in the direction of the commotion.

'That sounds like Luke,' I said, walking faster. Andrew ran ahead. My mind suddenly flooded with previous traumatic incidents and tediously long visits to the A&E – a catalogue of minor injuries and near-death experiences all merged together, like one big blurry exert from one of Flora's horror films. I imagined Luke lying prostrate, his bicycle a mangled wreck, blood gushing from a huge gash in his head. I started to run too, imagining the worst possible scenario.

It's always the boys who manage to mutilate themselves. I only had to take Flora once to hospital, when she was 6. She and Tom were playing 'Which Animal Am I?' and because Tom told her that real elephants have tusks, Flora promptly stuck a pencil up her nose which snapped off when Tom tried to assist with the insertion, leaving a piece of it jammed inside and a veritable river of blood flowing out. The nurse at the hospital finally managed to remove it after an hour of prodding and probing. Between them, the boys have notched up five broken fingers, three fractured toes, two broken ankles, two broken arms (one including a dislocation and severed artery), one broken leg, four eye injuries, a sliced finger, a bee sting resulting in a massively swollen tongue, an allergic reaction to a Mexican chorizo, and, last but not least – an enormous egg on Luke's head due to Tom swinging him round by his legs and letting him go near a lamp-post.

'How did your bike get up there?' I asked, when I saw Luke's bike stuck up in the tree.

'Tom put it there,' said Luke.

'What did you do that for?' Andrew said, wrestling with the handlebars to get it down.

'Luke said Tom's a loser at racing,' piped up Billy.

Finally, after a lot of pulling and pushing, we got it down. Luckily, the bike seemed to have survived its ordeal unscathed.

'Why do they have to fight like that,' I said to him as we resumed our walk.

'Well, you fought with your sister, didn't you? And I was always fighting with John – it's in our nature as human beings to try and get rid of the others so there's more food for us – it's a survival instinct. Natural selection is alive and kicking.'

It's at times like this when I envy people with only one child. They don't have to spend all their energy arbitrating over squabbles and skirmishes and ending up getting high blood pressure because they need to blot it all out with large quantities of gin. But, as I said earlier, it was my choice to go forth and multiply, and as Flora never ceases to remind me - it's no good whinging about the consequences is it!

Friday 4th January

I flew around the shops this afternoon trying to buy last-

minute school stuff such as; trainers for the boys, a myriad
of different sizes and styles of socks, underwear (same),
rulers, pencils, yet another calculator and a fountain pen for
Billy, now that he has his *Pen Licence* (do those teachers
realise what they have done giving him a new weapon of
destruction?) However, we must be happy for him now that
he has mastered joined-up writing and will hopefully take
more interest in his school work (who am I kidding!) Now
that Flora has started her A levels, she seems to need an
endless supply of lined paper, coloured pens, post-it notes
and large quantities of chocolate. Tom on the other hand,
who is supposed to be revising for his GCSE's, doesn't
seem to need anything at all.

What happens to all these things anyway – they seem to
vanish into thin air, just like odd socks, scissors, Sellotape,
spare batteries, today's newspaper, my make-up…. Anyway,
I felt quite smug that I'd remembered everything that
everyone had asked for, except of course the most
important thing – Andrew's suit from the dry-cleaners
which he needed tonight for a conference. This of course
resulted in a prolonged row later on about priorities –
suffice to say I will be in the dog house for a bit.

On the way home I collected Billy from my mother's
house – it's easier to leave him there than ask the others to
look after him, especially after the last time I left all of them
in the house together. The toasted toaster incident is
nothing in comparison. I mean, why Luke thought that Billy
would fit through the skylight in the bathroom ceiling I
don't know, because Billy is quite chunky for his age and
not particularly athletic. The paramedics were very good
about it though, and when they'd calmed Luke down and

checked Billy for any major injuries, they gave me good advice about claiming on the insurance for the window frame which shouldn't have come away from the roof so easily. They weren't so sure about the conservatory though, because we probably should have had shatterproof glass fitted when it was installed. It was a good job Billy landed on the new lounger I'd just bought and had a soft landing. By some miracle, he only had a few superficial cuts and bruises. Luke didn't even need the football which was stuck in the gutter, we've got several others in the shed. 'It was my best one!' he said in his defence at the time.

Of course, it's always with some trepidation that I leave him with my mother and I try not to do it too often. When I arrived at my mother's house, things seemed surprisingly calm and she told me that Billy had been very good.

'He's been no trouble at all – he played in the garden all afternoon and I hardly saw him,' she said smiling happily as we left.

'Well that was nice,' I said to Billy as we drove home. 'I think we'd better get you into the shower though,' I said, noticing how dirty he was.

'I've been digging for treasure.'

'Did you find anything?'

'Just these.' He held out the palm of his little hand caked in mud. On it lay a rusty hinge, a bit of broken pottery and a bottle top. I thought back to my own childhood and recalled nostalgically doing the very same thing in the same garden. Billy looked a bit disappointed though, with his unremarkable finds.

'Never mind Billy, you'll find something better next time…'

'I want to dig up a dead body!' he said, brightening up.

'That's not possible in a garden situation,' I said, - 'not normally anyway.' Billy's recent pre-occupation with death and dead things is slightly worrying, I think. Andrew says it's a phase. I certainly hope so.

Saturday 5th January

My sister Jess rang me up this morning in a bit of a state. Apparently, my mother was on her way across the lawn to hang out her washing when she fell into a large hole and broke her ankle.

'I can't take any time off work to look after her,' said Jess immediately. 'I've got 10 batches of Victoria sponge cakes, 500 meringues and 650 gingerbread men to make by Friday. My customers will just go elsewhere if I don't get these orders out to them, and I can't afford to lose any more customers!' I gritted my teeth. It was true of course – Jess had lost a few customers recently and it wasn't her fault that Patisserie Antoinette's were springing up all over the place taking all her business. 'Anyway, you are more flexi than me,' she said by way of further justification.

'Yes,' I sighed, - 'it makes more sense for me to have her.' Jess's relief was palpable. 'Oh good!' she said. 'I'll drop her round tomorrow morning when they discharge her.'

I decided to wait until later to break the news to Andrew – what was the point in spoiling an otherwise peaceful day.

Flora announced at lunch time that she was going to the cinema with her new boyfriend, Tom said he was going out on his bike, and Luke went to the park with his mates, so that just left Billy without anything to do. Andrew decided to take him into town with him, so I had a lovely afternoon walking the dogs on the common with my friend Suzie, followed by cinnamon toast and tea at her house. It's always so calm there. I sat back and savoured the peace and tranquillity of Suzie's conservatory - only momentarily dwelling on the fact that ours was still a no-go area. Apparently, some of the panes of glass are an unusual size and difficult to get hold of. That's so typical of us - I knew that builder Andrew wanted to use was cheap for a reason. Suzie's house is beautiful and perfect in every way, but then she does only have one child and a tiny dog, and her husband Warren is away all the time, and she doesn't have to go to work, and she has a cleaner …… I know, I can't help it – I *am* envious.

'I'm having a Ladies evening here next week,' she told me. 'Will you come Dora? It'll be lovely. Letty and Bunny have got some nice smellies and anti-aging stuff for sale, and Pierre is going to do some amazing food ….' I continued smiling though my heart sank a little.

'Well, you know it's not really my kind of thing …'

'Oh, come on Dora! It'll be sooooo much fun!' *No, it really won't, I thought to myself. For one thing, I don't want to buy stuff I don't need with money I don't have, plus some of Suzie's friends are unbelievably crass.*

'I'm not sure Suzie, Andrew might be working late that night …'

'But I haven't told you which night yet.'

'Well, he's working late a lot right now.' I said.

'Well, it's on Thursday – 7 o'clock till whenever. Please come – it'll be good for you to come out!'

'I'll try,' I said.

I told her about my mother's ankle and her impending extended visit, hoping she might offer to help me out, and although she was very sympathetic, she avoided offering any assistance.

'That Suzie is what you call a fair-weather friend,' Andrew always tells me when I complain about her. 'Why do you like her so much?' I'm not sure what the answer to that is. Sometimes I think that she's what I'd like to be if things were different – sophisticated, attractive, stick-thin, confident, and most importantly – well-off. Maybe I'm living an alternative existence vicariously through her ...OMG, could that be what I'm doing! I think I need to expand my circle of friends. That's definitely on my list of things to do this year.

Sunday 6ᵗʰ January

Last night's row with Andrew has left me feeling drained and anxious. What was I supposed to do? Anyway, I have my suspicions about that hole in the lawn. If Billy is responsible for my poor mother's accident, then we'll have to suffer the consequences. Of course, Andrew doesn't quite see it this way.

'Why didn't she look where she was going!' he said

unsympathetically.

'It was dark,' I said.

'Why was she hanging out washing in the dark?'

'I have no idea,' I said wearily.

'For God's sake! What a ridiculous thing to do. Why can't Jess help for once? Where are we going to put her? She can't get up the stairs can she!' And so it went on.

Anyway, by the time Jess turned up with Mum, Andrew had accepted that he was being pretty unreasonable, and had calmed down. We made her comfortable in his big armchair in front of the TV. Billy's eyes lit up when he saw his granny's plaster cast resting on the footstool.

'Can I draw on it?' he asked.

'Whatever for?' my mother replied.

'When Dan Herbert broke his leg in PE last week, we all signed his plaster – he had a green one!' Billy said enthusiastically.

'Oh well, I don't see why not. Can I get the *Archers* on this?' she said, pointing the remote at the TV. 'Oh, I can't work this – I need my glasses. Dora, could you fetch them for me, and a blanket, and a cushion would be nice, oh and a cup of tea would be lovely – I'm parched.' I can see that we will have testing times ahead.

Since school starts tomorrow, I had quite a lot to do today – ironing, searching for lost PE kit, naming bits of new uniform, making sure all four of them have their book bags ready. I realised I hadn't looked in Billy or Luke's bags since the end of last term. Based on previous experience, it's always a good idea to approach children's pockets and bags with a great deal of caution, and if possible - protective clothing.

'Don't you think you should be wearing gloves?' said Andrew when he saw me delving into Billy's school bag.

'Yes, with hindsight,' I said, showing him a squashed mouldy apple with a variety of rubbers, pencil sharpeners and sweets stuck to it. He recoiled in disgust.

'I don't know why you bother with healthy snacks – look what happens to them!'

'It's all very well for you to say that,' I told him curtly, 'but the school are having a healthy snack drive and I don't want to get told off by Mrs Pincher.'

'No …' Andrew agreed, 'I see what you mean.' Billy's teacher is an arch purveyor of Passive Aggressive, and has the ability to make you feel totally inadequate and utterly irresponsible with just a look. Ever since the launch of the *Change4Life Healthy Eating Campaign* by the Department of Health, and Jamie Oliver's boot camps for dinner ladies, Mrs Pincher has been like a dog with a bone. I know the nation is turning into a load of morbidly obese sluggards, but putting a salad bar in the school kitchen isn't going to cut it. Anyway, I didn't mean to send Billy to school with Haribos for his break-time snack. He was obviously throwing away a perfectly good apple on the way to school and cadging sweets off his brother. It's the way the woman smiles at you that is so irritating.

Luke's bag was peculiarly empty. I found a few dog-eared football cards, a couple of scruffy exercise books and a broken ruler.

'Where are your books?' I asked him.

'Dunno,' he said, gormlessly.

'Well, they can't just have disappeared!' I said. Luke looked blank. Then I noticed that the name on the front of the books wasn't his. 'You've brought the wrong bag home, you Charlie!' Luke shrugged. 'Can you please make sure that tomorrow morning you get yours back?'

'Yes, yes I will. Stop going on!'

'This isn't 'going on' If you want 'going on' you can sit there for an hour while I have a proper go at you!' He slunk off.

'I don't know how that lad got into grammar school,' said my Mum.

Monday 7th January

Well, I got them all off to school in time this morning – a major achievement on the first day of term. Tom forgot his packed lunch and Flora left her phone behind, but apart from that it all went to plan and when I closed the door on the last child to leave the house, I almost sat down. Then I remembered my mother.

'I didn't find that zed-bed very comfy,' she said, progressing slowly across the lounge on her crutches.

'Well, we'll have to sort something else out Mum. Come

and have some breakfast. I got you some of those muffins you like from Jess.'

We sat in the kitchen and chatted for a while which was nice because we don't get the chance very often.

'I'll have to get on with some work later,' I told her, hoping she'd understand. The trouble is, I don't think she does understand the concept of working from home and I have a bad feeling about it. We haven't lived in the same house together for twenty-eight years, so this isn't going to be easy. I'll have to be very patient. Of course, the dogs are a good distraction and can be walked any time of the day or night.

'These aren't as good as usual,' my mother said, discarding a half-eaten muffin and pushing the plate away. 'I think I'll have some toast instead please Dora.'

I managed to escape into the office for two hours while she read her book. I turned the computer on and clicked on my work emails. I was dismayed when I saw my inbox – how can there be 500 emails asking about silicone cheese puff cases and penguin-shaped salt-shakers? Who *are* these people! I really need to get a different job. This is almost as soul-destroying as the last one I had, selling 'variously styled' lumbar support belts.

Tuesday 8th January

I decided to take Mum out today for a change of scene – partly to give myself a break, plus she had interrupted me too many times and I'd lost the ability to focus on my work properly.

'Where shall we go?' I said to her mid-morning. 'We could go out for lunch – the weather isn't very good so we'll have to stay inside somewhere.'

'I'd love to go to Ikea,' she said. 'I've never been and I could do with a few things for the house. I saw a lovely orange and green stripy rug with matching lamp shades on the telly yesterday.'

'Right,' I said, slightly taken aback by both her snap decision-making and her sudden interest in gaudy colour combinations. 'Well, if we leave soon we can have lunch there. It takes about half an hour.' I quickly took the dogs out across the field at the back of the house while she got herself ready. Then I wrestled with the wheelchair the hospital had lent us. It weighed a ton. I finally got it into the boot of the car and then had another wrestling match with my mother's leg.

'I thought these people carriers were supposed to be spacious,' she complained as I wedged her plaster cast into the foot-well.

'Well they aren't built to accommodate invalids,' I said, getting slightly hot under the collar. Finally, we were ready to go. My mother switched the radio onto Classic FM, got out a bag of jelly babies and off we went.

Ikea was packed but quite wheelchair-friendly so once we managed to negotiate the car park and the lifts, we were soon swishing our way round the store.

'What fun!' my mother exclaimed as we rolled round the shopper track. We went for our lunch first - in the clean, airy and spacious café, where the food options were super-healthy and beautifully presented. We both chose the 'responsibly-sourced gravadlax wrap' followed by organic raspberry tarts and two UTZ-certified cappuccinos.

'Delicious!' said my mother, - 'proper food!' I chose to ignore this remark. I mean, I am a very busy person and can't always provide gourmet dinners on tap. My cooking is fine when I can be bothered, but after all these years of cooking for the five thousand one gets a bit kitchen-weary. We found our way to the bedroom department and my mother duly bought her blinkingly bright rug and lamps. Feeling pleased with herself, we packed everything back in the car and drove home. It was only then that I realised I'd meant to go food shopping today and now it was too late. Oh well, sometimes you just have to make do with what's in the cupboard. After a prolonged rummage, I came up with some couscous, a couple of tins of tuna, a tired cabbage, and some plum tomatoes. Well, if chefs on Netmums.com can come up with random cupboard food recipes that work, then surely I can manage it.

'This is a bit unusual,' said Andrew at dinner time.

'I don't like it.' said Billy.

'It's weird!' said Flora and Tom in unison.

'It tastes like poo!' said Luke.

'That gravadlax wrap in Ikea was good,' my mother piped up.

After I'd scraped most of the meal into the bin, Andrew went with Luke to get some chips. I obviously need to be a bit better organised in future, if only to avoid Billy going to school and telling Mrs Pincher that his mother made him something that tasted like poo for tea and that his Dad gave him chips.

After tea, we all settled down to watch a film together. This is a rare occurrence in our house as usually no one wants to spend much time with anyone who might be related to them, but this time they were in a convivial mood and agreed to watch *Tootsie* – a nice family film we could all watch together.

'What's it about?' asked my mother.

'Gender-bending.' said Tom, before I had a chance to explain.

'Oh …I'm not sure I'll like that sort of thing …'

Tom's description, though accurate, was of course completely misleading.

'You'll like it Mum, it's funny!' I told her. Of course, she fell asleep half way through as she always does but the rest of us enjoyed it – even Billy, who I thought might get bored when he saw that it didn't have guns or dying in it.

'Why does your mother have a pair of giant tits drawn on her leg?' Andrew whispered while we were watching the film.

'Oh – Billy tried to write his name on it but the pen ran out. Now that you mention it, it does look a bit odd. No wonder people were giving us funny looks in Ikea.'

Wednesday 9th January

I managed to get through lots of work today as Mum's friend came to take her out. My boss even congratulated me on the record number of orders processed in one day. I must say though, I fail to see how one average-sized B&B would need 150 yellow ladles, but it's not for me to question why, and what a nursing home wants with 20 novelty shark-attack bottle openers, I don't know, and it beggars belief that anyone would want to purchase a nutcracker in the shape of a penis complete with scrotum. Actually, on second thoughts, that would make a good present for my current boss Jarred Roach (or JR as he likes to be called). When he hired me three months ago, and discovered my full name, he was like a dog with two tails. I've heard all the jokes about Pandora's box a zillion times, but that didn't stop him.

I whizzed off to the supermarket to get the shopping, leaving my list on the kitchen table which is normal practice, and came back two hours later having spent a fortune on two-for-ones and discounted multi-packs.

'Did you get my shaving gel?' asked Andrew hopefully.

'Did you get *Chocosplits*?' asked Billy

'I hope you didn't forget my water pills,' said my Mum.

'Sorry,' I said, 'I'll do it all tomorrow.'

'Tomorrow's too late,' Andrew said.

'What do you mean?'

'I told myself that if you forgot my shaving gel again, I'd grow a beard. So, I'm now going to be the proud owner of a big bushy chin-warmer.'

'Don't be ridiculous!' I said.

'I'm not.'

'For God's sake Andrew!'

'It's been four days now! You know I can't get it easily myself. I wish you'd remember to get things I need – I had to go to that conference in my old suit last week because of you – I was a laughing stock! Everyone kept asking me if I was auditioning for a re-make of *Miami Vice!*' he said crossly.

'Why didn't you get your shaving gel when you were in town with Billy the other day then?'

'I forgot,' he said, - 'I can't be expected to remember everything!'

'And I need my pills too,' said Mum, 'or my legs will go up like balloons.'

Sometimes the responsibility of family life weighs very heavily. At this point, I took the dogs out for a long walk and left Andrew to make tea. If he grows a beard I might have to consider phoning 'Relate' – I really don't think I can stand for it.

Thursday 10th January

In preparation for this evening's 'do', I thought I'd better go and get my legs waxed and my hair done. I approach both these things with trepidation – waxing has it's obvious down-side, and although going to the salon fills most women with glee, my experience has often been a less than happy one. Anyway, I rang Anton at Les Cheveux to check that he was still expecting me and remind him what I wanted, although to be honest, I could hardly make myself understood over the radio which my mother had turned up loud enough to hear in the next street. Afterwards, I decided to get the waxing out of the way early in the morning. Sherry, who looks like she's had an all-over-body wax apart from her head, had a new girl in training today - just my luck.

'Hiya,' she said breezily. 'You don't mind if Angelica does you today do you – it'll be 20% off since she's still in training …. Now, is it half, or full?'

'Sorry?'

'Your legs.'

'Oh, half please.' Well, there's no point in paying for the bits no one sees is there? And I'm not showing my thighs to anyone thank you very much. Anyway, who has hairy thighs? When it was all over, I must say I was quite relieved – mainly because I didn't have to listen to Sherry chiming in a sing-songy voice 'remove and soothe' after every painful laceration. I went home and lay in the bath for an hour to recuperate. After having a quick lunch with Mum, I went off to the hairdressers with my mother's parting words of advice ringing in my ears –'get them to do a nice bob'. That's all very well, but my hair won't go into a nice anything – especially a neat stylish bob. Strangely, Anton seemed a bit on edge when he saw me enter the salon and I don't know why but his thin smile definitely looked a bit forced.

'Bonjour Dora! Ca va aujourd'hui?' He waved me over to sit by the basin and wait for an assistant, but I could see in the mirror that he was whispering to his partner Gaston, and pointing at me. Anyway, it all seemed to go perfectly well - until the end that is.

'But Dora,' he protested when he saw my face fall, 'It's what you asked for isn't it?'

'But I told you to 'trim the back and give me light highlights.' I said mournfully.

'I thought you said 'a trim with black and white stripes.'

'No!'

'Well, I'm sorry ma chérie, but you need to speak more clearly on the phone next time Dora.'

I blame my mother for this debacle. If she didn't insist on having the radio on 24/7, I wouldn't have ended up looking like a demented badger! I went home in an almighty strop.

'Don't say a word!' I said to my mother when I went in through the front door. Of course, that didn't stop the rest of them.

Tom didn't notice anything unusual, Luke sniggered, and Flora just looked stunned. Billy said 'I like your funny hair Mummy!'

When Andrew came home later, I had locked myself in the bathroom.

'Oh, come on Dora – it can't be that bad!' he shouted from the other side. When I decided to be brave and come out, he was very good and kept a totally straight face. I did see a twitch though, at the corner of his mouth.

'I'm not going out like this.' I said.

'Why didn't the salon do something about it?' he asked perfectly reasonably.

'Because you can't re-dye it straight away.'

'Why not?'

'Because all my hair could fall out!'

'In the circumstances, that might not be a bad thing......' Andrew said, and then he couldn't control his laughter any more. Flora very sweetly came out of her room and suggested we put it up in a bun. So, in the end I did go out, with my hair cleverly concealed (mostly) and wearing a new dress I'd bought the week before. After a quick make-up application, also by Flora (since my make-up bag seems to have gone missing again), I was ready to go.

Suzie's place looked fabulous of course, with the conservatory all lit up with white fairy lights. Her enormous kitchen was decorated with several carefully placed ornamental bushes and extravagant designer flower arrangements which she must have hired for the occasion. Lots of her friends were already there so I took a glass of pink Cava from the waiter and went to look at all the party plan stuff for sale. I didn't intend buying anything but I thought I'd better look at it so at least I knew what they were all talking about.

'Dora! How lovely to see you!' I turned to face someone

I hardly knew – I think her name is Cressida. She spoke with an unspecified foreign accent, rolling her 'r's – like Marlene Dietrich. In fact, she did look remarkably like her too. 'You simply must try zis stuff – it's absolutely amazing – I mean just look at my skin, not a blemish *anyvere*. I don't know how I managed without it!' I looked closely at her face. *With all that make-up, you wouldn't be able to tell how pock-marked she was, I thought.* She held up a large pink bottle. 'It's completely organic, cruelty-free, ethically sourced using environmentally responsible packaging, and manufactured using 100% wind power!'

'At that price, it should be!' I said, half choking on my fizz. 'Who on earth would spend £175 on foot moisturiser?'

'Oh, silly me,' she said, putting it down. 'I use zis one on my face.' She held up another pink bottle which looked the same but cost £200. '*Vat* do you use on *your* skin?' she asked, peering at me.

'Nothing,' I replied truthfully. She looked shocked, then terribly concerned, as if I had a terminal illness. She dropped her voice and went into confiding mode. Leaning closer, she picked up a smaller bottle and tapping it with a long red fingernail, said, 'I can let you have zis one for £50 but don't tell anyone.'

'Dora darling! There you are!' said Suzie, sweeping over to save me from Cressida's clutches. 'I say, that's pretty edgy make-up you're wearing!'

'Edgy?'

'You know – trendy bordering on mad!'

'Is it?'

'Well, yes! I mean glitter shadow *is* apparently back on trend, and I saw Lady Gaga wearing electric blue mascara on the *Graham Norton Show* last night!' (I hadn't actually looked at Flora's handiwork before leaving the house as I was in such a rush.) 'I hardly recognised you!' said Suzie, - 'especially with the Cruella De Vil thingy going on with your hair!'

'Fantastically gutsy darling!' butted in Suzie's friend Justine. 'My cleaner says mega-highlights are all the rage!'

I tried to change the subject. 'This Cava's nice!'

'That's Taittinger darling!'

'Oh, sorry! I can't tell the difference.'

'No, of course not,' said Justine with a superior smile. Feeling really out of my comfort zone, I began to think about making a quick exit, when a woman came over to me who I thought I recognised. Suzie introduced me to her and left us to chat.

'Melanie Stevens – my husband works with yours at Sharp Practice!'

I laughed. 'We call it that as well!' (*It's actually 'Sharp and Prentice'.*) 'Andrew has always liked your husband Geoff – says he's a good chap and very no-nonsense,' I said to her.

We got on rather well, Melanie and I. She whispered that she only came to please Suzie and get the numbers up. So, after that I relaxed a bit and actually ended up enjoying myself.

Friday 11th January

My sister Jess came this morning to take Mum to her house for the weekend. Mum had obviously pre-warned her about my hair because she didn't say a word, which was totally out of character - normally she can't help herself. It was a good job Mum was out of the way for a bit because we've got some friends and their two children coming on Sunday and I haven't done any housework for ages. In fact, I can't remember when I last did any proper cleaning. So, I spent the whole day going boldly where no person has dared to venture for at least three months. Under the sofa I found all sorts of things; a new supply of rubbers and sharpeners, hairbands and Kirby grips galore, a half-eaten sausage, several sticky sweets embedded in the carpet, three pens, a credit card and £5.80 in loose change. I also found two decomposing mice that our cat, Scratch, had brought in. God knows how long they'd been languishing there, rotting. I did wonder about the smell in that room, but when you have teenagers you assume it's them and just open the windows. I threw them in the bin and lit a joss stick.

I realised about lunchtime that I'd missed a call on my mobile from JR, so I listened to my messages. Unfortunately, he's not very happy. He's had a complaint from a B&B because we sent them 150 canary yellow ladles which they said they didn't order, and which are now blocking the corridor to the breakfast lounge and causing an obstruction and what are we going to do about it? And then, he said he'd had another complaint from a nursing home saying that they'd received in the post a particularly grotesque novelty nutcracker instead of the bottle-openers they'd ordered for raffle prizes. Strangely, the person who should have had the nutcracker hasn't contacted us yet. His message ended on a bit of a downer, saying that perhaps I wasn't cut out for this kind of work, and would I like to reconsider my position.

Andrew was very supportive about it. 'Well it's very easy to mistake label for ladle and as for mixing up the addresses – well, anyone can make that mistake, especially when they're both in Milton Keynes. I think he's being pretty unfair, and anyway he can't just get rid of you like that without giving you proper warnings. I'll get the Employment Law Department onto it.'

'No,' I said, I'd rather you didn't.

'Why?'

'Well, I don't really want to work for him any more anyway. And, well, the thing is – I've had two warnings already…'

Andrew looked dismayed. 'Why?'

'Well, I accidentally put a virus onto the company website and it started advertising sex aids to our customers. And then, last week I joked on Facebook that no one in their right mind would buy anything from a bloke who's namesake wears a 10 gallon hat …… and he got upset.'

'Well, yes he would. But why did you accept his friend request on Facebook in the first place?'

'Because I didn't want to hurt his feelings.'

Andrew looked at me with an expression of complete disbelief.

'Well, that's that them.'

'I'll find something else,' I said trying to cheer things up. 'I'm sure I can find something.' There was a long silence and then Andrew said he had to take Luke to football practice.

The trouble is, part-time jobs that are interesting and pay well are thin on the ground. Oh well, I'll have to be a bit thrifty for a while – I'm sure it won't be for too long.

Saturday 12th January

Today was Tom's birthday. He'll be 16 years old. He's changed so much in the last two years – gone from being a little boy to a young man in such a short space of time. He wanted to go to a rugby match for his birthday with some of his school friends, then onto Madras House in town for a curry. Andrew gave him some money and strict instructions to call us so we could come and collect them all later.

'They can't get into much trouble,' Andrew told me when I was nagging him to make sure he called us.

'Well, I know Tom's fairly sensible, but some of his friends most certainly are not!' I said.

'I'll be fine Mum,' were his parting words as he left the house. Half an hour later, I found his phone under a cushion.

'Look, we know where they're going, so there's no need to fret,' said Andrew.

We settled down to watch *Dragon's Den* followed by *Crime Night*, followed by a film about vampires. At midnight, I said to Andrew - 'He hasn't rung! Why hasn't he rung? He could have used his mate's phone! They must be finished by now!'

Even Andrew admitted that he was concerned. 'I'll go down to the restaurant.' After Andrew left I couldn't relax at all. Finally, he rang me at about 12.30pm.

'They didn't go to Madras House and I've driven all round town twice and can't see them,' he said, sounding very frustrated.

'Have we got any of the parent's numbers?' I suggested.

'No, have you?'

'No.' The trouble is, by the time they are this age, you don't really know who their friends are. I realised with horror that I had no idea who he was with, or what they looked like. I could barely remember what their names were. Then of course my imagination got the better of me. Oh my God! He could have been lured into a drug den down a dark alley and forced to take a cocktail of amphetamines and smack, or mugged in the street and left for dead. 'I'm going to call the hospital,' I said.

'That's a bit premature, isn't it?' said Andrew. I did it anyway and discovered that so far this evening, the A&E had only admitted four OAP's, an alcoholic and a child with a pin through his toe.

'See,' said Andrew, 'I told you he was OK.'

'No, he could be lying unconscious somewhere, bleeding to death and no one's found him!'

'You're getting in a flap unnecessarily,' said Andrew, ever the practical one in a crisis. 'Don't worry Dora, I'm sure he'll turn up soon.'

After another hour of driving round town, Andrew spotted him weaving along the road with a couple of other boys his age, and hauled them into the car. He deposited the other two with their grateful but unimpressed parents and then brought Tom home.

'It's 2 o'clock in the morning!' I shouted at Tom when they got back. 'I've been worried sick! What the hell were you doing?' Tom opened his mouth to speak and promptly vomited all over the cat who had been happily sleeping curled up on the sofa.

'Apparently, they used Tom's money to buy cider and went to someone's house after the rugby because they couldn't be bothered to walk across town to the restaurant.' Andrew told me as we immersed a reluctant cat in hot soapy water.

'Well, I suppose he's going to have his first hangover now!'

'Mine was when I was 14 and drank half a bottle of cooking sherry for a bet!' Andrew said, smiling.

'Mine was when I was 16 and drank four Crème de Menthes and three Dubonets at one of my aunt's soirees when no one was looking.'

'Well now he's been sick, he'll probably be fine,' Andrew said.

'I don't think Scratch is very impressed,' I said. 'Poor cat, look at him! I'll have to put him by the boiler to dry out.'

We finally went to bed at 3 o'clock in the morning. Thank goodness we don't have to be up early – it's Sunday - the day of rest!

Sunday 13th January

I woke up feeling very excited about seeing my old friend Candice from university days – I hadn't seen her for fifteen years and in that time she'd married Dan, had two children, and moved back to the States. Andrew was not as keen as I was to see them again though.

'What if Dan's really boring – what will we find to talk about? We have to spend five hours with them!'

'You liked Candice,' I said - 'don't you remember? You said she was nice.'

'Well, what I actually said was that she was nice-looking. Anyway, I thought you said that Dan was a plonker.'

'OK, I know I said that, but it was fifteen years ago. I'm sure he's matured since then – and he wasn't the only one involved in fake-tanning and shaving the eyebrows off Candice's brother on his stag night.'

I flew round the house plumping cushions, scrubbing toilets, hiding carpet stains with carefully positioned pieces of furniture, removing the cat litter tray from in front of the fridge, covering the sofa with a blanket (in an effort to contain the slight whiff of sick still lingering there), and instructed my discontented husband to clean the windows, unload the dishwasher and try to smile more. Flora, Tom and Luke all decided to take the dogs out (mostly to escape being asked to do any work). With beef casserole and baking potatoes ready to go, I felt fantastically well-organised and super-efficient.

'They're here, they're here!' shouted Billy when he saw a huge Winnebego Adventurer draw up in front of the house. When I opened the door to them, I barely recognised Candice. She was very thin and drawn-looking, her now mousy hair was scraped back in an unflattering ponytail, and she was carrying her youngest child in what looked like a straitjacket for babies. She and Dan wore matching tracksuits and golfing visors.

'Wow, what a quaint little place you have here!' said Dan.

'It's so great to see you!' said Candice. She handed me four bottles of milk to put in the fridge – 'my expressed milk for baby Ethan – I just put it in there before we got here. You do keep your fridge at the recommended temperature of 3 degrees don't you?'

'Er, yes of course,' I said. 'It's lovely to see you too Candice. Please sit down,' I said motioning them towards the sofa.

'This is Lauren,' Candice said, introducing their 7-year old daughter. 'Say 'Hi' Lauren!' Lauren scowled and said nothing.

'Right, who would like a cup of tea?' Andrew said, in an overly jovial way, rubbing his hands together.

'Oh, we don't drink tea, unless you have green tea – we don't like to contaminate our bodies with toxins, pesticides, or GMO's' said Candice.

'Oh, OK,' I said.

'We haven't got green tea, only toxic tea, 'said Andrew smiling.

I looked at him with slight panic, and tried to shush him telepathically. He followed me into the kitchen.

'What's a GMO?' I said.

'Gaseous Methane Overdose perhaps?'

I took the two mugs of hot water through to them and Andrew brought the biscuits.

'Perhaps Lauren would like to play with some of Billy's toys?' I suggested hopefully. 'Billy, come and see if Lauren would like to play.' I eyeballed him so he knew he had no choice. She followed him upstairs reluctantly.

Then the baby stirred. 'Oh, I'd better feed Ethan,' said Candice, unrolling him from his multi-layered wrappings. 'Could you warm one of those bottles up please, in a pan – not the microwave. Did you know Dora, that microwaves cause carcinogenic compounds in the food and destroy the nutrients? By the way, is this hot water bottled or tap?'

'So, Dan,' Andrew said, 'how's it hanging?'

'What?'

'How are things going – you know, business and so on?'

'Oh well, I guess it's going better than ever Andy. I started a health food business about three years ago. We promote healthy eating, and spiritual health and happiness. It's all in this brochure here,' he said solemnly handing Andrew a booklet.

'Great,' said Andrew, I probably need all three!'

'Guess you probably do,' said Dan, watching Andrew chomp his way through a Custard Cream.

'Of course, we're guided by the Good Lord in everything we do,' said Candice. 'We would never have found such personal fulfilment and spiritual happiness without the love of Jesus in our hearts.'

'I don't remember you being religious at university!' I said to Candice incredulously.

'I was walking in the valley of darkness Dora, but when I met Dan, he showed me the light. I got saved in October 1999 by Billy Graham himself in St Louis, Missouri - I'll never forget that night Dora – God entered my soul and took away my sins – I was washed in the blood of Christ. It was beautiful – I was born again!' She sat wide-eyed, telling me all this, while Dan looked at her with admiration and pride.

'Well,' I said, I think it's time to eat lunch, and escaped into the kitchen for a breather.

'They're completely nuts!' Andrew exclaimed, hot on my heels.

'Keep your voice down!' I said.

'Come on through and we'll have lunch,' I called.

'Why are we being posh?' said Flora loudly, on seeing napkins and more than one set of cutlery each.

'Because it's nice when we have guests,' I said.

'May I ask what we're having to eat?' said Dan - 'only we're vegans – sorry I should have warned you.' I saw Andrew roll his eyes at this point.

'OK, well you can have the baked potatoes, can't you?'

'Yeah, if they're organic.'

'Yes, of course they are,' I lied.

Lauren pushed her potato round the plate.

'Eat up honey,' said Candice.

'Would you like some Ketchup?' I suggested.

'No!' said Dan stopping my arm from lifting the offending article off the table. 'Ketchup is the devil's work.' Lauren looked thoroughly disappointed and scowled even more. I ditched the cheese and biscuits plan and substituted it with a fruit salad.

'Sorry but we can't eat the Kiwi fruit,' they said.

'Oh, are you allergic?' Andrew said a little too quickly.

'Any fruit that's come from the Antipodes has a carbon footprint which is unacceptable to us – sorry.'

The next three hours were interminable. Andrew took Cocoa and Fudge out four times.

To top it all, when Candice went into the kitchen to fetch her milk bottles out of the fridge, she stepped on a large, strategically placed cat poo, and freaked out.

When we finally waved them off, Andrew said, 'I never want to see those people again.'

'I don't think they'll ever want to see us again,' I responded.

'I heard Dan say our house is a spiritual desert,' said Luke, when they'd gone.

Monday 14th January

I must say, Andrew does *not* look good with a beard, particularly as it doesn't match his hair – grey with orange patches is quite off-putting I'm afraid. He probably only did it to see what it would look like because he's never grown one before. Anyway, I hope he gets rid of it soon.

Mum came back this morning – Jess dropped her off between delivering an orange and strawberry flan and 200 French Fancies. She gave us some left-over brownies Terry had made. We decided to go to the supermarket because, despite the fact that I did a food shop on Saturday, we seem to be out of loads of things already. My family seem to chomp their way through huge quantities of the stuff in record time.

'Haven't you got to work?' said Mum.

'No, I'm changing jobs.'

'Did JR's Bits & Bobs not work out then?'

'No.'

'Oh well, I'm sure you'll get something else.'

When we got to the supermarket, I got one of those disabled trollies for Mum to put on the front of her wheelchair and I pushed her along. We managed to avoid running over most people's feet and only barged into one set of ankles, which was pretty good I thought, for a first run.

'I need some hair dye,' said my Mum.

'Really?' I said, 'but you don't usually bother.'

'Well, everyone else is doing things with their hair, even Andrew, so I thought I might too!'

'OK, what colour?'

'Blue.'

'Really?'

'Well, I quite like Flora's pink hair, but I don't want to copy her, so I'll get blue instead.'

'Good grief, Mum, are you sure?'

'Well, yes! It can't be any worse than yours, can it?'

I was stumped. 'OK then, if it's what you want.'

I don't know what's got into my mother since she's been staying with us. She seems to be going a bit loopy. I'm beginning to wonder if Terry put something other than chocolate in those brownies...

At teatime, Flora asked if her boyfriend could come for tea on Wednesday after school. Whilst I am delighted that she has found someone who actually likes her, I am concerned it might distract her from her studies. Given that her A levels are only a few months away, I hope she gets her priorities right. It's hard enough these days to get anywhere in life without qualifications, particularly if you have fluorescent hair, a skull nose-stud, and your favourite accessory is a spiked slave collar. I will have to tell all the boys to be on their best behaviour, particularly Luke, who is the family prankster. Only the other day, Luke's form teacher had to call me because Luke and his friends had put a fish in one of Miss Vicker's drawers on the last day of term. Apparently, the Public Health Department were called in during the holidays to investigate and were less than impressed when they discovered the source of the noxious odour, and threatened to prosecute the perpetrators under the *1990 Environmental Protection Act.*

'It was only a sardine!' said Luke. This is the trouble with Luke, he can never see the potentially disastrous consequences of his actions.

Tuesday 15th January

'This milk tastes funny,' my mother said at breakfast this morning. I realised with horror when I looked at the bottle, that it was one Candice must have left in the fridge by accident.

'Let's throw that away,' I said, whisking it away and shovelling her cornflakes into the bin.

'It wasn't that bad!' she said, looking a bit startled.

Billy came into the kitchen and announced that it was a 'Show and Tell' day at school.

'That's nice,' I said. 'What are you going to take in?' My worst fears were instantly confirmed when he brought out a plastic take-away box and took the lid off. Laid in some straw was the pathetic, limp little body of a decapitated mouse.

'Uhh, GROSS!' said Flora.

'Where did you find it Billy?' I asked.

'In the garden.' I felt slightly relieved, thinking that at least I would not come across the other bit somewhere lurking in the house. 'Don't show it to Granny – she's trying to eat her breakfast.' I then tried to explain that I didn't think Mrs Pincher would be terribly enthusiastic about a rapidly decomposing half-chewed mouse in the classroom.

'He can take my dried scorpion or the sheep's skull I found last summer.' Luke offered.

Then Tom joined in – 'I've got a glass of milk in my room that's three months old and has gone all blue and fluffy....'

'Cool!' said Billy. 'Can I see it?'

'I don't feel very hungry now,' said Mum.

'Billy, just take something from the house – what about the starfish, or conch shell, or the air plant?' Billy looked disappointed, but reluctantly swapped his corpse for the conch shell and they all went off to school. I watched them shamble off down the road and wondered what life had in store for them. It was hard to imagine any of them becoming useful members of society at this point in time.

'Mum, what have you done with my Black Death T shirt? I can't find it anywhere!' Flora said crossly.

'What does it look like?'

Flora rolled her eyes. 'It's the one with the flayed skull on it.'

'I have no idea Flora. You'll have to wear something else, and hurry up or you'll be late for school.' She flounced off banging the kitchen door behind her.

'Do they let them wear things like that at school?' Mum asked.

'No – she hides it underneath her jumper.'

'Well, I wish she'd wear something pretty,' Mum said. I couldn't help remembering at this point that she used to say exactly the same thing to me when I was Flora's age.

'She'll grow out of it I expect,' I said, trying to convince myself.

After breakfast, I took the dogs out to meet Suzie on the common with her Chihuahua, Ping-Pong, and to hear all her latest news. She told me that she's decided to open a shop in town selling beauty products with a nail bar, massage and waxing etc.

'Lovely!' I said, trying to sound enthusiastic. Mind you, after my last experience, maybe it's not such a bad idea – I might even be her first client.

'I'm doing it with Cressida – she's terribly good at business you know – I'm really lucky to have such a wonderful partner.'

'What will you do with Ping-Pong?' I asked.

'He'll come with me, won't you darling!' Ping-Pong yapped enthusiastically.

'It all sounds very exciting!'

'It is Dora! Now, the other thing is that we need a receptionist, and now that you are unemployed, we wondered if you would be interested?'

'Umm, well, I'm not unemployed exactly, just resting between jobs,' I said, stalling for time. 'And of course, I've got my mother to consider – she won't get her plaster off for another four weeks.'

'That's fine, we won't be ready till then anyway,' said Suzie brightly.

'I'm not sure I'd be very good at it – I mean, I'm not very smart …'

'I'm sure you can manage answering the phone and greeting customers,' said Suzie.

'No, not that kind of 'smart', I said, smarting. 'I mean, most of my clothes are only suitable for walking the dog, my hair is a mess and my nails are past praying for!'

'Oh, we'll sort all that out,' said Suzie, which wasn't quite the response I was looking for. I decided to leave it at that for the time being, particularly as Cocoa and Fudge had disappeared over the brow of the hill along with Ping-Pong and wouldn't respond to being called. This is always a worry, since we've had a few unfortunate incidents involving the dogs, especially before they were neutered. The woman down the road with her prized pedigree King Charles Spaniels was certainly relieved when we finally told her they'd been done. Well, it wasn't our fault her fence wasn't high enough to keep out bigger dogs, was it? Andrew told her at the time that you can't prosecute dog owners for molestation by proxy. He probably shouldn't have said that her bitch, being 'open for business', should've been locked in the house if she'd wanted to protect her from unwanted admirers. Then of course it all got a bit acrimonious. She shouldn't have called our dogs 'ill-mannered mutts with no breeding' (although strictly speaking this was perfectly correct), and Andrew shouldn't have said that her dogs were poncy, over-bred, dim and an easy lay.' She's never forgiven us for having to pull out of Crufts, particularly as she won 'Best in Class' the year before. Anyway, the puppies were very sweet and she had no trouble at all selling them.

Suzie and I were beginning to get a bit concerned when after fifteen minutes, the dogs were still missing. Then a man and his dog came past and told us there was something going on down by the river. We hurried down in that direction and saw several people on the river-bank pointing, and I heard the unmistakable barking of Cocoa and Fudge. When we got there, my dogs were frantically barking at something in the water.

'There's a cat stuck over there on that log,' said a little girl. On closer inspection, we realised it was Ping-Pong clinging on to a branch in the middle of the river.

'That's my dog!' said Suzie, panicking. My two dogs were soaking wet and I knew exactly what had happened. They'd all gone in for a swim, but Ping-Pong being much too little for the strong current, couldn't get out again.

'Someone will have to go in and get him,' said the man, not moving. I looked at the water – it was freezing, and about 3 feet deep with an unappealing layer of creamy scum floating on the top. Knowing that my dogs were responsible for this, I felt I had no choice. I could see Suzie was torn between going in to save her dog in distress, and ruining her new, Gucci, lamb's leather knee boots, which had just set her back £700. There was nothing else for it, so I waded in and grabbed the poor little dog (he was now shivering and petrified), to a round of applause and gushing appreciation from Suzie. We wrapped him up in Suzie's woolly scarf and headed home. By the time I got back, my legs felt like blocks of ice.

'Did you have a nice walk?' my mother called out.

'Well, bracing,' I said. 'I'm going for a hot shower.'

Later on, when I told Andrew, he said Suzie should get a proper dog. 'I'm surprised she can find it in that vast handbag she carries,' he said, unkindly.

'When are you going to shave that beard off?' I asked him pointedly.

'I'm not – I quite like not having to shave,' he said.

'In that case, I'm moving into the spare room,' I told him.

'That's a bit extreme,' he said, looking slightly put out.

'Well, it's that, or I'll stop shaving too.' He thought about this for a minute and I could see the penny drop.

'Mm,' he said, 'well I suppose I might think about taking it off.'

'Good.'

Wednesday 16th January

Today, I decided, was a household chore day – well it has to be done before the chaos overtakes me and I feel I'm drowning in a giant avalanche of detritus. The ironing pile is beginning to resemble Snowdonia, the dogs have left mud-prints all over the house and clumps of their hair have gathered like an army of giant furry caterpillars marching across the living room carpet. I can barely face looking in either of the bathrooms, let alone actually cleaning them. We tried once to get a rota going with the children and it worked for a week, quickly disintegrating into a battle of wills and hours of bickering between them. I gave up when Tom and Flora had been arguing for two hours over who blocked the vacuum cleaner with a half-eaten muffin. Now, they are responsible for their own rooms and that is as much as I can hope for.

Mum offered to sit and do some of the ironing which was good, although I have a policy about ironing in my house: It's done on a strictly 'need to wear' basis. I also try not to buy things that require ironing. The main problem with this though, is that the family end up wearing predominantly cheap, stretchy and unflattering garments made of lycra and viscose – not a great plan either when combined with teenagers who struggle to perform the most basic rules of personal hygiene. Mind you, now that Flora has a boyfriend, she seems much more interested in being socially acceptable – at least in this department. So she has now happily acknowledged the existence of the humble soap and flannel. The boys on the other hand have to be marched at gunpoint into the shower and threatened with food-deprivation.

The other thing I had to do today was get my hair re-dyed at Les Cheveaux, so that I can hold my head up in public again without feeling like an extra from *Eastenders*.

By the time all the kids came in from school, I had achieved my aim with Mum's help, to have a house where you can actually see a few uncluttered surfaces, and which no longer resembles a reclamation yard for miscellaneous bric-a-brac and piles of lost property. I re-discovered several missing items too, including Flora's T shirt (which unfortunately, or not – depending on how you look at it, had been used to clean windows, and smelt strongly of Windowlene).

At around 6.30pm, Flora's boyfriend arrived, causing great excitement and curiosity. All three of her brothers suddenly appeared out of the woodwork to get a good look at him. They all grumbled 'Hi' to each other and then Flora disappeared upstairs with him to her room.

'Do you think you should let him be alone with her in her room?' asked Mum.

'Well, she's 17 …' I said in response. The thing is, I

hadn't thought about this scenario before today, but the thought of discussing the obvious consequences with Flora who could out-strop any teenager alive made me actually prefer the easier option of a possible unwanted teenage pregnancy.

'She's sensible enough to be careful,' I said to Mum, quickly touching lots of wooden things.

'Where is he then?' said Andrew when he came in from work, doing his rubbing hands and smiling routine. 'Flora, come on down!' he shouted up the stairs. After about ten minutes, Flora finally turned her music off and came downstairs, her new admirer drooping inauspiciously behind her.

'This is Gaz,' she said, introducing a person of ambiguous sexuality with a matching dog collar and black spikes through both ears.

'Hello Gaz!' said Andrew, trying to shake his hand. Gaz looked at Andrew as if he was asking him to perform some strange satanic ritual. 'Are you at school with Flora?'

'Yeah,' he said, looking sideways at Flora, who was finding the business of social interaction with her family both pointless and utterly excruciating. Andrew was not giving up though.

'What subjects are you doing?' he asked, while Flora rolled her eyes and puffed out her cheeks.

'None,' said Gaz.

'He works in the school kitchens Dad, OK! Not everyone thinks doing exams is the only thing in the universe – you're so old fashioned!'

I decided to intervene at this point, as I could see a dark cloud cast a shadow across Andrew's face. 'Let's have tea!' I said, 'Flora, please go and tell the boys to come down.'

'Gaz – that's an unusual name,' said Andrew, resuming. 'What's it short for?'

'Just Gaz,' said Gaz.

'OK, right, well Gaz, do you like toad-in-the-hole?'

'Uh?'

'It's sausages in batter. You know – don't they have it for school dinners any more?'

'Nah, it's pasta and salad and stuff like that.'

'So, Gaz,' said Andrew, pursuing a theme, 'what do you think you might do job-wise when you've finished working in the school kitchen?'

Gaz looked perplexed, and shot a glance at Flora for a possible answer.

'Dad thinks everyone should go to college Gaz, just ignore him, he's prehistoric.'

The boys all trooped in and sat down, so we all reverted to the usual scrum at meal times with Billy and Luke kicking each other under the table, Tom shovelling food in as fast as possible so he could go back to playing with his friends on X-Box, and Flora being prickly and confrontational.

'She's just really embarrassed,' I said in her defence, when they'd all left the table.

'I didn't bring her up to take up with a no-hoper like that! He's got less ambition than a suet pudding! What does she see in him?' said Andrew.

'There's no point in worrying about it,' I said. 'He's probably the first of many!' Anyway, he's just a youngster. Don't you remember what you were like when you were that age?'

Andrew scowled. 'At least I was trying to make something of myself!'

'What about when you failed your first year exams at university and went off with that girl you met on holiday in Brighton?'

Andrew was silent for a minute or two, then he changed the subject and said my hair looked nice and that he had to go and do some important work in the study.

Later, I went upstairs to get Billy to go to bed.

'Gaz is really cool,' said Billy. 'He can turn his eyelids inside out.'

'That's nice,' I said. 'How did you get on yesterday with the 'Show and Tell'?'

'Well, Ben said my conch shell was lame. He brought in a wasp's nest and a fossilised bird's claw, and Sam had a shark's tooth necklace.'

'Never mind Billy,' I said. 'I've got an idea - how about a trip to see a real mummy – you know, an Egyptian mummy?'

His eyes widened. 'Yeah, that would be brilliant. Ben

and Sam have definitely never seen a real live dead mummy!'

Thursday 17th January

I've decided that I really need to focus on saving money now I'm not working – there are lots of things I can do to be thrifty. So, for a start, I turned the heating down and put on a fleece. Then I made a list of meals I can make with the minimum amount of cooking and minimum expense. I put the washer on a 30 degree cycle instead of the usual hot wash, and hung out the previous load on the washing line instead of putting it in the tumble dryer.

'It won't dry outside today,' my Mum said, 'It's too cold and damp.'

'We'll see, I said. 'I'm trying to economise.' Then I went down to the pet shop and brought the Eco dog and cat food instead of the usual Gourmet-Mix for Pampered Pets. Then I needed to go to the chemist and get some toiletries. I resisted all the branded products and bought the Save Your Pennies range. When I got home I felt very pleased with myself. I'd already saved about £15. For lunch I made Mum a Pot Noodle.

'Did you know Mum, that if we lived on Pot Noodles for six months, I could save two thirds off my shopping bill? And I'd save on gas because there's no cooking.'

'I'm not sure I could eat one of those every day…' said Mum, looking slightly worried. 'It'll play havoc with my digestive system.'

It made me think though. I mean, all that time in the kitchen making healthy and nutritious meals would be a thing of the past – I'd have so much more time to do other things, and there'd be a lot less washing up to do so that's another saving on dishwasher tablets and electricity. There's another plus as well; the kids all love junk food so I'd be much more popular as a mother! It would be a win-win situation! What's the point in worrying about their health - when they leave home, they'll live on stuff like this anyway. After lunch, I went off down to Poundspreader to stock up on a variety of stomach-churning stodge and bumper packs of powdery biscuits and cakes. No more baking for me – no wonder our electricity bill is so enormous; the amount of cooking I have to do is probably sucking the National Grid dry.

The microwaved pizzas I gave them all for tea were a bit of a disaster though. The kids moaned that there was hardly any topping and that they were rubbery. They didn't seem to notice that they also tasted disgusting. Mum said she couldn't chew hers. Andrew retrieved the packaging from the bin and insisted on reading the list of ingredients out loud which took about ten minutes. 'There are enough chemicals in here to blow up the Houses of Parliament!'

'Well, healthy food is expensive and we need to save some money,' I said.

'I'd rather have what they're having,' Andrew said, pointing at the dog bowls. 'And another thing,' said Andrew, 'I don't know what all those piles of torn up newspaper are doing in the loo, but could someone please replace the toilet paper.'

'Yes,' said Mum, - 'it's not very good for blowing your nose on.'

Oh well, you can't win them, all. I'm determined to persevere. They ate the carob-chip muffins without too much complaining.

Friday 18th January

Jess came today and brought some left-over jam tarts which went down well. We took Mum out to the shopping centre in town and then for lunch at BHS.

'Can't we go to Le Petit Jardin?' complained Jess. I told her about my new economy drive on the catering front but she wasn't very impressed. 'Everyone in here is about 90!' she moaned. 'And it looks like an office canteen. It's all beige Formica and carpet slippers.'

'Don't exaggerate,' I said. 'Anyway, never mind the décor, tell us your news Jess. What's been happening at Paradise Bakery?' She never needs much encouragement to off-load.

'Well, Katy who does all the decorating was ill all last week with a septic toe so I had to do all the icing myself. I'm exhausted. You'd think she could have managed at least a couple of days – I mean it's only a toe for God's sake! I'm sure she could have hobbled in for a bit. Anyway, I struggled on. I'm going to be in the paper next week by the way – they're doing a special 4-page spread on local businesses in the community – I'm up for a regional award this year! If I get enough votes I could win 'Best Independent Baker'! I've told Terry that he's got to pull out all the stops now – this could be our big break!' Mum and I looked at each other. We both feel the same about Jess's husband – the poor man doesn't get a chance to breathe with Jess cracking the whip morning till night.

'Poor Terry!' we said in unison.

'What do you mean 'poor Terry'? What about poor me! It's no picnic running your own business you know Dora! You should try it now you're one of the two million unemployed.'

Feeling a sense of umbrage at this sideways swipe at my predicament, I foolishly announced that I had a new job already lined up.

'Oh, well I was going to ask you if you'd help me get the factory unit spruced up for the photos next week – Terry and I are flat out with baking and you're good at window-dressing Dora.'

'Am I?'

'Yes! You make that house of yours look amazing despite what you have to work with. You're a miracle worker Dora!'

I wasn't sure how to take this, but decided to be gracious and agreed to go and help her on Monday. She's very good at getting what she wants is my sister – always has been.

We wheeled Mum round the shops, where she bought some glitter hair slides, a pair of purple tights and a fishnet top. I am seriously concerned about her odd behaviour – Jess thinks it's just a bit of fun. 'Don't you think Mum's gone a bit funny in the head?' I asked Jess while Mum was in the disabled loo at the arcade.

'Maybe she has a bit,' said Jess, 'but we can't do anything about it if she is – I mean, she is getting on a bit now. Just humour her, Dora.'

That's all very well, but if my mother insists on wearing those things she just bought, people will think she's on an outing from Social Services.

We walked back through the park and fed the ducks on the pond. It's interesting that, although food is quite scarce at this time of year, the ducks didn't show any interest in the left-over pizza I threw in the water.

'Do ducks eat pizza?' asked Jess. The ducks swam round the doughy lumps, nudged them briefly with their beaks and swam off quickly.

'Obviously not,' I said.

Jess took Mum back to her house for the rest of the weekend and I decided to go and do the rest of the re-cycling which was getting out of control at home. I did get a bit carried away though. When I'd finished gathering together all the plastic, glass, paper and cardboard, I decided to get rid of some other things as well. It felt very cathartic rooting out old clothes, worn out shoes and books no one wanted any more. I filled up four bin-bags and went off to the local tip.

Tonight's dinner was a recipe of my own invention, and luckily there weren't too many complaints – not straight away anyway. I mashed up some tinned chick peas, lentils and beans, flavoured it with Ketchup, rolled it into balls and fried them. They went very well with a nice big pile of cabbage and a mashed swede that our neighbour gave us from his allotment.

'That was an interesting meal Dora – bit of a funny combination though,' said Andrew. By the way, have you seen my slippers anywhere - you know, the ones with a hole in the heel?'

'I can't find my *Dr Who* magazine,' said Luke. 'I know I left it on the kitchen table.'

'And I can't find my maths homework,' said Tom. 'I left it on the bookshelf yesterday.'

Then Flora joined in. 'Mum, where have you put my denim jacket with the ripped arm? I thought I'd put it in the wash, but it's not there.'

Oh dear! I suppose there was bound to be some fall-out. I looked blankly at them and feigned ignorance. However, I will no doubt be found out eventually.

Then Billy came into the kitchen and said that Cocoa and Fudge were both being sick on the lounge carpet.

'They must have eaten something,' said Andrew. This was the second time in two days that I'd had to clean up after them. 'They've never been sick before,' I said. 'They've got cast-iron stomachs.'

'I don't think the cat is very well either,' said Flora. 'He hasn't bitten me for two days and he just sleeps all the time.'

'Well it's obvious what's wrong with them isn't it!' said Andrew. 'It's that cardboard mush you've been feeding them on.'

Later on in the evening, Andrew was complaining again. 'It's freezing in the house Dora – it must be minus two at least! I can't find my old fishing sweater – you know, the blue one with the frayed collar and a hole in the elbow. It's the only thing I've got for these arctic conditions!'

'I've turned the heating down to save money,' I said. 'Our oil bill is huge. I'm following the Energy Secretary's advice to 'put another jumper on' instead of the heating.'

'That's all very fine and dandy – if I could *find* my jumper,' he said, crossly.

I suppose I can't expect them to embrace a new more frugal lifestyle without some complaining – after all, Rome wasn't built in a day.

Saturday 19th January

As it's quite cold in the house, we decided to go out for a family outing today. Traditionally, family outings are usually a hellish experience for everyone concerned, and I regret to say that today's was no exception. Since I had promised Billy that we would go and see a mummy, I suggested we all went to the British Museum and the National History Museum in London.

'Oh, brilliant!' said Luke. 'Can we go to McDonald's for lunch?'

'No, I've made a picnic,' I said.

His face contorted as if he was already being poisoned.

'Ughh, that sucks,' he said.

'Don't be silly Luke. I've made some nice sandwiches and a big Tiffin cake for everyone.'

'What's a Tiffin cake?' asked Tom.

'Cupboard sweepings mixed with chocolate,' said Flora. 'I'm not going.'

'Neither am I,' said Luke.

'You are *all* going,' said Andrew, firmly. 'It'll be fun!' I looked at him with raised eyebrows.

We eventually managed to coax our reluctant brood into the car by bribing them with sweets and some money to spend. Flora sulked all the way, Tom went to sleep, and Luke and Billy punched and kicked each other for most of the journey.

When we got there, they all wanted to do their own thing, hence defeating the purpose of a family outing, but I suppose this was inevitable. Flora wanted to go to the café, Tom and Luke wanted to see the stuffed animals and of course Billy wanted to go straight to the British Museum to see the mummies. What was left of the morning went by very quickly and we met up again for lunch at the café in the Natural History Museum. Inside, there was a special area set aside for families with their own picnic, or (according to Flora) 'sad, poor people'.

'We are not sad or poor, just temporarily disadvantaged,' I said to her.

'I saw real mummies in coffins,' said Billy, 'and a mummified cat that looked like Scratch.'

'They'll come and haunt you in the night,' said Luke, making ghost noises.

'They've got a life-size blue whale,' said Tom. 'It's awesome!'

'What have you been doing Flora?' I asked.

'Texting on her phone,' said Tom.

'Shut up scumbag,' said Flora.

'Well, it's true – you've been texting your Emo friend Gaz the whole time.'

'What's an Emo?' asked Billy.

'It's a saddo with issues,' said Tom, sniggering.

'Shut up Tom, or I'll smash your face.'

'All right, don't get your knickers in a twist.'

'I didn't want to come on this stupid outing anyway!' said Flora, scowling at Tom. She drew her finger across her throat and bared her teeth.

'For God's sake you two,' I said, exasperated.

'Flora, there must be something you like here – it's one of the world's biggest museums – it's got over 70 million exhibits!' Andrew said, equally exasperated.

This only served to annoy her more. 'I *hate* my family,' she said, and stomped off to get away from us.

'Tom, that was really unhelpful,' I said to him.

'It's not my fault she's so stressy!'

'I want to go to the Earthquake Zone,' said Luke.

'Yes – great idea, we'll swap one explosive situation for another!' said Andrew.

'It's not funny,' I said. 'What if we can't find her when it's time to leave?'

'They do sleepovers in museums now,' said Tom. 'She'll be fine.'

Later on we lost Luke for a while too, and I was just about to ask the desk to put out an announcement about a lost boy, when he turned up.

'Where have you been?' asked Andrew.

'In the Creepy-Crawlie room! Billy, you should see it – they've got tarantulas and giant cockroaches!'

I would have quite liked to see the Chinese Pottery collection and Oriental Artefacts, but Andrew went off with Tom to look at more fossils, so I had no choice but take Billy to my least favourite gallery in the whole museum. I tried not to look at most of the exhibits – after all, I have enough trouble with our own creepy-crawlies at home. Only the other day, the most enormous spider took up residence in the corner of our bedroom. Andrew named him Hercules and has been feeding him bits of bacon. I asked him to get rid of it but he said that all God's creatures have a right to a life. I didn't ask him to kill it though – just put it outside, but he said that would technically be manslaughter because he would die of cold. This was one of those late night conversations bordering on the ridiculous when everyone is tired and irrational. Actually, I think he was just trying to get his own back over the beard thing.

By the time we gathered at the museum entrance in the

late afternoon, we'd seen some amazing and mind-boggling things. I was relieved to see Flora and we made our way back to the car. On the way home, the boys gave marks out of ten for the exhibits which were: *Most Disgusting*, *Most Awesome*, and *Most Lame*. Flora sulked again because the battery on her phone was completely flat, and because she couldn't think of anything else to do. I suppose it won't be long before she leaves us and realises that we aren't the most awful parents in existence – then at least we might be appreciated retrospectively. Andrew keeps showing her prospectuses for universities abroad which is a bit unsubtle I feel.

Sunday 20th January

Jess and Terry brought Mum back today and we had Sunday Lunch together. I asked Jess if she would do a birthday cake for Flora as it's her eighteenth birthday soon. It's quite difficult to know what to do for it – she didn't want any of the things I suggested. She doesn't want a party – apparently her friend Carla tried to have one last week and no one turned up. After further questioning, I discovered that her parents had insisted on being there, so apparently that's not a party, that's a calamity. 'What about going bowling or to the cinema?' I said. Both these suggestions were spurned with equal disgust. It seems that organised trips are also unacceptable. She then had the bright idea of camping with friends in a field until I reminded her that it was January and unless she wanted to spend her eighteenth birthday in the A&E with frostbite and hyperthermia, it wasn't the best idea she'd ever had.

Then Terry had a brainwave - 'What about one of those haunted house sleepovers – there's one at Capthorpe Manor near us.' Flora's eyes lit up instantly. It was a brilliant idea.

'You're so clever, Terry!' I said. 'I'd never have thought of that!'

'Well, you like that kind of thing, don't you Flora?' said Terry.

Flora grinned for the first time in weeks. I could have kissed him. 'Terry, you are a genius!' I said.

'Don't overdo it Dora!' said Jess. 'I don't want him having any big ideas! He's got 300 Chelsea Buns to make tomorrow, and the unit to wash down for the papers coming.'

'What papers?' said Mum.

'The Citizen – they're coming to do an article and take photos of us on Tuesday.'

I don't know why, (call me psychic) but I have a bad feeling about this newspaper business. As a family, we seem to have more than our fair share of bad luck and any time we've had dealings with the local rag, something has gone wrong. The first time was when Flora was a baby and I put her in for the *Cute Baby* competition. She decided to have a purple fit instead of looking adorable and smiling so they published it a week later in the *Not so Cute* special edition. Then there was the time that Andrew was photographed outside the local courthouse with one of his clients, Barry (Slasher) McCormick and they muddled up the names. He couldn't go out in public for 3 weeks after that. The worst one though, was when they published Aunt Flo's Death Notice in the wrong section of the Classifieds. Under **Personal Services**, it said:

A hard act to follow
You were a trooper and a star
You gave it your all, dear Flo
And were the best by far

'I can't believe they did that!' said my Mum at the time. 'I told them poor Flo was with the angels now.

'They thought you meant Angel's Escort Agency,' said Jess – why didn't you say she'd died, or passed away like most people do.'

My mother has always preferred to use euphemisms and it does occasionally get her into trouble. Aunty Flo would have been delighted at the turnout to her funeral though – you've never seen so many people at St. Gregory's in one sitting.

Monday 21st January

As soon as all the kids had gone to school, the dogs had been walked and Mum provided for, I drove off down to Jess and Terry's little industrial unit on the other side of town. Paradise Bakery is squeezed rather unfortunately between a dental repair shop and a septic tank disposal firm, on a scruffy industrial estate full of pot-holes and littered with rubbish.

'Why don't you move somewhere nicer,' I asked Jess

once.

'Because it's cheap here,' said Jess.

'Actually, it's because Jess signed a 5-year lease that we can't get out of,' said Terry, much to Jess's annoyance.

Anyway, I got on with cleaning and sprucing up the outside first, with Jess directing operations of course. I must say, you do have to bite your tongue a lot when Jess is around. I'd forgotten how bossy she was. I don't know how Terry puts up with it.

For example, this is a snippet of a typical exchange -

'Terry, have you put the order in for flour yet?'

'No, I'm still doing the cleaning you asked me to do.'

'Well, hurry up – that order needs to be in by 2 o'clock. And Terry, did you use the blue or the green disinfectant?'

'Green.'

'You should have used the blue one. And Terry, can you prep the dough for the Chelsea Buns ASAP – we need to deliver them before 7.'

Terry just quietly puts up with this barrage of bossiness from Jess every day. One day, I like to imagine that he'll flip and dump a big bowl of cake mix on her head, or deliberately burn the cupcakes, or accidentally on purpose shove her into one of the massive bread ovens. I certainly was tempted myself.

There was quite a lot to do – the tarmac at the front

needed a good scrub with a soapy brush, as did the signage over the door, and all the windows. I decided to be really thorough and use some bleach on it all. I felt very pleased with myself afterwards – it all looked beautifully fresh and shiny. Inside, I arranged cakes on trays, put up posters, dressed the kitchen and counter with bunting and helped Terry make some dough.

'Dora, you don't need to help Terry,' said Jess when she came back after a delivery.

'Why not!' I said.

'Because you'll probably get it wrong – it's very tricky for a novice,' she said.

'It's Terry I feel sorry for,' I said to Mum later on. 'Why does he let her boss him about like that? She's a tyrant!'

'He obviously likes a domineering woman,' said Mum – 'you know, like Miss Whiplash.'

'Well, this is the last time I go and help her – even if she did give us a free box of Yum-Yums.'

Tuesday 22nd January

I'm going to have to give up on doing low temperature washes – everyone is complaining their clothes smell – even Billy. Andrew commented that his trousers were still damp after being on the washing line for two days and that he was in danger of developing piles if I continued with what he says is a 'ridiculous obsession' with saving money.

I suppose, given the fact that he's getting a pay-rise in March, and that I will probably be working again soon, I could capitulate. Also, I have to admit, that when mould starts growing on your sheets, it is a bit of a health hazard. Oh well, at least I won't have to listen to them all moaning about how cold it is in the house any more. I don't know – when I was young you just accepted hardships like this. There was no whinging and complaining about something as insignificant as damp socks or woodlice in the bath, or (God forbid) having to wear a vest! There were more important things to worry about. They'd be no good at surviving in hostile environments – none of them would last more than a day!

Talking about hostile environments, I had to go down to the factory unit today to get ready for the photo session. Jess was in her element of course, rushing round doing last minute titivating and barking orders at us.

'Terry,' she said, 'these buns are sub-standard – they can't be in the photos.'

'What's wrong with them?' we both said.

'They haven't got enough currants showing.'

'But no one is going to see details like that!' said Terry.

'I don't care – swap them for something else – put some muffins out instead. And Terry, your hat's on squiffy – you're not on Mary Berry's *Bake-Off*, you know. And Dora, don't wear your glasses – it doesn't give the right impression'.

'What do you mean?'

'I want *'young'*, *'exuberant'*, *'thrusting'* – you know – *'modern'* and *'dynamic'.'*

'So, that's why you didn't want Mum in the photos,' I said.

'Dora, these days you have to be business-savvy if you want to succeed. We can't be seen to be deficient in any way.'

'But I can't see without my specs.'

'Well, just take them off when the papers get here,' she said.

Honestly, I think this awards business has gone to her head a bit. Poor Terry looked quite vexed. Unfortunately, just as the newspaper people turned up, so did a lorry load of noxious and very smelly effluent from Septiclear Ltd. Jess was apoplectic.

'They promised me there would be no lorries this morning! For God's sake! How hard is it to be considerate just for once! It's not a lot to ask, is it?' She went stalking off to the office next door to try and get them to send the lorry away.

'We're trying to do the paperwork as fast as possible,' the secretary told her. I suspect Jess gave them a mouthful though, because the paperwork ended up taking twice as long as usual.

The newspaper people said it didn't matter, because they could start inside first, so we posed for the cameras holding up various combinations of baked goods on platters and baskets, smiling to order and sweating profusely under the hot lights. After an hour they'd finished and by this time the septic tank disposal lorry had gone, so they took us outside for a final photo.

'I think that went well,' said Jess. 'They seemed quite impressed didn't they?'

'I think so,' I said.

Oh well, I've done my bit to advance the fortunes of Paradise Bakery. I hope Jess is grateful.

Wednesday 23rd January

Andrew and I are feeling a little disappointed with Luke after attending his parent's evening last night. The sardine incident has of course put a dampener on things a bit and his teachers are right to be critical of his general behaviour, but we didn't quite expect there to be such a litany of mishaps and tomfoolery. We were put out to hear from his Geography teacher that Luke's answers to questions in a recent test included one on Iceland where he said it was a frozen food emporium next to Boots. He described The African Congo as a funny dance, said the Grand Canyon was a weapon of mass destruction, that the Northern Lights is a night club in Newcastle and that The Yangtze is a Chinese Take-away in town.

'He must try to be less of a clown in the classroom', his teacher solemnly told us.

It was the same story with his French teacher. Luke would be quite good at French if he applied himself, but regaling the class on a daily basis with jokes from *Allo Allo* wasn't going to advance his knowledge of the language very much, although as Monsieur Bonheur admitted, he is very funny. His chemistry teacher Miss Blunt had a similar story to tell.

'It's a shame he doesn't pay attention in class,' she said, 'because he didn't mean to set fire to Brian's hair with the Bunsen burner, he just wasn't listening properly to the safety instructions. Luckily we have a fire blanket close to hand, but it could have been so much worse – Brian's mother was quite upset that her son's nice curly hair is now a frizz-ball. Anyway, it will grow out eventually. I just hope that Luke has learned his lesson.'

The next teacher we saw was his P.E master, Mr Prosser and we hoped to have better news from him as Luke seems to enjoy most sports. However, Luke is apparently over-enthusiastic and his show-off antics have led to some unfortunate situations. Mr Prosser then proceeded to read from a list he'd made:

1. October 3rd – Luke Loveday was larking about on the beams and fell off, landing on top of Freddy Scarman, inflicting an unfortunate injury to Freddy's left ear and causing damage to school property (one tabard with torn seam).

2. October 17th – Luke Loveday was taking part in the school swimming gala when he took it upon himself to do a right turn and swim across all the lanes, causing the race to be terminated and himself to be disqualified.

3. November 7th – Luke Loveday scored 3 own-goals in the House Football match because he forgot which team he

was in.

4. November 14th – Luke Loveday threw the school rugby mascot onto the roof of the refectory at great inconvenience to the school janitor who had to hire in a special ladder long enough to climb up and get it back down.

5. November 21st - Luke Loveday, having started the cross-country race well was nowhere to be seen at the end of the course. He was discovered later to have taken a detour round by the Co-Op and was found eating a bag of toffees in the park adjacent to the school.

We stopped Mr Prosser at this point. 'I'm assuming December is no better,' said Andrew.

'Correct,' said Mr Prosser fixing us with a steely glare.

'Well, on the plus side, there is a two-week gap there with no incidents,' said Andrew.

'That was half term,' said Mr Prosser.

We said that we were very sorry Luke was not taking P.E. seriously enough and that we'd have words with him about it. I saw Mr Prosser shaking his head as we left the room.

'Let's go home, I said to Andrew, 'I don't think I want to see any more of his teachers today.'

'Yes, let's go,' said Andrew. 'I think we've got the picture.'

Of course, Luke had a plausible excuse for all the misdemeanours as I knew he would. The thing is, he doesn't mean any harm – he's a good boy really.

'You sound like one of those misguided mothers on the TV when their son is found guilty of a heinous crime,' said Andrew, when I expressed my feelings about Luke being misunderstood. 'He needs a firm hand – you're too soft,' he said.

'What do you propose we do then,' I asked him.

'Boot Camp.'

'That's a bit harsh isn't it?'

'Well you think of something then.'

'Well, we could withdraw his pocket money for a week or two…'

'I rest my case,' said Andrew.

Thursday 24th January

On the way back from taking the dogs out this morning, I stopped by the newsagents and bought a Citizen because the reporter had told me they were publishing the article today. Mum and I sat down with a cup of tea to read it. They'd done a whole half page on it which I thought was very good of them, with two big photos.

'Why does the sign say 'P IS Bake'?' Mum enquired.

'Oh dear, some of the letters appear to be missing - they've made the photos quite big haven't they!' I said, scrutinizing them.

'Dora,' she said, 'you've got your eyes all screwed up in

the photo and you're pulling a funny face.'

'Well, Jess wouldn't let me wear my glasses, so it's not my fault.'

We settled down to read the article, which was entitled:

'Paradise Bakery Rising Above the Rest' by Trudy Stoker.

Jess (47) and Terry (44) Philpot have good reason to be smiling this week, as their fledgling bakery has been nominated for a Regional Award at the Businesses of the Year Awards Evening next week in the Town Hall. Along with five other contenders, they will compete for 'Best Independent Bakers' in the South East. Despite being poorly located on Grimley's Industrial Estate next to a septic tank disposal company and Belcher's Dental Repairs, they have managed to flourish surprisingly well. Although admitting they had bitten off more than they could chew at first, they rose to the challenge and soon orders were pouring in.

"It's been an up-hill struggle," Jess told me, - "but we've fought tooth and nail for this business to stay afloat and now we're in the pipeline for an award – well, we're over-flowing with excitement!" Jess's sister Dora Loveday (45) -pictured right – said, "Yes, they've certainly had some disasters along the way but they've stuck together. The worst one was when someone found a J-cloth in a Victoria sponge – that was probably the low-point, but everyone's forgotten about that now,

thank goodness."

You can vote for Jess and Terry Philpot by telephone on: 011923 662554 or on line at www.citezanvotesforbusiness.co.uk

'Dora, did you really say that?' Mum said, sounding shocked.

'Yes, but it was off-the-record! I didn't expect them to print it!'

'Jess won't be very happy, will she?' Mum said, stating the obvious.

The blood drained from my whole head and I had to sit down. It wasn't long before the phone rang.

'You get it Mum,' I said, cowering in the kitchen.

'You'll have to speak to her,' she said. Sure enough it was Jess and she launched into a tirade instantly.

'Not only did you ruin my new sign with bleach, you had to ruin my reputation as well – I can't believe you told them about the Victoria sponge – it's taken us two years to get over that.'

'I'm really sorry Jess – Trudy Stoker said she wouldn't print it.'

'Never trust a journalist Dora – they're only interested in a good story. Anyway, I've got no chance of winning an award now after what you've done. Terry is devastated.'

'Sorry,' was all I could say and she hung up.

For the rest of the day I felt very despondent – after all, I hadn't meant to cause such a calamity. Later on, Andrew tried to comfort me.

'She'll get over it,' he said. 'Jess is Teflon-coated! Mud can't stick to her!' he joked, trying to make light of it. 'You know, there are quite a lot of similarities between you and Luke,' he pointed out. 'You meant well, I'm sure.'

'How will I ever make it up to her?' I lamented.

'Probably best to give her a wide berth at the moment,' Andrew said. 'You're Public Enemy Number One!'

Friday 25th January

I spent the morning making up a giant pot of lentil soup and a vegetable casserole for tea, plus some baking with Mum's help. We discussed Flora's imminent birthday.

'We should have a party for her – just a family one,' Mum said.

'Yes, we can have it next Friday because she's going to her Haunted House thing on Saturday night.'

'Who's she going with?' asked Mum.

'Her boyfriend and two others – it's costing us £40 each so we had to limit it.'

'That Gaz boy is a bit odd,' said Mum. 'He's got a tattoo on his chest that says 'Peas'.'

'How do you know?' I said.

'He showed me. Flora showed me hers as well.'

'What!' I said, almost shouting. 'What do you mean? Flora has a tattoo?'

'Didn't you know?'

'No! I hope hers is at least spelt correctly. What is it?' I asked, thinking the worst and imagining some grotesque sea creature plastered across her navel.

'It's a flower – on her shoulder.'

'That's bad enough,' I said, horrified at the idea of her marring her otherwise perfect young skin. 'I must say, I'm not very happy about her going out with Gaz. I wish she would find someone who's a bit more sensible, preferably with a name that doesn't give the impression the boy has limited brain function.'

'Well, she's only young – you had a few boyfriends like that Dora, before you met Andrew. Your father and I used to be very worried.'

'I don't remember,' I said, wishing I hadn't started this conversation.

'What about that boy from Watford who had an orange Mohican and wore a chain-mail vest over his bomber jacket and rode a rusty scooter – Ed wasn't it? You were besotted with him. I don't remember him being the Brainbox of Britain. And what about that lad at college you went out with called Eugene who kept ferrets and lived with his aunt over the chip shop? He wanted you to go and become an urban warrior in Bethnal Green of all places.'

Well, OK, but if Gaz is encouraging her to do things like get a tattoo – that's just unacceptable.'

'You got a nose ring and a mullet,' said Mum.

The trouble with living with your mother is that you feel like a child again. I know she's only trying to help but I was beginning to feel under fire myself. I decided to change the subject.

'We ought to go over to your house this afternoon,' I said. 'We could take your rug and lamps and check everything is OK there. I could fill the hole in the lawn so it's safe for when you go home.'

'Oooh yes, good idea,' said Mum.

Mum's house is part of a terrace flanked on both sides by troublesome neighbours. I've been trying to get her to move for years now, but she's very stubborn. On one side there's a grumpy old man called Reggie with a yappy Jack Russell Terrier and on the other side there's Mr and Mrs Frost who argue all the time and their charmless son who is 35 and still lives with them. When we got there, Reggie was out in his front garden with the dog.

'Hello Reggie,' I said. He looked at me and responded with a grunt.

'How's Tinker?' my Mother asked.

'Just the bloody same as before. What you dun ter yer leg?' he asked.

'I fell down a hole in the garden.'

'That's them blasted rabbits – if I still had my gun licence, I'd get out there an' shoot 'em.'

'Good job he hasn't,' I said to Mum when we got inside.

'He'd probably shoot you too.'

I went out into the back garden to inspect the hole. It was definitely man-made. I filled it and put the spade back in the shed. Mum had just made us a cup of tea, when the shouting started up next door.

'There they go again,' said Mum.

'Wouldn't you like to be somewhere less noisy with nice neighbours,' I said for the hundredth time.

'But I've been here for 40 years,' said Mum, as usual.

'I don't understand why she wants to stay in that house with such miserable people next door,' I said to Andrew later that evening.

'Old people get like that – they don't like change,' Andrew said.

'She could be so much happier somewhere else though – I wish we could persuade her to move.'

'It's what she's used to. Anyway, you won't change her mind about it. They get set in their ways, old people. They're not good at embracing new opportunities and trying new things. By the way, on another note, I don't like that new toothpaste you bought, or the shampoo, or that weird soap – what's happened to our usual stuff? The toothpaste tastes of Movicol, the shampoo makes my head itch and that soap has a very odd smell.'

'It's Avocado and Melon,' I said. 'I just thought that we could try some different things for a change.'

'Cheaper, you mean,' said Andrew.

'Well, OK, but what was that you were just saying about trying new things?'

'I don't think you can compare having to put up with second rate soap, to moving house!'

'Well, it's all relative,' I said.

'While we're on the subject of frugality – I'm sorry Dora, but all this vegetarian slop is giving me the trots.'

'Well, meat is very expensive Andrew.'

'I don't care. I'm having withdrawal symptoms.'

'Well, I can see you stomach has withdrawn a bit – you've lost some weight which is a good thing isn't it?'

'I'm being starved to death,' said Andrew grumpily. 'I'm not the only one complaining you know – the kids don't like it either. Billy calls it 'poo-stew'.'

'Great,' I said, imagining Mrs Pincher wagging her finger at me.

Well, no one can say I haven't tried, but all this negativity is depressing. I can see I'm going to have to re-think this whole economising thing.

Saturday 26th January

Melanie Stevens invited me over to her house for coffee this morning so I left everyone squabbling over who ate the last portion of Nutty Crunch and escaped to the less chaotic confines of Melanie and Geoff's house.

'I've been meaning to meet up for ages, but you know how it is with children and work – just impossible to find any spare time,' said Melanie when I arrived.

'I know,' I said, 'all my kids are demanding in different ways plus I've got my mother staying with me for another two weeks, plus Andrew seems to be doing a lot of long days at the moment.'

'Yes so is Geoff – I think they've got a big litigation case going on just now. How do you manage to fit in a job as well?'

'Because currently, I'm not working, thank goodness.' I said. Then I told Melanie about Suzie's offer of a part-time job at the new salon.

'God, you're brave doing that!' she said.

'Really?'

'Well yes – working with Cressida and some of those other women.'

'I must confess,' I said, 'I don't know Cressida very well.'

'Well,' said Melanie, - 'apart from looking like a corn-fed chicken with a blond wig and too much make-up, she's a bit bonkers.'

'Is she? Does Suzie know? When you say 'bonkers' – what exactly does that mean?' I asked, intrigued.

'Well, she used to run a wedding planning service with Anton at Les Cheveaux a few years ago. They used to quarrel all the time though and finally it all came to a head and they had a massive falling out. Apparently, the last straw was when Anton cancelled someone's wedding venue so his gay friends could hire it for a birthday Flamenco night. He only told Cressida a week before the wedding so the unhappy couple ended up in the skittle alley down at the Brown Jug instead of a posh function suite at the Priory Hotel. She went mad when he told her. She tipped a big bucket of iced water over his head and attacked his crown jewels with a cork screw.'

'Good grief!' I said, trying to imagine such a thing.

'Of course, that was the end of their partnership, particularly after the police came and arrested her for GBH.'

'So she's got a record then?' I said, amazed at this astonishing revelation.

'No, Anton didn't press charges in the end, but I think they came to an arrangement over the business and Anton got a bigger share.'

'What about him though – I mean wasn't he badly injured?'

'Just a couple of puncture wounds and a few ruffled feathers!' Melanie said, laughing.

'Does Suzie know about it?'

'Oh yes – she thinks it was all Anton's fault.'

'I wouldn't be so sure – Cressida looks a little scary to me.'

'Are you sure you want to go and work with those

women?' Melanie asked.

'Well, I need a job and Suzie's OK – I've known her for a long time.'

'I'm glad it's you and not me,' said Melanie. 'I think they'll be like a lot of cats in a bag, scratching each other's eyes out. Changing the subject – I saw you in the paper on Thursday with your sister. It was *meant* to be funny, wasn't it? It was hilarious! I really liked the bit about the J-cloth!'

Later on, I persuaded Tom to come with me to the common with the dogs for an hour. We don't get the chance to chat much, and of course he's fairly uncommunicative like most 16 year-old boys. I've always tried to engage my children in conversation though, even if they struggle to form coherent sentences. I think it's important to keep the lines of communication open at all times, whether they like it or not. Of course, mostly they'd rather not. Anyway Tom and I had a conversation which went like this:

'How are things at school Tom?'

'Ughh..' (shrugs)

'Is everything OK?'

'Uhugh.' (nods)

'Good. What are your mates up to this weekend?'

'Dunno.'

'Why don't you call them and arrange to do something – maybe go to the park to play football or something.'

'Mmmmm.'

'Sometimes you have to be pro-active in life Tom – you know, phone people up and ask them if they'd like to do something.'

'Uhh?'

'You are the master of your own ship Tom.'

'What?'

'Well, don't just wait around for things to happen to you, you can take charge yourself – you know, of your own destiny.'

'Mmmm.'

'Well, all I'm saying is you could be a bit more – well – dynamic.'

Tom looked at me as if I was talking in a foreign language.

'The teenage brain is a marvel of unchartered territory - even the experts can't fathom it out,' said Andrew at bedtime, - 'so how we are expected to, I don't know!'

'Well, I just worry that he seems so inarticulate.'

'What do you mean 'seems',' said Andrew. 'Anyway, there's no point in worrying about it. His pre-frontal cortex is still a work in progress. His brain will suddenly lurch into action when all the wires join up and we'll be astonished at the transformation!'

'I hope you're right. I wish I knew what was going on in

his head.'

'I'd rather remain blissfully ignorant,' said Andrew.

Sunday 27th January

'I don't want to do anything today except watch TV and chill out,' Andrew said, when he finally got up at 10 o'clock. 'I've had a killing week – you wouldn't believe this case we've got on at the moment.'

'Litigation?' I asked.

'Yes, how did you know?'

'Melanie told me.'

'Well, anyway I'm not going into it all now – suffice to say I'm fried. I need to switch off. I've got my day all planned out: Rugby, followed by football, followed by winter sports coverage, followed by *Die Hard 3*, followed by *Pulp Fiction.*'

'I see,' I said, 'so do you intend to lie on the sofa all day?'

'Yep.'

'How will you survive without food and water?'

'I'll pay the kids to wait on me.'

'Good luck with that idea,' I said, feeling fairly annoyed that he actually thought this was a perfectly reasonable way to spend his day. I mean, when do I ever get to lie around all day doing nothing but watch TV?'

'Why don't you join me?' he asked, perfectly innocently.

'Are you serious? Well, for a start there isn't one programme on your list that I would be remotely interested in, secondly – who is going to deal with all the laundry, take the dogs out, cook tonight's dinner, iron school uniforms, sort out PE kit, make packed lunches and make sure their homework is done? Thirdly – I can't just ignore the kids all day long, and lastly, I don't want to be accused of being a complete couch slug.'

'It's 'potato'.'

'I prefer 'slug'.'

'Well, suit yourself,' said Andrew.

'That's the whole point Andrew', I said, getting agitated. 'I can't suit myself, can I!'

'I hope you're not having a row,' said my mother.

'No, just a strong disagreement,' I said, - 'or rather a clash of cultures. Andrew thinks he can do as he pleases with no responsibilities, and I can't do anything I please, because I am responsible.'

'You should go on one of those all-girls holidays and get away for a bit,' said my mother.'

'That would be lovely,' I said, - 'but how could I?'

'I can look after the children,' said Mum.

'Really?'

'Yes, of course. We would manage wouldn't we Andrew?' she said, fixing him with a special look.

'Well, I must say, that's very tempting. I'll definitely

think about it.' I said, already imagining the shackles of domestic enslavement falling away from me.

I spent the rest of the day plotting and planning various possibilities. But who would I go with? That was much more difficult. Obviously, I couldn't go with Jess because she hates me at the moment. Suzie would be OK but she'd spend hours in the bathroom and would want to go shopping all the time. I thought about taking Flora, and then instantly dismissed the idea – the whole point of the holiday was to get away from the stresses and strains of family life, not take it with me. Anyway it is food for thought. I can take my time deciding what to do. I'm a bit surprised my mother offered to look after the children though – she's always avoided block bookings. I don't blame her either.

Monday 28th January

It was the usual scrimmage this morning trying to get everyone off to school without any dramas. Of course, Mondays are always harder than any other day.

Billy has become obsessed with breeding stick-insects recently because his friend Dan sells them for £2 each. He has a yogurt pot with eggs in it and is waiting for them to hatch out, so it's quite difficult to get him to abandon them every morning to go to school. Tom is always late because he can't find something essential, which is usually right under his nose. Luke seems to be a bit more on the ball at the moment and leaves on time – Tom says he's got a crush on a girl who he follows to school every day. Flora spends too long in the bathroom so is always rushing at the last minute and today was no exception.

'Mum,' she complained, 'Luke and Tom keep using my hair styling stuff – I can't find it! Why can't they get their own?' She stomped about banging doors. 'They've got my brush, my skin cleanser *and* my hair styling wax! You've got to tell them to stop taking my stuff Mum!'

I was tempted to say to her 'now you know how I feel', but I didn't. She finally banged out of the house ten minutes late.

Afterwards, I took the dogs out to meet Suzie and Ping-Pong for a walk and then to see Suzie's shop in town. The shop-fitters were very busy putting in shelving and a nice new wooden floor.

'It's coming on isn't it?' said Suzie.

'Yes, lovely!' I said, thinking that magenta and crimson is quite a strong statement.

'So, it's going to be called 'Pampers' then,' I said, seeing the pink neon sign above the door.

'Yes, it's cost an arm and a leg to get that sign done – it's custom-made of course.'

I wondered if she knew that Pampers is a well-known nappy brand.

'That's an interesting piece of artwork there,' I said, pointing at the curved pink glass counter at the front of the shop. It actually looked like a phallus, but Suzie said it was meant to be a water droplet. 'These seats are comfy,' I said sitting down on the sumptuous red velvet sofa, strewn with pink fluffy cushions.

'That's for the clients,' Suzie said. 'This is where you'll be sitting,' She showed me a high pink plastic moulded stool with hardly any seat to it.

'Where will I park my normal-sized behind?' I said, looking at it.

'Oh, you are funny Dora!' said Suzie. Come and see what we've done upstairs.'

We climbed the narrow, wrought-iron spiral staircase. I noticed Suzie kept getting her stiletto heels stuck in the fancy fretwork. The décor was equally impressive upstairs – they'd put some enormous replica Baroque mirrors on one side and there was pink and magenta floral wallpaper everywhere. A large red glass chandelier hung from the centre rose and a swirling red and pink rug filled the middle of the dark wood floor. At the three big Georgian-style windows they had put white blinds with their logo Pampers in crimson and a big motif of Eros in shocking pink. The by-line beneath said, '*Love Yourself*' in swirly writing.

'I'm very impressed Suzie! It looks amazing!'

'It's coming together,' said Suzie.

'There's quite a predominance of the colour red isn't there?' I said, daring to mention the obvious.

'It was Cressida's idea - it's supposed to imply luxury and extravagance – you know, give it an air of being a cut above the rest.'

'What are those for?' I asked, pointing at some doors on one side of the room.

'Private treatment rooms Dora – for massage and acupuncture – things like that.'

'Well,' I said when we went downstairs, 'I must say it all looks fabulous. I'm sure you'll get plenty of women wanting to come here.'

'And men,' said Suzie.

'Oh, really?'

'Yes, Cressida is very keen to encourage men as well – it's big business you know, men's grooming. They would come on separate days of course. You should send Andrew round when we're open – we could turn him into a new man!' she said.

'I don't think he could be persuaded to come to a place like this Suzie. No offence, but he's too much of a bloke.'

'Wild horses wouldn't drag me there!' said Andrew, when I suggested he'd like a make-over at Pampers.

'It's all the rage now you know,' I told him.

'I don't care. I don't want skin like a baby's bottom or my eyebrows re-shaped, or ….. what's that?' he said, looking at the list of treatments on Suzie's pamphlet.

'Oh, BSC – that's 'back, sack and crack' – you know, a Brazilian for blokes.'

'Now I've heard it all!' he said.

'They do acupuncture and massage – you could go for a de-stressing session Andrew.'

'I'd rather watch the rugby with a beer. That's my idea of de-stressing. Anyway, all these things cost a fortune – look how much it is just for a manicure – that's practically £5 per finger! I can't believe people pay for some of these things. Haven't they got better things to do?'

'Don't let Suzie hear you say that,' I said, 'she's very excited about this new business. Cressida has been pounding the streets all week handing out leaflets ready for the Grand Opening – which by the way, we are both invited to.'

'I'm busy that night,' said Andrew pulling a face.

'Well, I have to go to your office do's and listen to lawyers boring on about torts and affidavits, so you're not getting out of this Andrew. The girls will be very disappointed if you don't come.'

Andrew groaned. 'OK, but don't let them get their mitts on me – I don't want to be oiled, boiled, pricked or pummelled by some stranger lurking in a dark room.'

Tuesday 29th January

Scratch has gone missing. The children are quite upset about it – we made some posters with a photo of him last night and I went round today sticking them up on lamp posts and in shop windows. I don't think anyone could have taken him because he's not the friendliest cat you could hope to meet. He attacked the on-line delivery man once, just as he was bringing our basket of fruit and veg to the door. The man threatened to call Pest Control because Scratch bit his ankle. Another time, Scratch left a nasty claw mark on Tom's hand when Tom and Luke were arm-wrestling in the kitchen. He had a go at me once as well and nearly bit my finger off. Andrew thinks he's a bit psychotic. We could be partly to blame though, because when we got him as a kitten, a few things happened which might have affected his mental health. We should never have left him unsupervised, for instance, near that desk fan - it took us ages to get all the fur out of the mesh. I don't think falling into the bucket of Jay's fluid did him much good either, even if it was diluted. But, the worst thing that happened was when Billy accidentally flushed him down the loo and Andrew had to get the manhole cover off outside the house and fish him out of the sewerage pipe. Luckily for Scratch, there was another blockage further along the pipe because Billy had also dropped a flannel down the loo, so the flow was slow or he would have ended up at Beckton Treatment Works in the bottom of a sludge tank. I'm not quite sure what Billy thought he was doing, but he said something about potty training. He was only three at the time. Anyway the poor cat has had a traumatic kitten-hood one way and another. It would be very sad to lose him now though when we have all got used to his quirky personality. The lady in the Co-Op was very helpful and said she would tell everyone about it.

The kids went out this evening for three hours to look for him but came back empty handed.

'Never mind,' I said. 'I expect he'll turn up in a day or two. Sometimes cats go off for a bit to be by themselves.'

'What if someone's kidnapped him!' said Luke.

'What if someone's caught him for his fur,' said Flora.

'I've heard of people doing that.'

'Or homeless people if they're hungry,' said Tom.

'For goodness' sake Tom!' I said -'stop being so morbid! He's probably just gone off for a bit. I'm sure he'll come back soon.'

'If Scratch dies, can we have a proper funeral for him with a coffin and bury him with his toys like the Egyptian mummy cats?' said Billy.

'He's not dead Billy,' I said, getting annoyed with them, 'he's just lost.'

'Your cat Fudge went missing once – do you remember?' Mum said. 'She came back a week later with her tail missing.'

'Yes Mum – I don't think that's particularly helpful right now though.'

'Urghh! What happened?' Flora asked, horrified.

'We don't know but she made a good recovery. I did have to keep explaining to people she wasn't a Manx cat though.'

'What's a Manx cat?' asked Billy.

'It's a type of cat that is born without a tail,' I told him.

'Cool!' said Billy. 'I want one of those for my next pet when Scratch dies.'

'Have you checked your stick-insects today?' I asked, trying to change the subject.

'Yes and they haven't hatched yet,' said Billy. 'When they

do, I'll have 50 baby ones – that makes £100!'

'Only if they actually hatch,' said Luke.

'Of course they will,' I said, scowling at Luke.

'Well I'm just saying…'

'Well don't 'just say',' I said.

Wednesday 30ᵗʰ January

'I need to get a present for Flora,' I said to Mum this morning, 'and I don't know what to get her. It's quite difficult - I don't just want to give her money. I'd like to give her something enduring – maybe a locket or some nice earrings.'

'She wants another tattoo,' said Mum. 'That'd be enduring.'

'Well, I'm not paying for that! The trouble is, that she only likes skulls and daggers and things like that, so I'd be wasting my money on jewellery.'

'She won't be like that for ever,' said Mum. 'She'll grow out of it – you did.'

'Well perhaps I could get her something nice for later on when she's more normal.'

Then I remembered that Jess was supposed to be making a cake for Flora. 'Mum, could you speak to Jess about the cake – do you think she's still going to make it now she's fallen out with me?'

'Of course she will Dora – she won't let the fact that

you are her current worst enemy stop her from making Flora's cake.'

'Can you speak to her about it please Mum. I don't want another earful.'

'I expect she's forgotten all about it now,' said Mum.

'Not according to Trudy Stoker, the Citizen's number one reporter and all-round trouble-maker,' I said.

'What do you mean,' asked Mum.

'Well, she rang me up yesterday because apparently they're doing a piece on the dynamics of family businesses – you know, the ups and downs, pros and cons. Anyway, she interviewed Jess the day before and she told Trudy that having a sister as incompetent as me was a terrible handicap and she'd be better off with her 75-year-old mother with one leg helping.'

'She never did!' said Mum. 'What did that Stoker woman want then?'

'To know what I thought of what Jess told her.'

'I hope you told her to get lost,' said Mum.

'Not before I told her that Jess is a bossy control freak who's a victim of her own success.'

'Oh dear! Look Dora, don't you think Trudy Stoker has caused enough trouble without you adding to it? I mean, I'm not condoning what Jess said, but it's all getting a bit out of hand isn't it?'

Later, when Andrew finally rolled in very late from work, he suggested that he got his firm to slap an injunction on Trudy Stoker to stop her printing the article.

'That seems a bit over-the-top,' I said to him.

'No Dora, she's got to be stopped before she causes world war three. The woman's a first class menace. We can get her on *Defamation* and *Intent to Incite Violence Between Two Factions*. We'll get her bang to rights.' Andrew was in his element and on a roll. 'I can get it served tomorrow first thing, as soon as she arrives at the office, before she has time to slurp from her double espresso or take a drag from her first Gauloise of the day, before she has time to park her bony ass on the coffee-stained swivel, before she's blinked at her emails or checked her pigeon hole. Oh yes, she'll live to regret slur …slurring my wife,' he said, slurring, - 'in that two-bit rag of thing she calls a newspaper. How dare she defame the good name of my lovely Dora, light of my life…'

'Are you drunk?' I asked, finally realising that he was talking what's commonly known as 'utter bollocks'.

'Only a bit,' he lied.

'You had me going there for a bit,' I said.

'I meant all of it,' he said, getting undressed and threatening to trip over his trousers.

'Why were you in the pub on a week-day?'

'Celebrating.'

'What?'

'That litigation case went to court yesterday and we won.'

'Oh good,' I said. 'Scratch is still missing,' I said to him, but he'd gone to sleep and was already snoring.

Thursday 31st January

Andrew looked positively peaky this morning and said he couldn't face his usual bowl of Shreddies. I'm not surprised, after a bottle of champagne each, followed by three chasers. As far as I can gather, all they had to eat between the four of them was a bowl of peanuts and some Pork Scratchings. Still, it's good for business winning a big case like that – it all helps to cement Andrew's future at Sharp & Prentice. Andrew says they'll be in the Sunday papers as they've set a legal precedent. Although I feel very proud of his achievements, I have to admit that I am envious. There's Andrew, realizing his ambition to be a top lawyer, hobnobbing with the best legal minds in Britain, enjoying a champagne life-style in the company of glamorous and brilliant people, while I on the other hand, am cleaning out dog bowls, scrubbing toilets, collecting up an endless supply of cheesy socks, removing scummy tide-lines from the bath and wiping up spilt milk, spilt fruit juice, spilt tea, coffee, toast crumbs, cake, crisps – I'm definitely at the sharp end of this marriage.

'Mum, I've got a hole in my trousers,' said Billy, ten minutes before he was supposed to leave the house.

'Well, I haven't got time to sew it up now Billy – why didn't you tell me last night?' I looked at the hole – it was more of a large split. His spare pair was still wet on the washing line outside. The only thing to do was to put a couple of safety pins in and hope for the best.

'I need £5 for lunch today,' said Tom

'And I need £2 for the sponsored silence, Mum,' said Luke.

'Do you need anything Flora?' I asked - 'because you might as well join in.'

'Only my iPod,' she said, scowling at Tom.

'I haven't got it,' he said.

'OK – Luke then!'

'I haven't seen it!' said Luke.

After more stomping and banging, they all went off to school. Sometimes I feel as if I have run a marathon before I've even had time to eat my own breakfast.

I think I need a project to keep myself sane – something creative – something to broaden my horizons. I don't think working at Suzie and Cressida's pampering parlour is really going to help matters. Besides, it wasn't for nothing the four years of hard slog it took to get my Fine Art Degree. Or was it?

FEBRUARY

Friday 1st February

Mrs Pincher rang me today to let me know that a safety pin had become dislodged from the crotch of Billy's trousers and embedded itself in his groin. The school nurse had administered some antiseptic cream and dressed it with a Spiderman plaster, but thought I should check with our GP to see when Billy last had a tetanus jab. Mrs Pincher suggested I sew the split seam without delay to avoid further mishaps of this nature. She also suggested that if I felt unable to manage some simple sewing, there is a very good seamstress in town who does little jobs like that. My excuses fell on deaf ears of course, and she ended our conversation by saying, 'well, we're all busy people Mrs Loveday – it's a matter of managing one's time efficiently.' I bet she doesn't have any children herself, the old bag.

I tried to put it out of my mind and concentrate on Flora's birthday party. Mum and I went off out to the supermarket to buy everything and came back laden with balloons, party food, wine, paper hats, and a big Happy

Birthday banner. Terry appeared looking sheepish with Flora's birthday cake which looked fabulous – it was a number 18 covered in pink icing with shocking pink piping on a glittery pink cake stand.

'Thank you Terry,' I said. 'It looks amazing.'

'Jess did it,' said Terry.

'Well thank her for me please,' I said. 'Flora will love it!'

'Well, I'd better get off,' he said, escaping as quickly as he could.

Actually, Flora probably thought it was hideous and would have preferred a black cake piped with dripping blood or something like it.

The rest of the afternoon, I spent preparing all the food and blowing up balloons, which the dogs thought was a great game and managed to burst half of them before I could rescue them. They also ate half a plate of sausage rolls before I wrestled it off them and put them outside in the garden. I suddenly realised that I hadn't seen Mum for quite a while so I went to investigate. I found her in the bathroom with her head over the bath dying her hair blue. I'm doing this for Flora's birthday,' said Mum. 'I thought it would be fun. The only thing is, I think I've managed to dye other things as well as my hair.

'Why didn't you let me help you?' I asked.

'Because I wanted it to be a surprise,' said Mum.

'Well, it certainly is that,' I said, looking at her matching blue face, ears and neck.

Flora was unusually civilised and almost a pleasure to be with during her birthday tea. The boys stuffed themselves silly, the dogs had a ball hoovering up underneath the table and Andrew was happy because he'd come home early for a change. Flora opened her presents – a Death Metal CD from Tom, a fake dog poo from Luke, a matchbox with five stick-insect eggs from Billy, and Mum's present was the fishnet tunic, purple tights and glitter slides (*Of course! How silly of me to think she'd bought them for herself!*). Andrew and I presented her with a silver bracelet engraved with '*Happy 18th Birthday Flora, love from Mum and Dad*'. She pretended she thought this was cheesy and old fashioned, but I think she was secretly pleased.

'Nan, you know that blue dye is permanent, don't you?' Flora said.

'Oh, is it? I thought it would wash out again.'

'No, you're stuck with it until it grows out.'

'I hope I'm not going to be stuck with a blue face as well, I'm getting my plaster off next week.'

'I like it,' said Billy – 'you look like a Smurf.'

'So, Flora,' said Andrew - 'now you're 18, you are officially a grown-up! There's a whole list of things you can do, like; buy fags and alcohol, see an 18-certificate film, get a piercing, get a tattoo…'

'She's done all that,' said Tom.

'OK, well – she's allowed to vote now, and apply for a mortgage, and get married of course …'

'Yeah, you could marry Gaz,' said Tom.

'We've split up,' Flora said. 'He was two-timing me with a girl from Lower 6th.'

'Oh dear!' I said, trying to sound sympathetic. 'Never mind – plenty more fish in the sea!'

'Not like Gaz,' said Flora, looking down in the mouth.

'No, he was definitely a one-off,' said Andrew. 'But Flora, there must be some nice lads in your year at school aren't there? You know, ones with names like Richard, James, Christopher ...'

'No, they're all idiots.'

'Oh well, never mind. You've got your sleepover to look forward to tomorrow night – who have you invited?'

'Nat, Tash, Tori and Pen.'

'Are they all girls?' Andrew enquired.

'Yes Dad!' Flora said, rolling her eyes.

Later on when Andrew and I were clearing up in the kitchen, Billy appeared with his yogurt pot.

'Why aren't they hatching?' he complained.

'They're just not ready yet,' I said, looking at the hundreds of eggs. They can take months to hatch out.'

'Oh.' Billy looked crest-fallen.

'I had a stick-insect once,' Andrew said, 'but the cat ate it one day when I was at school.'

'How do you know he ate it?' said Billy.

'Because the jar had got knocked over and there were

leaves everywhere.'

'I'll make sure mine are safe,' said Billy, wandering off.

'Actually,' Andrew said, when he'd gone, - 'the cat sicked it up later.'

'Yuk! I'd rather you kept stories like that to yourself Andrew!'

'Good news about Gaz though isn't it!' said Andrew, grinning.

'Don't let Flora hear you,' I said, shushing him.

Saturday 2nd February

Jess rang Mum this morning – she was going past Mum's house yesterday and Reggie stopped her to say that Tinker keeps barking at the house all the time and he reckoned there was someone inside.

'I hope I haven't got squatters,' said Mum. 'I've only just put that nice Ikea rug down.'

'We'd better go and investigate,' I said.

When we arrived at Mum's house, Reggie saw my car and came out of his house.

'That bloody dog of mine's been barkin' like mad and trying to get under the fence to yer garden – I don't know what e's after but sommat's not right.'

'OK Reggie,' I said. 'We're going in to have a look.'

I put Mum's key in the door feeling very uneasy, but I couldn't hear anything. Anyway, we opened the door and went inside. After looking in all the rooms, we were non-the-wiser until Mum spotted something lying on the kitchen floor. It was a half-eaten rabbit – the head was still intact with its protruding eyes looking up at us in a very disconcerting way.

'It's freezing in here,' I said to Mum. 'Did you mean to leave the window open?'

'The kitchen needed airing – I opened it when we came last week. I must have forgotten to shut it when we left.'

'Well, it looks like a cat's been coming in,' I said. I was just closing the window when a cat did indeed appear at the back door. I would recognize that squeaky mewing anywhere. 'Scratch!' I said, - 'what are you doing here you silly cat!'

'He must have hitched a ride in the car when we came last week,' said Mum.

'Well, at least you're safe now – a bit thinner though. We'd better take you home and give you something nice to eat.'

'Ahhh – it's a damn cat!' said Reggie, seeing us emerge from the house with Scratch, whose tail immediately turned into a bottle-brush on seeing Tinker. Tinker yapped frantically while Scratch dug his claws into my arm and hissed violently.

'Tink don't like cats,' said Reggie. 'I've never liked 'em either – unfriendly, selfish creatures they are.'

'So are some people,' I said, unable to resist.

'Well, thank goodness for that!' I said to Mum on the

way home. 'I'd better take down all the posters and let everyone know we've got him back.'

When we got home, Andrew had just come back with Luke and Tom who'd been playing rugby. The boys were caked in mud and still had their rugby boots on in the kitchen. Andrew was oblivious of course.

'It was freezing on the pitches this morning,' said Andrew, running his hands under the hot tap. Then he saw Scratch.

'Where was he?'

'At Mum's house.'

'Oh, really?'

'We accidentally took him there last week,' said Mum, - 'but he seems fine. He had a supply of rabbits from the garden.'

Luke and Tom were tearing into a box of biscuits with their muddy hands.

'Boys – please go and get washed and changed before you contaminate the food supply,' I told them crossly. 'And take your boots off before you go upstairs, and put your kit by the washing machine, not in a trail along the hall floor, bathroom floor or bedroom floor.'

'But we're starving!' they said.

'You're always starving so you can starve for a bit longer. Go on, hurry up!'

They went off upstairs, grumbling.

'Luke scored a try,' said Andrew proudly. 'And Tom played really well too. There are some awful parents there though – they should be banned from going to matches. There was this one bloke – I think his name is Jim Scarman. Anyway, he kept shouting and swearing at the side of the pitch – it was completely inappropriate. I'm surprised Jim Prosser didn't ask him to leave. When I approached him and requested perfectly politely that he desist from his aggressive behaviour, do you know what he did?'

'No,' we all said.

'He actually threatened to have me banned from matches!'

'That's Freddy's Dad,' said Luke, coming back into the kitchen. 'He's a school governor, so old tosser Prosser won't say anything to him.'

'Don't call your teacher a 'tosser' please Luke!' I said.

'Well, you did,' said Luke – 'after the parent's evening.'

'You shouldn't have been listening!' I said, embarrassed. 'Anyway, I'm an adult and that's different.'

'Well, anyway,' said Andrew, - 'I complained about him to the school.'

'Oh no, did you?' said Luke. 'That's so embarrassing.'

'Well, I'm sorry Luke, but people like that are setting a bad example to the boys – I want you to learn to respect other people and be sportsmanlike. You've been brought up to behave like a gentleman and not go around shouting and swearing and losing your temper.'

Luke grabbed a handful of custard creams and left the kitchen looking less than happy.

Flora's friends turned up in the afternoon and they spent several hours holed up in her bedroom listening to her new CD which just sounded like several cats being strangled at once.

'What's that awful racket,' asked Mum. 'Is Scratch all right?'

'Yes, it's Flora's music,' I told her.

'I'd rather listen to the Frosts next door shouting at each other, than that.'

'I know. She's off out soon thank goodness. Andrew is taking them all up to Capthorpe Manor at 5 o'clock.'

'I hope they won't get too frightened up there tonight,' said Mum.

'Oh they'll be fine!' I said, - 'they love scaring themselves half to death at this age – Flora's been talking about it all week – she even posted on Facebook that she couldn't wait. They'll have a ball!'

Sunday 3rd February

Well, I didn't expect to have to get up in the middle of the night (3am to be precise) and be made to drive to Capthorpe Manor by a snooty receptionist. Honestly, what did she expect my reaction to be like when she'd woken me up out of a nice deep sleep. I was having a lovely dream about moving to a desert island with George Clooney.

'No, I'm not 'bloody joking',' she said. 'You must come now and fetch them.'

So I put my coat on over my pyjamas and drove down in my slippers. The girls were waiting in reception when I arrived.

'Sorry Mum,' said a tearful Flora.

'What's happened,' I asked the cross-looking receptionist behind the desk.

'They refused to stay in their room and I'm afraid they've been disturbing the other guests.'

'But our room is really haunted – we can't sleep.'

'That's the whole point!' I said. 'That's why you came!'

'But we got too scared and then she (Flora pointed at the woman behind the desk) wouldn't let us have another room.'

'We're full,' the woman said, - 'and anyway, all the rooms are equally haunted so you wouldn't have wanted another room. Basically, you didn't enjoy our 'Haunted House Experience'. We do understand that some clients are not expecting it to be quite so unsettling, but most people are very satisfied with our service. We've been voted 'Best Haunted Hotel' in a recent survey,' she said, getting quite uppity.

In the car, the girls told me that it had all been great fun until they tried to go to sleep in their room.

'Things were going bump in the night!' said Flora.

'I saw shadows moving on the wall,' said Pen.

'There was definitely someone in our room – I heard breathing,' said Tori.

'And I'm sure I heard a voice whispering,' said Nat.

'I just want to go home,' said Flora.

I fell back into bed at about 4 o'clock, and having been woken up, struggled to get back to sleep. Thank goodness I didn't have to get up early.

'Wakey, wakey! Rise and shine!' shouted Andrew at 7 o'clock in the morning.

'What?' I said, still asleep.

'It's time we made more of our free time,' said Andrew. 'We should be more active – everyone in this family needs to do more exercise. I've decided we all need to do more.'

'Well, you can do more of whatever – I'm going back to sleep. Besides, *you* didn't have to go out in the night on a rescue mission did you?'

'Oh, sorry,' said Andrew. 'They didn't like it then?'

'No.'

'OK – I'll just go out by myself – I'll take my bike out.'

I drifted off to sleep again, wondering what this sudden interest in springing out of bed early on a Sunday was all about.

Actually, it wasn't true to say the girls didn't like the haunted house because when they finally emerged from their room at lunch time, they spent a long time telling the

117

boys how incredibly scary it was and how it was definitely genuinely haunted and how they'd never, ever want to go back there again.

'Did you actually see a real live ghost?' asked Billy, enthralled.

'Not exactly, but you knew they were there. You could hear them and feel their presence,' said Flora. She'd regained her composure of course now she was back at home, and really laid it on thick.

'We had a poltergeist in our room - moving stuff around and moaning.'

'Are you sure that wasn't Mum?' said Andrew when he came back in.

'Seriously Dad – it was moving the curtains and trying to pull the duvet off me.'

'That was definitely your mother,' said Andrew.

Monday 4th February

Jess came this morning to take Mum to get her plaster off and we are friends again – well still a bit cool, but we are talking. She said that Trudy Stoker didn't publish her article in the end anyway. Apparently she upset a number of people and some of them threatened to sue her paper. She also said that my remarks about the J-cloth incident hadn't put people off voting for them and Paradise Bakery had won the award by a whisker. Terry has purchased a better quality hard-wearing sign for the front of the unit as well, so all in all, a good outcome.

I went out with the dogs to meet Suzie and Ping-Pong on our usual walk over on the common and we swapped our news.

'I need a project,' I told her - 'something to get my teeth into, like you have with Pampers.'

'What sort of project?' asked Suzie.

'That's the problem, I don't really know.'

'Well, what about something arty – that's what you're good at.'

'I think I need to learn a new skill,' I said suddenly realising that's what was holding me back - 'it's so obvious, I don't know why I didn't think of it before.'

'Probably because your life is already busy enough,' said Suzie.

'Yes, busy with drudgery – the lack of stimulation is shrinking my brain. If I don't act soon – the damage could be irreversible. Only the other day I put the milk in the oven and the car keys in the microwave.'

'Well, you have had a lot on your plate,' Suzie said.

'Now Mum's gone home, I think I'll be able to focus better.'

'What about the job at Pampers then?'

'Sorry Suzie, but I think I'll give it a miss – I'm not cut out for that sort of thing.'

Suzie looked a bit hurt but said she understood. 'You don't know what you'll be missing!' She picked up Ping-

Pong who was beginning to flag and put him in her handbag.

'I hope you'll be OK going into business with Cressida,' I said.

'Well, between you and me,' Suzie said, - 'I'm not entirely sure of her – I think she has issues.'

'Oh I know about the business with Anton,' I said.

'No, not that,' said Suzie, lowering her voice.

'What do you mean?' I asked.

'Well, there are large chunks of time in her past she can't account for.'

'Maybe she was unemployed,' I said, giving Cressida the benefit of the doubt.

'Well, she can't remember what she was doing between October 1999 and March 2004.'

'I see ….. that's curious,' I said. 'Perhaps she had some sort of accident and got amnesia.'

'Dora, you don't really think that do you? She's obviously got something to hide don't you think?'

'Well, it is a bit strange.'

'The thing is,' said Suzie, - 'she's been very good at setting up the business and we get on well together, even though I've only known her for a few months.'

'Just make sure you have a good lawyer looking after your interests.' I said.

Tuesday 5ᵗʰ February

Luke came home from school saying that Freddy Scarman told him 'my Dad's going to punch your Dad'.'

'Really?' I said, 'Why is that then?'

'Because,' said Luke, - 'Dad complained to the school and Freddy's Dad might have to go on an Anger Management Course.'

'Does he know where we live?' I asked.

'No, I don't think so – why?'

'No reason.'

I've been giving my idea of doing something new some thought and have decided to enrol on a pottery course. I saw it advertised at the local college. There weren't a lot of creative courses to choose from - it was either that, or sock puppets. Our local college doesn't offer much in the way of part-time leisure courses, although I did notice there are quite a few for beauticians and builders – sort of similar skills really when you think about it. Cressida certainly relies on a good bit of rendering and buffing up. I feel quite relieved that I've ducked out of the receptionist's job at Pampers – I imagine there will be a continuous stream of Cressidas queuing up for refurbishment and renovation. Don't get me wrong – I don't mind these women wanting an improved version of themselves – it's up to them, but equally I don't think I want to be reminded every day that I am heading down the road to Wrinkle Town myself and it's not too long a journey either. I'd rather pretend it's not happening which is probably why I haven't replaced my glasses with the stronger magnification ones which I need, and why I haven't replaced the bathroom mirror light which shorted out three weeks ago.

Andrew came home after work today and went straight out on his bike again. I'm wondering whether he's having one of those mid-life crisis experiences. He did after all, go out at the weekend and buy some lycra cycling shorts and a high-viz anti-sweat vest. When I asked him about it, he just said he's always wished he was fitter. The thing is, he's never shown the slightest interest in being healthy before now, so I'm not buying it. Melanie says she thinks it's because Sharp and Prentice have taken on two more young lawyers and our husbands are trying to impress them. Particularly, Melanie says, because one of them is a very pretty Indian girl with beautiful teeth and long sleek hair, called Shama. This news is no surprise to me, as Andrew is both easily flattered and slightly deluded. However, I think I'll put any thoughts of going on a girl's holiday to one side for a while, just as a precautionary measure.

When I mentioned what Luke had said about Jim Scarman to Andrew, he brushed it off saying that the man was a 'prat' and needed to be taught a lesson.

'All the same,' I said, - 'I don't think you want to antagonize him any further.'

'Don't worry Dora, he's all mouth and no trousers – it's just bravado because I made a fool of him.'

I can't help having a sinking feeling about this though – something tells me Andrew is being a little too complacent.

Wednesday 6th February

Andrew's parents Bob and Barbara have announced they'd like to come down at half-term to see the children. I can hardly refuse them since we virtually never go to visit them. The trouble is, the children refuse to go there. Andrew's parents are New-Age hippies, or rather old-age hippies now of course. They live in a tepee in a commune near Coventry with a bunch of other old hippies. When they first went there, Andrew had been away from home for a couple of years. They told him and his brother John that they wanted a new life away from all the trappings of a modern consumerist existence. They wanted to disassociate themselves from bourgeois values and denounce capitalism, so Bob gave up his job as a geography teacher and Barbara jacked in her job with the Civil Service. They gave everything away – the TV, computers, the phone, all electronic gadgets, washing machine, fridge, cooker, dishwasher, all their furniture and all their accumulated possessions. Interestingly, they didn't give up their favoured mode of transport – their rusty old camper van. They kept a few personal things like photos and family jewellery, and Barbara couldn't part with her collection of ceramic owls, but apart from that they kept very little.

They wanted to grow their own everything, including cannabis (which got them arrested twice). Andrew had to work quite hard to avoid them being convicted the second time. They pleaded mental impairment due to the onset of Alzheimer's, saying they'd forgotten it was illegal and were let off with a caution. How they managed to get a doctor to say they both had the same condition I don't know. Anyway, as far as I can tell, there's nothing much wrong with either of them in that department. Their lifestyle is really only possible because they sold their house and have been living off the proceeds ever since, much to Andrew and John's disgust as they watch their inheritance dwindle away. Bob and Barbara still need money to live on of course - all that organic food costs money and you can't grow avocados in an allotment, or Blue Mountain coffee beans. We went to the commune a couple of times and took our tent. The children thought it was fun at first and in the summer it's not too bad. The winters are awful though. When we went two years ago we only lasted two days. The children's hair froze to the inside of the tent in the night and Andrew's big toe only just survived the onset of frostbite. The nature of a commune is of course to help with the workload – this goes against my children's philosophy of life, which is basically to be as unhelpful and un-cooperative as possible. They also found the complete absence of technology impossible to bear. So, after two days of collecting and chopping firewood, fashioning furniture out of recycled plastic and being offered barbequed road-kill and unidentifiable soup to eat, they demanded to be taken home.

'Well, that was an interesting experience,' said Andrew, as we drove back to our lovely warm house.

'How can Nan and Grandad live like that?' Flora had asked.

'They're used to it,' said Andrew. 'They've toughened up – become accustomed to their harsh existence like mountain goats or highland cattle.'

'More like they've blunted their ability to feel the cold by smoking tons of weed and drinking Barbara's home-brewed cider,' I said (which, incidentally, tastes like fusty parsnips).

'Why do they smoke weeds?' asked Billy.

'It's a sort of medicine,' said Andrew.

So after that, the children weren't very enthusiastic about visiting them again. Luckily, Andrew's parents are quite happy to come to us. I suppose it gives them a chance to enjoy a bit of luxury for a change, although you wouldn't know it – they spend a lot of time complaining about the excesses of modern living and in particular, our lifestyle which according to them is thoroughly materialistic and appallingly wasteful. I am inclined to agree with them but they should try telling Flora she doesn't need a phone or a laptop, or an iPod, and Tom would have to have his X-box surgically removed. No, they have no idea what they're talking about. Anyway, they will be arriving next week, so I'd better sort out the spare room which will no doubt be full of chocolate wrappers, crisp packets, discarded juice bottles and spilt popcorn from when Flora's friends stayed at the weekend. Mind you, perhaps I should just leave it like that – Andrew's parents would probably see it as a foraging and recycling opportunity. It's always interesting to get a different perspective on life I suppose.

Thursday 7th February

Tom came home from school with a letter about the *Duke of Edinburgh Award Scheme* today. He will be required to undertake about fifty hours of voluntary community work. I pointed this out to Tom who of course shrugged and curled his lip.

'Well, if you want to do this, you have to do the helping people bit too,' I said. 'Don't you remember that Flora had to go and help Mrs Dodds down the road with her shopping and walk her poodle every day.'

'I'm not doing that,' said Tom suddenly becoming articulate.

'Well, you think of something then.'

He went off upstairs.

'That was a nightmare,' said Flora.

'What was?'

'Helping Mrs Dodds – don't you remember me complaining about it Mum!'

'No, not really – you complain a lot so I probably didn't notice.'

Flora scowled at me. 'It was awful – the house smelt horrible and there was rubbish everywhere – she never threw anything away!' I resisted the temptation to say 'not unlike your bedroom then Flora.'

'Well, when people get old Flora, they can't tidy up after themselves very well.'

'I'll never get like that,' said Flora.

'Talking about old people,' I said, - 'your Nan and Grandad are coming on Sunday to stay for a bit.' This went down like a lead balloon.

'Oh God! Really! Why?'

'Because they want to see their grandchildren of course!'

'Last time they came, they made us give all our pocket money to a beggar sitting by the HSBC cash machine.'

'I know, but they're only here for a few days so I'm sure we can all put up with them for a short time can't we?'

'I like it when they come,' said Billy magnanimously. 'They made a fire pit in the garden and we cooked things on it. Can we have roasted marshmallows again?'

'Yeah, that was fun,' said Luke.

'As long as we don't have to listen to Grandad singing with his guitar,' said Flora.

'It's not that bad,' I said. Bob's singing is actually quite good. Barbara's is a bit off key though. Of course any music that isn't to Flora's taste should be consigned to the dustbin according to Flora, and is doubly unacceptable if performed by members of her own family.

'Not that bad!' said Flora. 'Mum, it's terrible – it's the worst thing I've ever heard! They're so embarrassing!'

'Well, you obviously haven't heard your father singing *My Way* then,' I said, with a wry smile.

Flora looked at me with an expression of horror and revulsion.

'Oh yes Flora, you father has been known to do quite a bit of singing in the dim and distant past – at university - before you lot came along.'

Flora was plainly mortified by this revelation. 'What, do you mean - in a band?'

'Yes,' I said, - 'he was in a band called Snake-hips – they weren't very good though.'

'Oh my God Mum, you can't be serious!'

'Of course I am – ask him when he comes in.'

Andrew didn't come home until 10 o'clock this evening, which was late even by his standards. He said he had extra work on at the moment because one of the others is on holiday. It's not inconceivable that he's avoiding being at home – I mean lots of husbands are experts at dodging out of family responsibilities - anything to avoid the bickering children, irritable wives and piles of washing-up. I will confer with Melanie and see what she thinks.

Friday 8th February

I went along to college today to enrol on my pottery course. I am very excited about it and can't wait to start. It's been so long since I did anything creative, I'm not sure if I've got it in me any more. Anyway, Pat Handy (our tutor), was very encouraging and said he thought I'd take to it like a duck to water, and that with his expert guidance, I'd soon get the hang of it. He seems a very nice chap and I must say, very good-looking. No wonder his queue was the longest and he had the biggest take-up. I was lucky to get a place I think. Anyway, the course starts on next Tuesday afternoon. I am so pleased to be renewing my interest in the creative arts – my artistic sensibilities have been repressed for far too long. How did I let this happen? How did I allow my own intellectual and creative needs to slide so far down the list of priorities? Well, I'm doing something about it now, and who knows where it could lead!

In the afternoon I met Melanie in town for a coffee between stocking up on food for the five thousand, and collecting worm pills from the vets for the dogs. I asked her about this working late business and she said that they were in the pub from 7 o'clock.

'Have you heard the latest?' Melanie said.

'I don't think so ...'

'They're doing a 30-mile charity cycle ride in two weeks' time – it was Shama's idea apparently.'

'Oh, I get it – that's why Andrew's suddenly taken up cycling.'

'Snap,' said Melanie. 'Geoff has been going out four or five times a week practicing. Mind you, he's so unfit – I saw him walking his bike up the hill near our house. I don't know how he thinks he's going to manage 30 miles through the Chiltern Hills.'

'Well, the only exercise Andrew normally gets is climbing up the stairs at bed time.'

'Last night they had a planning meeting in the pub to decide on the route,' Melanie said. 'It's going to be in aid of a new rehab clinic.'

'I wonder why he hasn't mentioned it to me?' I said, feeling a bit foolish that I didn't know about it.

'Well, I only just found out,' said Melanie, - 'because my friend's daughter Maggie works in the King's Head which is where they were last night.'

'Why all the secrecy?' I asked her.

'Maybe they think we'll laugh at them.'

'Well, that's a strong possibility,' I said, laughing.

'Geoff said he hadn't told me because he thought I might try and stop him doing it since he has high blood pressure.'

'Oh, I see. Well I don't know what Andrew's excuse is but I do know that Shama is a very persuasive young woman, with some outstandingly seductive assets – if you know what I mean.'

It was the big opening night at Pampers tonight and despite Andrew's complaints about being too tired to go, I cajoled him into action and we turned up half an hour into the proceedings which seemed to be going well. There were loads of people there, including Trudy Stoker, who I spied furtively leafing through the guest list. Andrew made a beeline for Geoff where he could feel the slight benefit of safety in numbers.

'Dora darling! There you are!' Now you must come and meet Brad and Jed – Brad is into hot-stone treatments and Jed does acupuncture and aromatherapy massage – zay are so talented!' Cressida gushed as she thrust a glass of fizz into my hand and pulled me towards two extremely fit and attractive young men.

'Oh, hello,' I said, trying to avert my eyes from their bulging pectorals and finely honed biceps. Tanned, clean-shaven and freshly showered, I had to agree with Cressida - they were indeed 'talented'. I discovered they are Australians here for six months and they know Cressida from a previous business venture.

'Do you work out a lot?' I said, trying to think of something to say.

'Sure,' they said, flashing their blindingly white teeth. 'We go to the gym about four hours a day and we have a protein-based diet – it helps to build muscle strength.'

'Doesn't that get a bit tedious?'

They frowned, not understanding the question.

'I suppose the compensation for all the hard work is the end result,' I said.

'Oh, it's OK, we take laxatives for that,' they said.

'Right ......' I tried another tack: 'What do you do in your spare time?' I asked. (I could hear Flora in my head saying *that's so lame mother*.) They looked a bit blank and then one of them said they watched TV or played video games. Brad said *Zombie Killers* and *Candy Crush* were his favourites. Luckily Suzie came along at this point with someone else and I escaped.

'Those guys look like Barbie's friend Ken,' said Melanie.

'They're called Jed and Brad – from Australia,' I told her. 'They spend half their day in the gym and the other half playing games. I'm afraid they're not great conversationalists.'

'Well, they look ripped,' she said.

'What?'

'Ask Flora – it's urban slang,' said Melanie. 'I tell you what – even if they are one sausage short of a barbeque, I'll be first in the queue for a massage.'

Throughout the evening, the photographers for the Citizen snapped away and Cressida and Suzie spent a great deal of time posing with various VIP's. I noticed the mayor looking particularly pleased to be pressed up against them – being about a foot shorter. Andrew and Geoff barely shifted from the drinks table all evening so when it came time to go they were both fairly inebriated.

'Thanks so much for coming,' Suzie said, as Melanie and I guided our well-oiled husbands out onto the pavement.

'Who was that woman who looked like a cross between Joan Rivers and a piece of old string?'

'That was Cressida,' I said.

'Well, she said that Geoff looks pasty and he ought to get one of her spray tans, and that his eyebrows are out of control and need serious re-shaping,' said Andrew, sniggering.

'She said you need to lose weight and get someone other than your wife to cut your hair,' retorted Geoff.

'What a cheek,' I said – 'that's all very well for her to say, but she doesn't have to tighten her belt does she!'

'No, just everything else she's wearing!' said Andrew, and they both fell about laughing.

He went straight to sleep when we got home. He's going

to regret drinking all that champagne when he has to take the boys to rugby in the morning.

Saturday 9th February

I spent the morning getting the house ready for Andrew's parents coming, although I don't know why because they are pretty untidy and wouldn't notice. When Andrew came back at lunch time with the boys, he looked as if he'd been in a scrum himself.

'What happened to you?' I asked, grabbing a wad of kitchen paper to stem the flow of blood from his battered nose. He had a black eye, another cut on his chin and a red, swollen cheek.

'Dad was fighting!' said Luke.

'He needs to get some skills,' said Tom. 'Jim Scarman gave him a right pasting. If old Prosser hadn't come over, Dad would have been mincemeat.'

'That bloody nutter went for me!' said Andrew.

'Well you did say he was a pea-brained Neanderthal with less intellect than a chicken,' said Tom.

'He shouldn't have called me a fat, pompous twat,' said Andrew.

'But that was after you asked him how his lessons were going,' said Luke.

'Andrew! Honestly! What did I say to you about

antagonising him?' He's probably lost his place on the Board of Governors because of you.'

'Dad's been banned from all the matches,' said Tom.

'It's ridiculous,' said Andrew – 'I'm not the one who said I'd re-arrange his face for him, and I didn't throw the first punch. It's not fair!'

'Mr Prosser said that Dad and Jim Scarman were behaving like kids and setting a terrible example to the boys by not controlling their behaviour, and that they were a disgrace to their families. He said he'd never witnessed anything like it in all the years of coaching rugby …'

'Yes, yes, all right Luke,' said Andrew, - 'I think Mum's heard enough.'

I was worried about how the boys might react to their father's ridiculous behaviour and after I heard them talking about it by listening on the other side of their bedroom door, I decided it might be a good idea to talk to them about the importance of resolving issues in a non-violent way.

'Freddy's Dad nearly killed our Dad!' Luke was saying.

'Nah,' said Tom, - 'our Dad's tough – he kept getting up again didn't he – and he tried to hit him, it's just that he couldn't see out of his bashed eye.'

'But Jamie Tapper said our Dad's a loser and fights like a girl.'

'That's crap,' said Tom. 'Don't listen to him – he nearly

fainted when he saw all the blood on Dad's face!'

'Oh yeah, that was awesome!'

'Sorry,' Andrew said to me later when we went to bed.

'Well, you will be, when you have to face your clients on Monday looking like that,' I said. 'That's a real shiner!'

'I've got three days off remember – because Mum and Dad are coming.'

'That's fortuitous isn't it!' I said.

'Depends how you look at it,' said Andrew.

Sunday 10th February

Bob and Barbara have arrived, and they've brought with them a fellow hippy from the commune, called Stan.

'Don't worry Dora, he's going to sleep in the camper van. He needed a change of scene so we invited him along. You don't mind do you?' said Barbara, but this was more of a statement than a question. I looked at Andrew and said nothing. Last time they brought someone, it all ended in tears – an old lady called Jemima who plainly hadn't washed in years and didn't intend to change the habit of a lifetime just for us. We put her in the shed on a camp bed but if the wind was blowing in the wrong direction, we still had to close all the windows. Bob and Barbara thought that we were over-reacting, but even the cat avoided her. Andrew reckons his parents have lost their sense of smell from smoking so much pot. I think they've lost their senses full stop.

'What happened to you?' they both said, when they saw the state of Andrew's face.

'I had a disagreement with someone.'

'And came off the worst by the look of it,' said Barbara.

'Violence never solves anything,' piped up Bob.

'That's not what you said when you used to whack me and John with a garden cane for eating all the strawberries you'd just grown,' said Andrew.

'I don't remember,' said Bob.

'Well, I've still got the marks to prove it!'

'Would you like some tea?' I asked them quickly, before the fireworks started.

Stan stared blankly at the wall and said nothing.

'We will thanks,' said Barbara. 'Stan will have what I'm having – just black tea please.

'Stan's a bit depressed so we thought we might cheer him up a bit,' said Bob, lighting a roll-up.

'Dad, please will you smoke outside,' Andrew said, already showing signs of exasperation. We have to tell them every time.

'Oh, OK,' said Bob, and he went out into the garden, leaving a trail of a certain pungent aroma behind him.

'So what's new at Tepee Valley?' asked Andrew.

'We're being evicted Andrew – we were served with a

notice last week. Everyone's very upset.'

'Oh dear, that's bad news,' said Andrew.

'When do you have to go?' I asked, when I came back with the tea.

'In a month.'

'Cripes – where will you all go?' Andrew asked.

'We don't know, do we Stan?' Stan slurped his tea but didn't answer.

'It's had a terrible effect on Stan; we think he might be in shock,' Barbara said, patting him on the arm. 'He hasn't spoken since we got the news.'

Bob came back in from the garden. 'You could make better use of that lawn you know Andy,' said Bob.

'What do you mean?'

'It's a waste of a good space – you should put it to work – get some veg growing out there.'

'But we like our lawn.'

'Son – that amount of grass is indecent, it's typical of the sort of middle class extravagance that we dislike so much – it's wasteful. You could feed the whole family with that amount of space.'

'He's right Andrew,' said Barbara.

'Where would the children play if we got rid of it?' I said.

'On the street like we did.'

'Yes, but Dad,' said Andrew, - 'that was back in the 1950's when there was only one car and a horse and waggon in the street. Things are different now!'

'Not for the better.' Bob sat back in the big arm chair that used to be his, and looked around. 'Is that a new TV?' he said.

'Yes Dad, it is,' said Andrew. I could feel the tension building. It's always like this. I offered a plate of chocolate biscuits round, hoping to distract Bob from the usual denunciations. The kids all trooped in dutifully to say hello to their grandparents, and quickly dispersed once this was accomplished and they'd eaten enough biscuits.

'How have you been?' I asked Barbara.

'My arthritis is bad,' she said. 'I struggle to get up in the mornings these days.'

'Maybe you should think about getting a council house Mum - living in a tepee is damp and bad for your health,' said Andrew.

'Nonsense son,' said Bob. 'People have been living in them for centuries.'

'Yes, but not in England with an average rainfall of thirty inches a year. You're not a Sioux Indian Dad!' Bob got up and went to roll another fag.

'Try not to fall out with your father Andy,' said his Mum.

'Well, he's being selfish wanting to live like you do – you're not getting any younger Mum.'

'Why don't we all go for a nice walk,' I suggested. 'We could take the dogs out.'

'Don't rise to the bait,' I said to Andrew as we left the house.

'I know, but I can't help it – he's infuriating!'

Teatime was a bit of a trial. I'd made a beef stew followed by Eton Mess which the kids love.

'Just think of all that fat and sugar,' said Barbara. 'I can't eat anything like that – I can feel my arteries clogging up just looking at it.'

'Well, you can have an apple or something like that instead if you like. We don't eat this all the time you know – it was supposed to be a treat,' I said, feeling exhausted by them already.

'They've only been here for half a day – how will we get through another three days of this?' I moaned to Andrew when they'd gone to bed.

'I'm worried about the eviction,' he said. 'Just imagine if they pitch up here with all their vagrant chums.'

'Stan is a bit weird isn't he?' I said. 'Your Mum thinks he's just a bit down, but he looks mentally ill to me – I hope he stays in the van. We'll have to think of something to do with them tomorrow or we'll all go mad.'

Monday 11th February

'Mum, what's Grandad doing?' said Billy this morning. I looked out of the lounge window and saw a pile of bricks on the front lawn.

'I don't know,' I said, watching Bob disappear up the road with a Tesco shopping trolley.

'Is he going to build a house?' asked Billy – 'that'd be cool – he and Nan and Stan could live in our garden!'

I went and woke Andrew up and opened the curtains.

'What's he doing?' I said.

'I have no idea, but it looks as if he's up to his usual tricks…' Andrew said.

'I've been up for hours,' said Bob when Andrew shuffled into the kitchen still in his dressing gown.

'Yes, I heard you banging around at six o'clock this morning,' said Andrew, slightly narked. 'What are you doing Dad?'

'Well, I was looking around yesterday and saw some builders demolishing a garage down the road. They said I could have the bricks if I wanted to move them myself.'

'I bet they thought you were the best thing since sliced bread Dad - it'll save them paying any landfill tipping charges – they must have been delighted you took it off their hands,' said Andrew. 'What on earth are you going to do with it all?'

'I don't know yet – couldn't see it all going to waste though Andy – there's some good stuff there.'

'But it can't just be left there,' said Andrew, pointing at the pile of rubble now obliterating the view from our bay window.

'Don't worry Andy, I'll move them. You need to chill son – don't get so worked up about things. They won't be there for long.'

We've heard this before – several times. Last time Bob came, he found an old abandoned ambulance and towed it onto our drive where it sat for six months until Andrew paid someone to take it away. The front garden has been a depositing ground for a myriad of foraged items over the years, rescued from certain death where they would otherwise have been consigned to the crusher at the local tip. Bob has salvaged things from skips, building sites, side streets, back gardens, parks and industrial estates – things which he is certain someone will find useful. Unfortunately, none of these things have ever been any use to us, despite the fact that they end up on our little patch of grass, blocking out the light. We've had window frames, cans of paint, discarded furniture, old mattresses, bags of clothing, even a pile of brushwood which Bob thought we could use on the fire.

'But we don't have a fire,' I told him at the time.

'Well, let's have a bonfire then,' said Bob.

'Where?'

'Here!' he'd said, pointing at the huge pile of twigs in front of the house.

'But the people next door will complain,' I'd said.

That didn't stop him of course. I told him it was too near the hedge and pointed out to him that it was quite a windy day, which he totally ignored. It took us two years to get back on friendly terms with our neighbours after Bob's inferno engulfed everything within close proximity. Replacing their copper-beech hedge and mahogany swing seats complete with luxury cushions, cost us a fortune - never mind the herbaceous borders and rustic rose arbour. The fire brigade were very rude to us too, saying that we should have had more sense than to set light to a twelve foot high bonfire in a confined space, particularly when there was a stiff breeze blowing that day. They said we narrowly missed being prosecuted. Andrew was furious with his Dad and banned him from lighting any fires ever again. We gave in though last year and let him have a small fire pit in the back garden to cook on.

'We'd better go out somewhere,' I said to Andrew, - 'before Bob makes that pile any bigger.'

'We'll go down to the coast – he can't do any harm there, can he?' said Andrew.

We parked our car right by the beach. It was lovely to get out and breathe in the salty air. We'd even managed to persuade all the kids to come with us. Bob and Barbara took out a couple of bin bags from their pockets and went along the beach collecting things. This kept them busy for at least three hours. Stan refused to get out of the car though, and stayed steadfastly looking out of the window across the bay.

'He's alright,' said Barbara, - 'he just wants to sit quietly and look at the view.'

I watched him as I pottered about on the shore. He was muttering to himself and pulling at his clothes.

We went for lunch in a little café beside the harbour. The sea air had made us all ravenous but I must say, it was a little off-putting trying to eat my chilli con-carne and chips with the smell of rotting seaweed coming from Bob and Barbara's bin bags which they'd stashed under the table.

The kids spent the afternoon playing pool in the recreation centre.

'We're not going on a boring walk,' they all said in unison. The dogs on the other hand, had a fabulous time getting drenched in the sea and running on the sand. Unfortunately, Fudge found a dead seagull to roll on which made the journey home quite unpleasant. By the time we got home, everyone was frozen stiff from having to drive along with all the windows down on the motorway.

'We need a fire,' said Bob.

'No,' said Andrew quickly, - 'I'll turn up the heating.'

'Who volunteers to shampoo Fudge?' I asked - (silence). 'OK – who would like to earn £5?'

'I'll do it,' said Luke.

Bob and Barbara offered to cook tea and disappeared into the kitchen with their booty. I tried to tell them that the children probably wouldn't be very keen on that sort of sea food, but it fell on deaf ears. To be honest, I was pretty lukewarm myself. After about an hour, I went in to investigate how the culinary activities were going. When I opened the door, I was engulfed in a cloud of hot, fishy steam. Barbara was intently stirring a pot of boiled winkles and seaweed stew.

'Urgh! I'm not eating that!' said Billy.

'Gross,' said Flora.

'I had snails once in France on my exchange trip,' said Tom. 'They were disgusting.'

'I'll eat one if you give me a fiver Tom,' said Luke.

'I'm sorry Bob,' I said, 'but I did warn you they wouldn't touch those molluscs with a barge-pole.'

'Kids these days have no sense of adventure,' said Bob, disappointed. 'This is a modified version of a Rick Stein classic. You'll have some won't you?' he said to Andrew and me.

'I'm not keen Dad — sorry. Bivalves aren't my thing — especially when gathered within spitting distance of a sewage outlet pipe. I know I'm being fussy, but I think I'll give them a miss this time.'

I made everyone else egg and chips, including Stan, who shook his head vigorously when Barbara offered him a plate of green slime and a pin.

'Well, we got through our first day with them relatively unscathed,' said Andrew cheerfully, when we went to bed.

Tuesday 12th February

We were woken suddenly in the night by Flora banging on our door and shouting, 'Mum, Dad, come quickly – it's Stan…'

Andrew fell out of bed and stumbled across the carpet looking for his slippers and dressing gown.

'What the bloody hell's going on!' he said.

'It's Stan,' shouted Flora from the other side of the door. 'He's on the roof.'

'Oh, for Christ's sake!' said Andrew. 'What time is it?'

'4 o'clock,' I said, squinting at our radio alarm.

'How in God's name did he get up there!' exclaimed Andrew, shining a torch up onto the apex of the roof. Stan was sitting astride the roof and clinging to the chimney, his face white and wincing in the strong beam of light from Andrew's torch.

'Come on old chap,' said Andrew, 'you'd better come down before you do yourself a mischief.'

'He's depressed,' I said, - 'he might jump! I'm calling the fire brigade.'

By the time they arrived half the street had gathered on the pavement outside in front of our house.

'Mr and Mrs Loveday?' said the Fire Officer.

'You were quick,' said Andrew.

'Well, there's not much call for us at this hour of the night usually - plus, this is the fourth time in the last six months that the emergency services have been called to this address, so we know our way here quite well.' He surveyed the scene. 'Those bricks are obstructing access to the front of the house so we'll have to use the aerial ladder from the driveway.'

'Boys,' he signalled to his firemen. 'Someone will need to move that antiquated rust-bucket off the driveway,' we heard him say to one of the lads.

'Have you got the keys for this,' he said, pointing at the camper van. Bob and Barbara appeared in their nightclothes, backed it off the drive and parked it on the road.

Barbara shouted up to Stan and tried to talk him down. 'Come on Stan, it'll be all right you know. We'll find somewhere else to live – we could stay here for a while couldn't we, Andrew?' Barbara looked at Andrew expectantly. Andrew looked stricken. I could see a slight twitch appear at the corner of his mouth.

One by one the children came outside, having been woken up by all the noise and the flashing blue lights.

'Come on Stan, let's be having you,' the fireman was saying to him as the ladder swung up to the roof. Stan clung on to the chimney even more tightly.

'Wow,' said Luke – 'that's a really big ladder.'

'Why won't Stan get in the basket?' said Billy. 'He could fall off there like I did when Luke pushed me through the bathroom window. He might hurt himself.'

'I didn't push you, you twit,' shouted Luke. 'You wanted

to go on the roof – it's not my fault you were stupid enough to fall off.'

'Shush,' I said, - 'people are listening.

Eventually, after what felt like an eon, Stan agreed to go with the fireman and was brought down safely.

'He should see a doctor,' said the Fire Officer, - 'he's obviously got some mental health issues.' Stan was now sitting on the garden wall, wrapped in a foil blanket, looking like an oven-ready chicken. He was muttering again and shaking his head.

'We'll sort him out,' said Barbara. 'Thank you for all your help.'

'That's OK,' he said, 'but you should think about moving those bricks – they're a temptation for the local youths (he looked at Flora and Tom). Someone will lob one of those through your window if you're not careful. Another thing – someone could easily climb up that pile of bricks and gain access to the roof where they can get in through those open windows – there are a lot of burglars about you know just waiting for an opportunity like that.'

'Right, thanks – we'll do something about it tomorrow,' said Andrew, desperate for everyone to go away. 'Nothing more to see here,' he said to the gawping crowd. 'Off you go home now.'

Bob and Barbara assisted the pathetic-looking Stan into the van and everyone went back to bed, although I found it quite difficult to settle.

'I hope he doesn't try that stunt again, 'said Andrew - 'by

the way, have you seen my watch? I'm positive I left it in the bathroom this evening.'

'No I haven't. Funny you should mention that – I've lost my silver bracelet too. I don't know what I did with it.'

'What are you all going to do today?' I asked everyone over breakfast the next morning.

'There are things I need to do here,' said Andrew, 'while I've got a couple of days off. I need to mow the back lawn for a start.'

'I'll sort that out for you,' said Bob.

'Well, I've got my new class this afternoon,' I said. 'So you'll all have to fend for yourselves.'

I was a bit nervous about leaving my family with a trio of crazed old hippies for an entire afternoon – especially after last night's dramatic events. Anyway, I tried to block it all out and focus on Pat's introductory talk which was very informative and really quite inspiring. By the end of the afternoon I felt quite invigorated and Pat was very complimentary about my first attempt at a coil pot. He said it had real promise and I showed a lot of potential. He's obviously a very perceptive man and very charming with it.

When I got home, the atmosphere between Bob and Andrew was tense to say the least.

'What's the matter?' I asked Andrew.

'Look outside,' he said.

I did as he asked, and the sight which greeted my eyes

was not a happy one.

'What happened?' I asked when I saw a ploughed field instead of grass and a patio outside the kitchen window. 'Where's my garden furniture?' I said in a shocked whisper.

'Ask him!' Andrew said, pointing at Bob.

'Don't worry Dora – it's all quite safe. Barbara lent it to the builders round the corner so they can sit and have a nice cup of tea and a biscuit – as a sort of 'thank you' for the bricks.'

'Where were you when all this was going on?' I asked Andrew in an accusatory tone.

'Down at the garage getting my car windscreen replaced, because last night someone lobbed a brick through it, and in the process stole all my Bob Dylan CD's.'

'Oh, no!' I said, trying to sound sympathetic, but secretly delighted. Not because the windscreen was smashed of course, but at the thought of travelling in Andrew's car without being subjected to *Tambourine Man* for the millionth time.

'Well,' he said, 'the good news is that I've managed to get discounted replacement cd's delivered within three days, but the bad news is that my windscreen is going to take two weeks.'

'What's happened to our garden?' asked Flora, who'd been hibernating in her room all day, and finally come up for air. 'It looks like the Somme.'

'Well, you're not far off it,' said Andrew crossly. 'I nearly considered committing a homicide and burying the body out there. If nothing else, he'd make good compost.'

'Andrew, don't be like that,' said Barbara. 'Your Dad's got your best interests at heart – he wants you to be self-sufficient like us. That supermarket food is full of chemicals and additives – it will be much healthier to grow your own crops, and you've got so much space here.'

'Does this mean we have to eat more poo-stew?' asked Billy.

'I'd rather have the chemicals,' said Andrew. 'Anyway Mum, you can't tell me those winkles were healthy. They were probably radioactive – they certainly smelt like it.'

'Hey,' said Luke, - 'we can make mud slides – my friend Jake had a mud-sliding party last year. It was awesome!'

'That's the spirit Luke,' said Bob. 'I don't know why everyone's being so negative.'

'Where's Stan?' I asked, suddenly wondering where he was.

'He's been out and about today,' said Barbara. 'He's been going off on walks around the neighbourhood – he must be feeling a bit better.'

'Well, I'm glad someone feels happy,' said Andrew, 'because I don't. In the space of two days, my house looks like a demolition site. It's probably lost a third of its value overnight.'

Wednesday 13th February

'I know we should have told you about Stan and his

Kleptomania,' said Barbara, when the police brought him back to the house this morning, - 'but we were hoping the cognitive behavioural therapy he's been having had worked.'

'Would you be able to identify any of these stolen items?' asked the policeman, emptying a large grubby hold-all onto our kitchen table.

Immediately, I recognised several things, including my bracelet and Andrew's watch.

'Look – all my cd's!' said Andrew.

'Those are my shoes!' said Tom.

'That's my purse!' said Flora.

'Have you arrested him?' asked Andrew, hopefully.

'No, we haven't. We know all about Stanley Mitten – he's been half-inching stuff like this all his life. His whole family are notorious criminals. Unfortunately for Stan, he's not very good at it – he's not the full shilling you see. We try to avoid arresting the poor bugger if we can.'

'I'm going out on my bike,' said Andrew, when the police had gone. 'I need to get away from this mad house for a bit.'

Great, I thought – someone has to stay and hold the fort and that'll be me of course!

'What's he doing in all that fancy gear?' asked Bob when he saw Andrew's new cycling clobber. I explained about the charity cycle ride and saw Bob's face contorting. I'd opened a can of worms.

'Charities should be outlawed,' said Bob, getting on his political soapbox. 'They're the product of a capitalist system which refuses to take responsibility for its people and their needs. Charity is the scourge of our modern world Dora – if there was no such thing, governments would be forced to spread the wealth and give it to those who need it most.'

I should have seen this one coming – it was only last summer that there was a bit of an embarrassing scene at the school fete, over whether Andrew should have put £2.50 in a charity collection box for *Rescue A Hedgehog*, or not. The worst thing about it was trying to explain it to Billy, who thought that his Grandad was mean and horrible.

'Grandad thinks that other people should look after the ill hedgehogs,' we said, - 'and not us.'

'Why?' asked Billy.

'Because the other people have got more money than us and can look after them better.'

'Then why don't they?' said Billy.

'Because they want to spend their money on other things.'

'Don't they like hedgehogs?'

'No, Billy.'

'That's stupid,' said Billy.

While Andrew was out, I tried to get Bob to understand how important my patio was to my general well-being and that it would be a shame if his camper van met the same fate. You can get quite good money for those old VW vans – there are a lot of people out there who would be very happy to collect the same day as well. I think Bob got the gist of what I was saying because he decided to enlist Stan's help and re-construct my patio forthwith. Unfortunately, the grass cannot be so easily restored – the lawn had been scattered liberally with bald patches, mainly due to football games, so there is no thick, luscious turf to roll back onto the dug-up garden.

'We'll have to either re-seed it, or fork out for turf,' said Andrew when he reappeared. 'Well, at least we don't have to entertain them this afternoon – it'll take Dad all day to re-do the patio.'

I decided to take Barbara and the boys out to the park after lunch and give the dogs a good run. It was cold but sunny, and spring was definitely in the air. Flora had refused to come of course – parks are for old people and babies according to her. The boys took their football and had a good kick around. Barbara and I sauntered over to the duck pond while the dogs chased each other into the water, scaring the ducks.

'Look,' said Barbara, - 'someone's been throwing pizza in there! That's just terrible!' She tutted disapprovingly. 'Honestly, some people haven't got a clue - they're completely divorced from the natural world.' I nodded in agreement. *How could that pizza have lasted so long in the water? It was astonishing – you'd think it would have disintegrated by now.*

'People are poisoning the world around them,' continued Barbara, - 'they are ignorant and selfish and need educating.'

'Yes,' I said, - 'I couldn't agree more. What's going to happen about Tepee Valley?' I asked, quickly changing the subject.

'Well, Stan says he's got a friend out on the Costa del Sol who's got a villa that's empty at the moment. He says we could go out and stay there for a while. We thought it might be quite a nice little break. The weather will be better for my health. Bob says you can grow oranges and lemons there.'

'That sounds like a great idea!' I said, delighted at the prospect of them moving far enough away for it to be unfeasible to visit. I wondered what the locals there would make of them.

'There are a lot of ex-pats out there,' said Barbara, - 'so we will be in a commune of sorts.'

'Ex-cons more like,' said Andrew, when we were getting the dinner ready in the kitchen. 'They'll probably all get along like a house on fire,' he said, smirking.

'You're in a good mood this evening,' I said.

'Well,' he said, - 'they're leaving tomorrow, the patio is almost back to how it was before Dad re-arranged it, and I've found a home for the brick mountain – but don't tell Dad.'

Thursday 14th February

We waved our visitors off this morning with slightly more enthusiasm than is politely acceptable, but it was a great relief to see them go.

'Thank God for that!' Andrew and I said to each other.

'Why?' said Billy.

'Because they are what you call high maintenance guests,' Andrew said. Billy looked blank.

'People who require a lot of looking after,' I said.

'Like the hedgehogs?' asked Billy.

'No, not really – they can take care of themselves – it's just that your grandparents manage to cause a lot of trouble wherever they go. A bit like you lot,' I said.

'The difference is,' said Andrew, 'that you are children and we expect a certain amount of hassle from you – although less would be good.'

'When are they coming back?' asked Luke. 'I like it when they're here – it's fun.'

'Well, I think there's been enough excitement for a bit. We don't know when they'll be back. They might be going to live in Spain for a while.'

'Cool,' said Luke. 'Can we visit them there?'

'We'll see,' I said, envisaging nothing but nightmare scenarios. God knows what Stan's been up to in the past. I imagined a dark underworld of seriously scary people all living together on a dry, rocky outcrop on the Spanish coast with nothing to do except drink too much sangria, and gamble their ill-gotten gains away. Andrew's parents would hate it – living amongst all those dodgy criminals and retired office workers. Where would they erect their tepee? Anyway, they'll hate the heat – it's boiling in summer. Oh well, I certainly won't be trying to stop them from going - I just hope they realise that Stan probably has some very unsavoury friends and they should watch their backs.

Today's date didn't go unnoticed – well not by me anyway. When the postman came, both Flora and Tom hovered around by the front door to see if there was anything for them. Luckily, they each had a card but no one was allowed to see what they'd been sent. Andrew and I have long since stopped bothering – the last time he gave me anything on Valentine's Day was in 1996, just after Flora was born. We both agree that we don't need to indulge in big romantic gestures – after all, we have been together for a long time. However, although I did agree with him that it is a ridiculous lot of commercially cynical nonsense, I can't help feeling slightly miffed that the pragmatic, undemonstrative side of his character seems to have taken him over completely. I wish he'd make a bit of an effort sometimes.

Andrew went off to work and I decided to take Luke and Billy swimming at our local pool. Flora has lost interest in most physical activities unless it involves the opposite sex, and Tom will only play football or have the occasional wrestling match with Andrew over who's in charge of the TV remote. Luke and Billy are still young enough to enjoy playing in the water and I need to do any exercise I can at the moment, before Suzie starts suggesting that I sign up for the body-wrap and vacuum massage sessions they are offering at the salon for rapid weight loss.

At the pool, the boys and I went our separate ways. I

gave them strict instructions not to go in until I came out – Billy can vaguely swim with a sort of flailing thrashing stroke but it's not reliable. Unfortunately, when I got to the female changing rooms, I realised with horror that I'd brought Flora's swimwear instead of my own. I weighed up the pros and cons of wearing something that was two sizes too small and made me look both sadly deluded, and completely lacking in self-awareness. I decided (against my better judgement), to go ahead and squeeze into it rather than ditch the swimming plan and go and sit in the spectator's gallery – mainly because I needed to watch Billy closely. With hindsight, staying out of the water would have been a much better idea. *If I get into the water quickly, I thought, no one will really notice that I look like a jelly in a sieve. Anyway, I probably won't see anyone I know.* Then, just as I was stuffing my clothes into my locker, I heard someone shout my name.

'Dora!' said the voice, - 'fancy seeing you here!' It was Justine, Suzie's friend, looking tanned and beautiful in a white one-piece.

'Oh, hello,' I said, regretting my rashness instantly.

'The water's lovely – but I'm just getting out – facial appointment.'

'Oh good – I mean great that the water's good – my boys will be waiting – I'd better go. See you.' I virtually ran round the corner to get away from what she was probably thinking, but didn't say. Unfortunately, my boys don't have any such inhibitions and certainly like to call a spade a 'spade'.

'Mum! Why are you wearing Flora's bikini?' said Luke. 'It's tiny!'

'You look like a hippolotomas,' said Billy.

'It's Hippopotamus!' said Luke, really loudly.

'Thanks,' I said, - 'just go and play please.' I plunged in quickly before people started looking at me pityingly or worse, pretending not to look.

'Stay in the shallow end,' I told them both. I felt protected by the water once I was in and did a few lengths before having a rest at the side. There are always a few keen ones ploughing up and down the lanes – making people like me feel like a lost cause, and today was no exception. As I watched them, I realised that one of them was Pat Handy. There he was, coursing through the water like a knife through butter! What a powerful front crawl and such stylish movement! I wonder if people are born with that kind of self-assured panache, or whether it's something you can learn. If only I was young and single again, I thought, wistfully. Just my bad luck though! Of all the people I least wanted to bump into right now, it would have to be him, looking all toned and tanned and sporting a very nifty pair of bathing trunks. I decided I would have to make a quick exit when he was swimming in the opposite direction. I waited until he turned and made for the steps at the side of the pool.

Suddenly I heard Luke shouting, 'Mum, Mum, come quickly – it's Billy!' I'd been so busy admiring Pat's progress through the water that I'd forgotten to keep an eye on my children. I lunged up the steps and as I ran down the side of the pool, I saw Pat swim across the lanes at speed, scoop Billy up and lift him heroically out of the pool – the lifeguards were crowded round him so I couldn't see anything until I got there. Thankfully he was alive. He was spluttering and coughing, and slightly blue, but definitely alive.

'This gentleman just saved your son from drowning,' said one of the lifeguards. 'What was your boy doing up here in the deep end though? He obviously can't swim properly.' He looked at me with measured disdain.

'Dora, is that you?' said Pat. 'I'm sorry – I didn't recognise you!'

I did momentarily toy with the idea of saying 'no' and that I had a twin sister called Dora. 'Yes, it's me,' I said, weakly.

The lifeguard was still looking at me crossly. 'I did tell him not to go in the deep end, didn't I Billy!' I said, but he was still coughing and couldn't answer. 'Thank you Pat – I don't know what to say – except that I am very grateful of course.'

'No worries – glad to have helped. See you on Tuesday - great bikini by the way!' He winked, waved, and swam off.

'You should probably cover yourself up Madam,' said the cross lifeguard, handing me a polystyrene float and indicating with his eyes that something was amiss. I looked down and realised with horrific clarity exactly what he meant.

'Well at least it wasn't the bottom half that came adrift,' said Andrew, in an effort to alleviate the pain.

'I can never go back there again,' I said, in a trembling voice. 'I feel so humiliated …. I'm a laughing stock!'

'It'll all blow over in time,' said Andrew. 'No one will remember you in a few weeks.'

'That's what you said about Slasher McCormick, but people still give you funny looks. And people always remember things like boobs making a public appearance – who could forget poor old Judy Finnigan.'

'Look, you just have to put it out of your mind Dora – there's nothing you can do about it. Anyway, you're not a public figure – who cares that you flashed your knockers at a few old geezers – it's not going to be on national TV is it!'

Friday 15th February

I decided to keep a low profile today after yesterday's disastrous episode. Anyway, I had to stay around at home for the pick-up truck that was coming to collect the bricks. We promised the boys if they helped, we'd pay them. I don't know what Andrew's doing with them, but I'll be glad to see them go. I'll be able to see across the road again, and people won't keep asking if we're having building work done. Flora came with me to walk the dogs on the common in the afternoon. This is a very rare occurrence – she doesn't like to use up too much of her energy on things low on her priority list, in case she needs it for something more important. I've tried to explain to her that the more you do, the more energy you have. 'It's like charging your phone,' I tell her – 'active bodies make active brains'. She doesn't believe me of course.

'If that was true,' she says, 'then what about Stephen Hawking? He can't even move his eyelids and he's a genius.'

Well, I can't argue with that can I?

'So,' I said to Flora, as we followed the dogs down to the river, -'how's the revising going?'

'OK.'

'Not long now till the exams is it?' I said.

'Yes, I know,' said Flora, irritably.

Flora's idea of revising is to wait until the last minute, panic, and then stay up all night cramming. Apparently that's what Andrew did. He foolishly let this slip once in Flora's hearing so she now uses this piece of invaluable information as justification for her own approach to studying.

'Do you still want to do Criminology?' I asked, suspecting that she'd probably changed her mind again. She's gone from English Lit (which she has a place for if she gets the grades) to Philosophy, to Brewing and Distilling, to Circus Skills, to Criminology.

'I don't know – I might just get a job instead. I'm bored with learning stuff.'

'OK,' I said, trying to stay calm. 'It's a good idea to try your best though isn't it? And then you can decide later, once you've got your exam results.'

'God, Mum! You and Dad are so *Bourgeois!*'

'Do you even know what that is?' I asked her, feeling my hackles rising.

'Grandad said it,' she said.

'Oh I knew that,' I said. 'Some of Grandad's ideas are not very practical,' I said, trying not to have a row.

'You'll miss all the fun of student life if you decide not to go to university. Think of all the parties and great social life – it's not just about learning things you know!'

'Gaz says you can go to college here and learn things like cooking. He's doing baking – I wouldn't mind doing that.'

'Is he back on the scene then?' I asked, knowing the likely answer.

'Maybe,' Flora said, in an off-hand way. I stopped myself from saying anything derogatory either about the disappointing re-appearance of Gaz, or about Flora's cooking. As far as I know, Flora has never cooked anything apart from some scrambled eggs once and she burnt the pan so badly I had to chuck it out.

'You could try doing some cooking at home,' I said, - 'that would be good practice.'

Flora looked at me in disbelief. 'Why would I do that?'

'Because if you think cooking might be a potential career choice, you might want to actually have a go at it …'

'Our kitchen is useless for cooking,' she said. 'At the college where Gaz goes, they've got a proper professional kitchen with all the proper stuff.'

The thing is, Flora has veered dramatically from one idea to the next, depending on who she last spoke to – or (as is currently the case), whoever her latest boyfriend happens to be.

'You mustn't be influenced by other people,' I said. 'You've got to think about what you want to do yourself.'

'Well, you and Dad try to influence me don't you?'

'Well, I know, but that's different.'

'No it isn't.'

'Yes it is.'

We walked in silence for a while.

'Have you thought about having a Gap Year Flora?' I said, after a bit. 'You could spend a year working while you decide what you want to do – you'd be able to save up some money.'

'Yeah, maybe. Or I could go travelling – that'd be cool,' she said, looking more animated.

Later, I tried to discuss Flora with Andrew.

'What do you mean a 'Gap Year'!' he exclaimed. 'You do realise what that might mean don't you Dora – she'll be here for another whole year!'

'She did say she'd like to go travelling,' I said, in an attempt to placate him.

'That'll last about three days,' said Andrew. 'She'll be back here as soon as she realises that travelling involves some unpalatable things, like: uncomfortable beds in dodgy places, frequent food poisoning, catching obscure infections, having to wait around for hours for buses, trains, and boats, and meeting lots of weird people who want to be your new best friend.'

'Speak for yourself Andrew,' I said, -'you're so cynical! Anyway what do you mean 'infections'?'

'Oh just something that happened years ago,' he said, brushing it off.

Andrew has never liked roughing it, so his experience of student travelling is bound to be biased. Even camping for one night is something to be endured rather than enjoyed.

'If you'd grown up with my parents, you'd understand,' he says quite often.

'Well, don't discourage her,' I said. 'She needs to find out for herself.'

Saturday 16th February

'Social networking is the way to go,' said Jess, as we sat and had coffee in her kitchen this morning. 'I've been beavering away to get our business advertised as effectively as possible – it's not easy with all the competition around. What we need is something to catch people's attention – you know, make them sit up and take notice.' She had her laptop open on the table. 'Look at this for instance,' she said. 'This YouTube video's gone viral – some ridiculous woman whose bikini top 'accidentally' came off is suddenly one of the most watched videos on YouTube overnight! I mean, how daft is that?! If only I could think of something that would get Paradise Bakery noticed like that – we'd be laughing!'

'Let me see that,' I said, almost choking on my croissant. 'Oh my God!' I gasped.

'It's not that shocking is it?' said Jess. 'I mean – you've

seen plenty of sagging breasts before – just be glad they're not yours!' she laughed.

Thank Goodness no one can see my face, I thought. Someone's fat arm is obscuring it. Good grief, that was a close call - and luckily, no sign of Luke or Billy on it. Whoever filmed it focused the camera very precisely.

'You've gone red in the face Dora,' said Jess, – 'are you OK?'

'Oh yes, I think I might be a bit menopausal – I've been getting hot flushes recently.'

'Really Dora! That's come on suddenly.'

'Yes, I know. I could do with a bit of air – I'll just go outside for a minute or two.'

'Where's Dad,' asked Tom when I got back home.

'On his charity cycle ride – he went off at 6 o'clock this morning.'

'It's raining though,' said Tom.

'He'll be fine. He's got all the latest hi-tech gear. We can go and watch his progress later – I've got the route here.' I showed Tom the map.

I am quite amazed that Andrew actually agreed to do this charity thing. Shama has obviously got them all wrapped around her little finger. It's quite funny really – all the boys in the office flexing their muscles and showing off to her, but they're living in Cloud Cuckoo Land - they're all at least twice her age, and none of them could be described as 'a catch'– not these days anyway. When I think back to Andrew's younger self, it's remarkable how much a person can change physically in such a short time. When I showed Flora a picture of Andrew in his band at University the other day, she couldn't believe it was him.

'But he's got long black hair Mum, and he's skinny!'

'People change,' I said, - 'sadly'.

'Is that you?' she said, pointing at the person right on the edge of the photo.

'Oh, umm, yes – I've never noticed that before.'

'Mum, you look like a bloke – is that a mullet? God Mum – that is *such* a bad hairstyle – and what *are* you wearing! I've got to show this to Gaz – it's insane!'

'For your information, that metallic spandex cat-suit was very trendy at the time,' I said, feeling slightly miffed that my former self was being so vehemently ridiculed. 'Those emerald green platform boots were my pride and joy – my girlfriends were always trying to borrow them.'

'David Bowie has a lot to answer for,' said Flora.

After lunch we all got in the car and set off in the rain to look for the cyclists. Melanie said she'd meet me at the finish where they were doing refreshments but the children wanted to see where he was in the pack first. It took us about an hour to find the end of the trail of cyclists and I was pleased to see that Andrew wasn't bringing up the rear. We drove slowly along, trying to spot him.

'I can't see him,' said Luke.

'Maybe he fell off,' said Tom.

'He could be at the front,' said Billy hopefully.

'No,' we all said in unison, - 'that would never happen.'

We carried on past them all, battling uphill in the rain. There was no sign of Andrew. I parked up at the finishing post, 7 miles on, where there was a village hall and lots of people milling about. Melanie waved at me to come across to the hall.

'He's in here,' she said. 'Don't worry, he's fine.'

'What happened to you?' I asked him. He was sitting on a rubber ring looking miserable and dripping wet. The children all followed me in, hoping for biscuits and squash.

'Is Daddy going swimming?' asked Billy, when he saw him.

'No, I don't think so,' I said, trying not to laugh.

'Geoff didn't last past the first post either,' said Melanie. 'He got a puncture.'

'Why are you sitting on that weird cushion?' said Flora.

'Can we go home?' asked Andrew mournfully. 'I need to get out of these shorts.'

Shama came over as Andrew got up. She looked immaculate and sleek in her black shiny Lycra and matching hydro-pack.

'Shama came 5th,' said Andrew.

'Wow,' I said, trying to sound enthusiastic, - 'that's really good.'

'Thanks,' she said, her long dark ponytail swinging jauntily. 'I'm so sorry about Andrew – I've heard saddle sores can be very painful. Sudocrem is very good, apparently.' She smiled, flashing her whiter than white teeth and disappeared.

'I feel so humiliated,' said Andrew, as I applied antiseptic healing cream to his very raw looking posterior later that evening. 'Now I've got to face everyone at work and I'll never live it down.'

'Never mind,' I said. 'People soon forget these things – today's news is tomorrow's fish and chip paper – it'll all blow over – it's not as if it's going to be on national TV is it!' I said, savouring the moment.

'Do you have to rub it in so hard?' said Andrew, wincing.

Sunday 17th February

Thank Goodness the kids are back at school tomorrow. It's always such hard work having them all at home together and they eat so much food – they even cleared out some stale Tiffin that'd been hanging around for at least a fortnight. I decided to go to the supermarket to replenish supplies. Andrew's stayed at home nursing his chaffed behind while the kids tormented him.

'Is it a pain in the arse Dad?' asked Tom, - 'that's a bummer!'

'Leave your poor old Dad alone,' I said.

'Hey – leave out the 'old' part please!' said Andrew.

'I'll get you some of those padded pants while I'm out,' I said.

'Thanks,' said Andrew. 'You really know how to make a man feel special.'

In the supermarket, I pushed my trolley round in a kind of trance-like state. There's something about the lighting and the overwhelming selection of products that sends me into a sort of catalepsy. It was while I was in the vegetable section trying to decide between curly kale and purple sprouting, that I was suddenly aware of someone shouting at me.

'Hey, you – you're Luke Loveday's Mum aren't you?'

I looked up to see a stocky, balding man with a round red face and piercing blue eyes. He didn't look happy.

'If I find out it was your husband that dumped those bricks in my driveway, I swear I'll kill him!' said Jim Scarman, waving his forefinger at me.

'Why would he do that?' I said.

'Because he's a bloody idiot, that's why!'

'Hang on a minute,' I said, - 'you're lucky I didn't call the police after you hit my husband the other week – he's still got a fat lip.'

'Oh, yeah? Well he started it, and as far as I can see, it runs in the family.'

'I beg your pardon,' I said, getting irate now. 'What do you mean by that?'

'Your son Luke – he attacked my son.'

'What are you talking about?'

'He jumped on him in PE – ripped his clothes and nearly tore his ear right off! He's out of control, just like his Dad.'

'How dare you!' I shouted. 'Luke fell – it was an accident – he didn't mean to hurt Freddy!'

At this point an assistant marched up and told us take it outside or go our separate ways.

'Don't forget,' were Jim's parting words as he exited past the parsnips, - 'you tell him from me!'

I did the rest of the shopping in a state of perplexed agitation and went home two hours later with only half the things I needed.

'What's for tea?' asked Andrew when I got back.

'For you: Nothing!' I said, fixing him with an evil stare.

'What's the matter?'

'Bricks!'

'Oh that,' said Andrew.

'Yes – that!' I said. 'What were you thinking? I've just been verbally abused by that horrible man because he suspects you!'

'He can't prove anything,' said Andrew.

'I don't think it'll be that difficult for him Andrew! Everyone in our street saw it all in our garden! It wasn't exactly a big secret was it! Of course he'll know it was you.'

'So what if he does,' said Andrew, - 'he can't do anything about it.'

There must be a law about dumping stuff on people's driveways,' I said, - 'and anyway, he says he's going to kill you.'

'Well, that puts a slightly different perspective on things,' said Andrew, with less bravado.

'If he does,' I said unsympathetically, - 'you've only got yourself to blame.'

When I confided in Melanie on the telephone later, she suggested that Andrew ought to be careful because if he did anything illegal, he could be struck off.

'Sometimes, I feel as if I have no control over my life at all,' I said to her. 'It's as if I'm being tossed about like a rubber ball.'

'I know the feeling,' said Melanie, but she didn't

elaborate. I don't think she does know really – I mean she isn't married to an impetuous fool is she? Geoff doesn't go around inciting violence and behaving like a complete prick - and I bet his parents are normal people who stay in and watch TV. Melanie and Geoff were sensible enough to stick to two children, and their only pet is a goldfish called Frank. But it's too late now – I've 'made my bed' as they say. I wondered how I'd feel if Andrew got murdered, and later, as I drifted off to sleep, I speculated about how long one should respectfully wait until it would be acceptable to re-marry. Pat Handy's face swam in front of my eyes – a sainted vision of male perfection with his flawless personality and unrivalled good looks. I fell asleep and my dream was of unparalleled bliss – my life transformed in an instant as I shunned my responsibilities without remorse.

Monday 18th February

Andrew went off to work this morning with a face like a beaten spaniel, and walked with a pronounced limp to his car. I heard him groan as he sat down in the driver's seat and despite these recent shenanigans, I did feel a bit sorry for him. The kids were all late leaving the house – our usual practice on the first day of term, and most other days truth be told. It's so difficult motivating four individual personalities at once – maybe I should employ someone else to do it. Personal Trainers are not cheap though, and I think they only have one or two victims at once, not four. Perhaps I'm the one who needs a trainer – I could benefit from someone motivating me – I mean, sometimes life can seem a bit depressing. I know one should try to be positive but at the moment I must say, the negatives seem to be out-weighing the positives.

I decided to go and see Suzie after breakfast and walk the dogs with Ping-Pong. Suzie, if nothing else, is a vibrant, happy sole and she does have a good effect on me. Of course it's easy to be positive, when your monthly clothes budget is about the same as Andrew's entire year's salary, and you never have to hoover behind the sofa or scrape a casserole dish clean.

We met at her house and as I waited for her to emerge, I noticed that she'd had her front garden re-configured for the third time in a year.

'I like your new look,' I said, when she stepped outside.

'Oh thanks – I just bought this last week – it's Armani.'

'No! Not your jacket Suzie - the garden!'

'Oh yes, it's good isn't it! The boys from the salon came and did a marvellous job – you've met Jed and Brad haven't you? Come and see this new addition.' She pointed out a mound of earth and randomly placed stones.

'Ah – a rock garden,' I said, hoping this was a correct assertion.

'Isn't it wonderful!' said Suzie. 'We haven't put the plants in yet, but it's going to be in the style of a Japanese Zen garden – it'll be great when it's finished.'

'Yes, I'm sure it will,' I said, as Cocoa ran across and peed copiously on the rocks. Luckily Suzie wasn't looking.

'I didn't know those two did gardening,' I said, surprised that they would have even the faintest idea what a weed was.

'Well, they don't really – I just get them to do all the hard graft.'

'Oh, of course,' I said.

'This is my new water feature,' she said, as we followed the path round towards the gate. I hadn't noticed it before as the view from the drive was obscured by last year's topiary extravaganza. A large stone statue of Eros was squirting water from his elevated foot. It sprayed upwards in an arc, enveloping the figure on its way back down with a fine curtain of water which fell back into the little pool he stood in.

'Very impressive,' I said, 'but why is he painted pink?'

'It was Melanie's idea – a reference to Pampers – I wasn't sure at first. It's a bit bonkers.'

'You can say that again,' I said, raising my eyebrows. 'It's fairly spectacular isn't it? What does Warren think of it?'

'He hasn't seen it – he's away in Singapore for a month,' she said, grinning.

'Well, I suppose it's lovely to have the odd decorative objet d'art in the garden – makes it more fun doesn't it!'

'Do you mean this, or the boys?' She said, laughing.

'Ideally, both!' I said. 'Maybe I should get them to come and sort my garden out. I could do with a nice view from my kitchen window.'

We headed off down the road. I already felt my spirits improving in Suzie's company, until we turned the corner towards the end of the estate where she lived, and the sight of someone else's front garden made my heart sink again. Suzie was chattering away about the salon and she noticed me looking over at number 53.

'That's the Scarman's place,' she said. 'Apparently someone dumped all those bricks across their drive in the middle of the night. Imagine that! They don't know who did it – so they say anyway. To be honest, I think it's quite funny – no one likes them. Jim's car is in the garage and he couldn't get to work the next day, or take the kids to school. They all had to get the bus. His wife was furious –

she was an hour late for work. The police are very sticky about punctuality.'

'The police!' I said, slightly too loudly.

'Yes, she's a secretary in the office.'

'So she'll be able to find out who did it do you think?' I said. I felt my stomach churning.

'I suppose so – but the whole street heard them rowing about it – she blames Jim – says he's always courting trouble.'
'I know how she feels,' I said, pulling the dogs along more quickly to get past the house in double quick time.

'I wish they'd move away,' said Suzie. 'They're not the sort of people you want as your neighbours.

I tried to put it out of my mind and asked Suzie about the salon. She told me it's been going from strength to strength.

'Business is booming,' she said. 'Cressida has brought us a lot of clients – I don't know how she does it – she's a miracle worker. The boys are very popular too – they're booked up for three months solid. We're getting a lot of men coming in too – Cressida was right about appealing to the male population. And Bunny's skin products are selling well – you should try some Dora. It helps to replenish and rejuvenate the skin cells so your face looks more radiant – I use it all the time.'

'I looked at Suzie's face. She had so much make-up on, I couldn't tell.

'Oh, yes,' I said, 'you always look amazing.' This was certainly true.

'Come down to the salon Dora, and have some treatments. It's worth it – you'll feel fantastic afterwards.'

'OK,' I said, - 'when?'

'We've had a cancellation on Wednesday – in the afternoon. It's at two thirty.'

So, I agreed to go and experience the hot stone treatment, have a deep cleansing facial and a reflexology session. I tried not to think about the cost – after all, it's quite a while since I spent anything on myself. With this thought to comfort me, I told myself that the end would justify the means.

Tuesday 19th February

I spent the morning consumed with apprehension and anxiety. I tried to block out the unremitting flash-backs from the swimming pool fiasco, but to no avail. I considered not going to my class and dropping out.

'But you've only just started!' said Melanie, when I rang her for moral support.

'How can I face Pat now?' I lamented.

'I wouldn't worry so much Dora, he's seen it all before – he is an artist after all! Don't let a silly thing like this spoil your fun,' said Melanie, - 'just be brave and act as if it was funny – you know, just try and laugh it off.'

'Oh, I suppose you're right – I wish I could turn back the clock though.'

'Don't we all,' said Melanie. 'Only the other day I was chatting to Suzie about her garden and she showed me a photo of her fountain – I suggested she had it painted pink to match the Pampers logo. I was only joking but she actually went and did it! Now everyone thinks it was my idea – I mean that's pretty embarrassing isn't it?'

Not compared to flashing your tits in public by accident and then having them aired globally in high definition, I thought – not unreasonably.

'Talking about Pampers – did you know there are a lot of rumours going around? Apparently the police have been.'

'No, why?'

'Geoff says he thinks they might be employing illegal immigrants.'

When I hung up, I realised how terrible that could be for Suzie. The fines are enormous if you are guilty – it certainly put my worries into perspective.

After lunch I went off to my class feeling less sorry for myself. It was a good session today: My coil pot had fired successfully with no cracks. Pat very gallantly commented that he appreciated its lustrous finish and shapely form, and that my next challenge would be a slab pot. There was an embarrassing moment when I misheard him:

'No Dora, it's slab - with a 'b'.' He winked at me and smiled knowingly. I noticed some of the others in the class sniggering. Well, of course they don't know the connotation, thank goodness. Although, when Pat handed me Flora's bikini top at the end of the class, saying - 'I think this belongs to you Dora,' I must say, I thought he could have been a bit more discreet.

Later on, when Andrew came home, I told him about the police.

'I'm not surprised,' he said. 'I thought there was something a bit dodgy going on there.'

'Really?' I said. 'What makes you think that?'

'All those foreign girls who can't speak any English, is a bit of a clue,' he said, - 'plus, a little bird told me.'

'But what will happen – what about poor Suzie?'

'Well she'll be liable, being joint owner I'm afraid,' he said, matter-of-factly.

'This is terrible Andrew,' I said, - 'can't we do something?'

'No, not really – I can represent her in court if she wants. Of course, we don't know all the facts yet, so there's no point in worrying about what might or might not happen.' He had his lawyer's hat on – cool and collected and thoroughly detached.

'But she's my friend!' I said to him.

'Well Dora, I'm not sure you should be friends with someone who's committed a serious crime – it reflects badly on you. Don't you think you should keep your distance? - at least until it's all blown over.'

'Certainly not!' I said crossly, -'Suzie is my friend and I don't think she's guilty anyway. And besides, who are you to cast aspersions – fly-tipping is a criminal offence – I looked it up.'

'Those bricks were a present – an olive branch - a gesture of reconciliation. I even put a bow on the top. He's a builder isn't he? Those bricks are handmade Victorian Reds – best quality you can get.'

'I might have known you'd find a way round it. Well you can apply the same cunning to Suzie's situation can't you – outfoxing the opposition is obviously second nature to you. I'm sure you can think of something – I'm counting on you Andrew.'

'We'll see,' said Andrew. I gave him a very hard stare and carried on cooking tea. I accidentally burnt his sausages on purpose, but he didn't notice. I suppose it happens quite a lot. How dare he suggest that my friend is a common criminal! I decided to wait until the next day to speak to Suzie. It might have all blown over by then anyway. People are too quick to jump to conclusions – there could be a perfectly innocent explanation.

Wednesday 20th February

I popped round to see my mother this morning and found her front door ajar. She was in the garden drinking tea with Reggie of all people.

'Reggie's been very helpful Dora – he's been doing some mowing and hedge clipping for me.'

'Oh, that's nice of you,' I said, noticing Reggie looking a bit smarter than usual.

'Well, with 'er leg still mendin' I thought I'd 'elp 'er a bit, see.'

'Well, that's very kind Reggie.'

'Ahrr, well – I'll be on my way then….'

'Oh, you don't have to go yet,' I said, but he got up and hobbled off.

'He's not much fitter than you!' I laughed. 'What's all this sudden friendliness about then?'

'I don't know,' said Mum. 'Since I came back from hospital, he's been coming over a lot.'

'I'd be careful if I were you Mum – he might have his eye on you.'

'That's ridiculous,' said my mother.

Later, while I was getting ready to go out to the salon for my appointment, I thought it might be a good idea to talk to her about her will, and make sure that mine and

Jess's inheritance is properly protected. You can't be too careful these days – anything could happen. I mean, people get lonely by themselves, and Reggie polishes up quite well. Anyway, Mum's eyesight's not as good as it used to be so she probably thinks he's agreeable enough. I think I'll get on to it quickly though – I'm sure I detected a glint in his eye which I haven't noticed before.

I realised I hadn't given much thought to what to wear to my debut Pampers visit and after a quick rummage in the wardrobe I remembered I hadn't ironed anything for weeks. In the airing cupboard – the destination for all dry washing on the ironing waiting list, I found a dress to wear (thank goodness for Crimplene). Strangely, as I yanked it out, a discarded yogurt pot fell out onto the floor. Honestly, the kids are so lazy, they'll do anything rather than make the effort to go downstairs and put something in the rubbish bin.

I put my coat on and decided to walk to the salon since it's only half an hour – a chance to burn off a few more calories. As I walked along, I began to regret my choice of garment – it felt itchy, as if something was crawling about on my skin. My mother always warned me about static build-up with this sort of fabric – if there's too much friction, apparently there's even a slight risk of combustion. With this in mind, I decided to walk with my arms at a 45-degree angle from my body until I got to the High Street. I couldn't believe my eyes when I turned the corner next to Pampers. There were four police cars, a big silver van with blacked out windows, and crowds of people gathered on the street. I stopped at the newsagents and spoke to Mr Jafari.

'It's a raid,' he said, - 'they've been here since early this morning.' He was giving me a funny look. 'Did you know you've got ants in your hair?'

Suddenly I realised there were hundreds of them crawling all over my arms. I let out a very loud screech and tried to shake them off. Poor Mr Jafari didn't know where to look – but what was I supposed to do? I did at least run into his shop *before* I stripped off. The little blighters were everywhere! Billy was going to be very upset, but he really should have put a lid on that pot to stop them all escaping.

'I don't want all those ants in my shop!' exclaimed Mr Jafari.

'It's OK – they're not ants, they're stick insects,' I told him, as I pulled on my coat over my underwear and ran back out of the shop. I ran across the road and tried to find Suzie.

'Sorry Madam, but you can't enter the premises,' said the policeman blocking the doorway to the salon. 'Please go and stand over there with the others,' he said, pointing at a group of the salon girls mooching around on the pavement.

'But I need to find my friend Suzie.'

'Just do as you're told Miss and no one will get hurt.'

'But I need to find Suzie,' I said, getting a bit irate.

The policeman got a bit stroppy at this point and told me to do up my coat and at least try to look respectable, since there were children and old people in the vicinity.

'If you don't move over there pronto, you'll be escorted down to the local Nick along with those two over there.' He pointed to another policeman who was manhandling Jed into a car, handcuffed and complaining loudly, - 'you've got it all wrong, mate. I'm just visiting my Auntie.' Brad was already sitting in the back seat looking glum. I reluctantly went and stood with the girls. I must say, I thought it was a bit heavy-handed not to let the girls go and get a coat or something – they were barely wearing any clothes which at least made me feel less conspicuous, I can tell you. Honestly, young people these days don't seem to feel the cold at all. I saw Trudy Stoker making copious notes on the side-lines and when she recognised me, she came straight over.

'What's going on?' I asked her.

'Don't you know?' she said. 'It's a raid. What can you tell me about Suzie Small?' she asked.

'Oh, no, I'm not telling you anything, not after last time.'

'Suit yourself,' she said, - 'only your friend has just been arrested for money laundering, employing illegal immigrants and running a house of ill-repute. Any comments?'

'Oh my God!' I said. 'I don't believe it! That's completely outrageous! Poor Suzie – she didn't have anything to do with this,' I said, - 'she's completely innocent!'

'Can I quote you?' said Trudy.

The girls were starting to get a bit rowdy by now. They'd been kept waiting outside for some time and they wanted to go home.

'Move along,' said the policeman, directing Trudy away from the girls.

'Oi! Flatfoot! When are we going home?' one of the girls shouted.

'You'll shortly be taken down to the police station for questioning,' he told her, smiling.

'Stuff that – I'm off,' she said, discarding her cigarette and squashing it with her stiletto. 'You can't keep me 'ere.'

'Me neither!' said another one. Someone threw a missile

and there was a lot of pushing and shoving. Some of them started to move off. Straight away, Flatfoot blew on his whistle, and three officers stepped forward, grabbed the girls and helped them into a waiting police van.

I tried to tell them I wasn't anything to do with it, but they didn't listen. The journey to the police station was not very comfortable at all. Those seats are really hard and the strong smell of pee mixed with cheap perfume was quite overpowering. I was almost relieved to be put in a cell at the other end. When I was finally allowed to ring Andrew, it was nearly four hours later.

'Bloody hell Dora! What *are* you wearing! Or rather *not* wearing!' said Andrew, when he was let in to my cell.

'Oh, well, I did have a dress on, but I had to take it off because it was infested with Billy's stick insects ....' Andrew rolled his eyes heavenward.

'OK ... let's just get this over with as quickly as possible,' he said, wearily.

Andrew was very patient during the interview, because I do have a tendency to offer more information than is required. Anyway, eventually they realised that I really was just in the wrong place at the wrong time, and that despite my scant attire, I was a perfectly respectable wife and mother. I waited another hour while he went to see Suzie, and then eventually we went home.

'It's not looking very good for her,' he said, pouring us a couple of large gin and tonics. 'For a start, Cressida is not who she claims to be. Her real name is Dasha Shadrova – a Ukrainian citizen travelling on a false passport. She was sent to Holloway prison for four years for her involvement in people trafficking, and money laundering. She's also been done for miss-selling, embezzlement and tax evasion, and she has a couple of convictions for GBH. Her husband is

182

and there was a lot of pushing and shoving. Some of them started to move off. Straight away, Flatfoot blew on his whistle, and three officers stepped forward, grabbed the girls and helped them into a waiting police van.

I tried to tell them I wasn't anything to do with it, but they didn't listen. The journey to the police station was not very comfortable at all. Those seats are really hard and the strong smell of pee mixed with cheap perfume was quite overpowering. I was almost relieved to be put in a cell at the other end. When I was finally allowed to ring Andrew, it was nearly four hours later.

'Bloody hell Dora! What *are* you wearing! Or rather *not* wearing!' said Andrew, when he was let in to my cell.

'Oh, well, I did have a dress on, but I had to take it off because it was infested with Billy's stick insects ....' Andrew rolled his eyes heavenward.

'OK ... let's just get this over with as quickly as possible,' he said, wearily.

Andrew was very patient during the interview, because I do have a tendency to offer more information than is required. Anyway, eventually they realised that I really was just in the wrong place at the wrong time, and that despite my scant attire, I was a perfectly respectable wife and mother. I waited another hour while he went to see Suzie, and then eventually we went home.

'It's not looking very good for her,' he said, pouring us a couple of large gin and tonics. 'For a start, Cressida is not who she claims to be. Her real name is Dasha Shadrova – a Ukrainian citizen travelling on a false passport. She was sent to Holloway prison for four years for her involvement in people trafficking, and money laundering. She's also been done for miss-selling, embezzlement and tax evasion, and she has a couple of convictions for GBH. Her husband is currently doing ten years for armed robbery - so, all in all – a really nice person to know!'

'Jesus!' I said, gobsmacked.

'No – not quite!' said Andrew.

'What about Jed and Brad – they were taken away too.'

'Those two have outstayed their welcome I'm afraid. Their visas ran out a year ago. They've been on borrowed time.'

'I can't believe I've been so naive!'

'Well, Dora – you weren't the only one. Suzie fell for it all - she provided the money but wasn't there herself much, so she had no idea what was going on. By the way, she asked if you could get Ping-Pong and look after him for a bit.'

'Andrew – this is really serious isn't it?'

'I'm afraid so.'

Thursday 21st February

'Have you seen the front page of the Citizen?' asked Melanie, when I went round to her house straight after the kids had gone off to school. She held it up. I could barely look. Cressida and Suzie were pictured being propelled into an unmarked van with blacked out windows, by two stony-faced, thick-set policemen. Suzie looked like a rabbit in the headlights, confused and in shock. Cressida had her coat over her head, but you could tell it was her because of her scrawny fake-tanned legs and large quantities of jewellery adorning the two-finger gesture to the photographer. In the background the girls from the salon were being escorted out of the premises, along with a couple of hapless clients. Melanie made us some coffee while I looked at Trudy

Stoker's alarming exposé with the unambiguous headline:

DAWN RAID AT LOCAL MASSAGE PARLOUR (it made depressing and disturbing reading):

Early yesterday morning, acting on information received, our local police swooped in and successfully carried out a raid on a massage parlour known as 'Pampers Beauty Salon': 35, The High Street, Shillingsworth. A number of occupants were arrested along with several members of the public for affray and attempting to obstruct the enforcement of the law. PC Rob Wilko refused to comment, saying that at the current time, the owners are under investigation and it was not appropriate to jeopardise any future trial. However, I spoke to Jack Spiller, the owner of the neighbouring business- 'Jack's Hardware Store'. He said: "Ever since that lot next door opened up, I knew there was something funny going on. My flat's right next door, and the noise coming from there at night was terrible – I couldn't get to sleep some nights. I've complained hundreds of times to the council and they've done nothing about it. And some of those girls I've seen coming out – well, I know modern girls don't wear much, but I've seen more cloth on a peg doll......"

The police removed several items from the premises, including two computers, some files of documents, mobile phones and a variety of other unidentified objects. Several girls from the salon were heard to protest loudly, one saying – "Get yer 'ands off my stuff – what do you need more handcuffs for?" Others uttered expletives and one was seen throwing a missile at a policeman's head. It turned out to be a box of multi-coloured contraceptives which bounced off his helmet and landed in the road where a passing car hit it, resulting in an explosion of condoms plastering the length of the High Street. More officers were called in to contain the protesting women who were arrested and taken down to Shillingsworth Police Station. Five people remain in custody pending further enquiries. The proprietors of 'Pampers', Cressida Knightly and Suzie Small, have been arrested on several counts of employing illegal workers, money laundering, and running a house of ill-repute. They remain in custody until their bail hearing on Friday22nd. A close friend of Suzie Small's – Pandora Loveday, was quoted as saying: "She didn't have anything to do with this -she's completely innocent!" Meanwhile, 'Pampers Beauty Salon' will be closed until further notice.

I can't believe Suzie didn't know!' said Melanie. 'She must have been aware of something.'

'I know it seems like that, but she didn't get involved in the day-to-day running, did she? I mean, she just stumped up the cash didn't she!'

'She's going to lose it all isn't she? Crikey, what a mess!'

'Well, Trudy hasn't left any stones unturned has she!' said Melanie. 'Talking of stones, it's a pity about Jed and Brad – I was looking forward to some special hot-stone treatment!'

'Hot stud, you mean,' I said. 'I bet they weren't qualified in *anything.*'
'Experience is worth so much more,' said Melanie, smiling.

'Suzie told me that Cressida – I mean Dasha – might have had a dodgy past because of the suspicious gap on her

CV.' I said.

'Well if she had a CV at all, you can guarantee it's a work of fiction entirely. She's obviously spent a great deal of time in the clink. Poor old Suzie's been well and truly stitched up,' said Melanie. 'I thought Cress – I mean Dasha – had a hard-nosed, mean, sort of face and did you notice her eyes? She looked right through you. I didn't trust her from the start. That face cream she was peddling was re-packaged cheap stuff that was past its sell-by date – I saw it being delivered to the salon. My friend Jane got a rash after using it.'

When I'd left Melanie's house, I went round to Suzie's neighbour to collect Ping-Pong. I noticed with some relief that the pile of bricks was finally gone.

I decided to ring my mother when I got home to tell her about Suzie and the unfolding nightmare, hoping for some pearls of wisdom, or at least words of comfort. I was surprised and taken aback when Reggie answered the phone.

'I'll just go and get 'er,' he said, cutting me off.

I rang back and got Mum on the phone. 'Mum,' I said, 'why is Reggie answering your phone?'

'Oh, well, I was just in the kitchen making us some lunch, so I couldn't get to the phone.'

'Is everything all right?' I asked.

'Of course it is Dora. I'm feeling quite chipper,' she said, much to my dissatisfaction.

'If you are sure,' I said.

'Yes Dora, why wouldn't I? My leg is much better, and Reggie is going to take me to Blooming Miraculous after lunch.'

'What's that?'

'It's a garden centre Dora - we're going to get some nice bedding plants – Reggie has offered to plant them in for me.'

'Well, just be careful,' I said.

'My leg is fine Dora – I've told you! There's no need to fuss!'

'I didn't mean your leg,' I said.

'I'll have to go Dora - our Welsh Rarebit is getting cold.'

Well, really! I thought - now she's making Reggie my favourite childhood lunchtime treat! This doesn't bode well, not at all.

Since there was really nothing I could do about Suzie's predicament, or my Mother's peculiar choice of companion, I decided to distract myself from recent traumatic events and go down to our local library. As part of the course requirement, I am supposed to keep a scrapbook of ideas. So far all I've got in my folder is a photograph of the pond in the park with some bored ducks and a magazine cutting of some dolphins. Truth be told, I'm struggling to feel inspired. I just can't seem to focus. Pat says I need to learn to *empty my mind of everything cluttering it up and go to a still, quiet place where I can be creative and true to myself*. It's easier said than done though. I mean, he probably doesn't have five other people, three animals and a loose cannon for a mother all clamouring for attention – and he certainly doesn't have a criminal investigation threatening to ruin his best friend's life (not that I know of anyway).

The library seemed like a good idea – a nice calm environment where I could find some peace and quiet. Shillingsworth Library is not very big and since the advent of computer access for all, there are even less books than before. However, I located the Art section, and was surprised to find that there actually was one still, and sifted through the motley collection in search of my next amazing pot design. After a nice long peruse, I chose a few to take home and approached the stiff looking librarian at the desk. I realised at this point that my library membership card was missing from my purse, but the librarian said rather solemnly, that I could give him my details instead, which I did.

'I'm sorry,' he said, 'but you have quite a few overdue books to return and we can't let you have any more until they're brought back and the fines are paid.'

'Oh,' I said, - 'how many and how much?'

'Well, let's see,' he said. He seemed to take an age totting it all up. 'It seems you have twelve books outstanding, five from as long ago as June 2006.' He arched his eyebrows over his glasses and gave me a teacher-like glower.

'Oh dear!' I said.

'Oh dear is quite right!' he said. 'That amounts to five hundred and sixty five pounds and thirteen pence.'

'But that's ridiculous – what sort of books are they anyway?' I said. 'Can't I just buy some more?'

'Some of them may be out of print now Madam,' he said, - 'so they'll be irreplaceable.'

'I think I'll put these books back and go home and look for them,' I said, feeling embarrassed now that there was a queue building up. 'Just give me the titles and I'll write them down,' I said, somewhat foolishly. He proceeded to honour my request, but in an unnecessarily loud voice, I thought.

'How to Lose Weight and Gain Friends'

'Skinny Bitch'

'Does My Bum Look Big in This?'

'Salvation – a Handbook For Desperate Parents'

'40 is The New 30'

'Not Dead Yet – a Guide to Staying Active in Middle Age'

'Lumber Support Magazine Issue 15'

'Big Bertha's Naked Fantasy'

'Revelations of a Vicar's Daughter'

'Confessions of a Window Cleaner'

'Alex Ferguson's Football Highlights'

'Compendium of Infectious Diseases'

'Could you slow down a bit,' I said, prolonging the agony. 'I can't write that fast.'

As I slunk out of the library, feeling several pairs of eyes boring into the back of my head, I thought to myself that I should have stayed at home and saved myself from this latest humiliation. Anyway, I don't remember half of those books – I'm sure there must be a mistake. Now I'll have to spend ages looking for them, and in my house that could mean weeks.

Later when I showed Andrew the list, he denied all knowledge of any of them, particularly the latter half, but suggested Tom's room would be a good starting place.

'How long is it Dora, since we went out together?' he suddenly asked. I tried to remember, but apart from the opening night at Pampers, I couldn't think of any.

'Well,' he said, 'tomorrow evening we are going out.'

'Oh, lovely,' I said, - 'where?'

'It's a surprise,' he said, grinning.

Friday 22nd February

I do wonder sometimes, if it's possible to wake up in the morning and have a peaceful breakfast. As usual today's first hour and a half was as un-relaxing as ever. Flora has lost her phone again, which resulted in her banging round the house for the best part of an hour, blaming everyone else and still not finding it. Tom got up late, left the house in a rush and forgot his PE kit, so had to come back in a temper and get it. Luke and Billy were fighting. Today it was over who had taken the last Waggon Wheel.

'But that was mine!' said Billy. 'I wanted it for my snack at school - you've already had three!'

'No I haven't,' said Luke. 'Anyway – you ate all the Chocosplits.'

'Didn't!'

'Did!'

'Didn't'

'DID!'

Then Billy threw a spoon at Luke. Luke ducked and the spoon hit Tom on the head. Tom then cuffed Billy, who started to cry. Luke called Billy a baby, so Billy punched Luke. By now, I was yelling at all of them.

'This place is a nut house – I'm going!' shouted Flora, banging the door extra loudly as she left the house.

No wonder I got out a book on the challenges of modern parenting, I thought, looking at the list of books. It's like a war zone sometimes and I'm caught in the crossfire.

After a strong coffee and a crumpet for extra sustenance, I decided to risk entering Tom's room.

Gingerly, I opened his door, half expecting a crabby voice shouting, 'get out Mum!' I didn't need the sign on the door to tell me I was entering *'at my own peril'* or that there could be *'toxic waste within'.* Tom painted his room a violent red colour about a year ago and I'm sure it must be having an effect on his psyche – I mean, B&Q isn't that colour for nothing is it? Because of a sudden preference for Beyoncé and Rihanna in favour of Cristiano Ronaldo and Wayne Rooney, there are quite a few holes in the plaster where ancient blue tack failed to peel off with ease. Consequently, his room resembles a break-out from a prison cell with bullet holes scattered across the walls – Spaghetti Westerns like *The Good, The Bad, and The Ugly* come instantly to mind. You can at least see the floor in Tom's room, which is more that you can say for Flora's. His X-Box and TV dominate the space, where there is a sort of invisible magic ring around it - nothing invades that inner sanctum. I looked around at the piles of books and clothes, scattered CD's and empty Lucozade bottles by the over-flowing rubbish bin. At what point, I wondered to myself, does a man decide that a bin needs to be emptied? Is it when there is more rubbish on the floor than in the actual bin? Or are they waiting for it to bio-degrade without assistance? I opened the window to let some much-needed air into the room. It did feel slightly furtive, creeping round Tom's room, upturning things and opening drawers, but asking him to look for the missing books would be pointless. Apart from the obvious embarrassment of having to admit he had them in the first place, at sixteen he has the memory of an amoeba. How on earth they pass any GCSE's I don't know. Anyway, I rummaged guiltily around his room and managed to find four of the books Andrew suggested would almost certainly be there, plus my missing library card. So, I still had to locate *Big Bertha's Naked Fantasy*. Before I left his room, I did quickly look under his pillow, where I found a Valentine's card from a girl called Lucy who very sweetly promised to love him until she died, but no Bertha.

I closed the door on his room, hoping that he wouldn't notice the intrusion. It's amazing how they do notice – they must memorize the exact location of everything, even though it looks to us like a chaotic heap. I found the other books eventually, propping open the conservatory door, covered in dust and dog hairs.

Deciding that currently, I didn't feel brave enough to encounter the stern librarian again, I thought I'd postpone a return visit for another day or two, plus of course, there was the mystery of the elusive Bertha book to solve.

Andrew called me at lunch time, to let me know that Suzie had been given bail and would be home by 2 0'clock, so I decided to go over and take Ping-Pong back. He was probably extremely relieved to be going home. Scratch has been tormenting the poor dog ever since he arrived and it was only by pure chance that I noticed him hiding underneath Andrew's car this morning. What a terrible thing that would have been if Andrew hadn't heard me shouting to him not to drive off. The thought of having to present an already traumatized Suzie with a squashed, lifeless Ping-Pong doesn't bear thinking about. When I arrived at Suzie's house, I saw Trudy Stoker's orange Mini Coupé parked at Suzie's gate. *God, she doesn't waste any time! I thought – poor Suzie! I hope she knows what that woman's like. She'll turn Suzie's story into a sensational piece of dramatic fiction in no time.*

'Oh, hello Mrs Loveday,' Trudy said brightly, as she stepped out of the house. 'We're just leaving.' She tootled off down the garden path as her photographer took various snaps on his way out.

'Suzie!' I exclaimed when I saw her. 'You look terrible!'

'Well, it's been a gruelling few days,' said Suzie, tearfully. 'Do you know, they didn't even let me have my hydrating skin lotions – my face looks like one of your crumpled un-ironed shirts – I don't think it will ever recover, and my eye-bags are the size of Mount Fuji.' Ping-Pong leapt from my arms and was scooped up instantly by Suzie, who clutched him to her bosom as if she thought he'd died but miraculously hadn't. (How true that was, she'll never know).

We went into her vast kitchen and I made us both some tea.

'What was Trudy here for?' I asked her.

'Oh, she's very sweet isn't she!' said Suzie. 'She came to see how I was and if I needed anything.'

'Like a shoulder to cry on maybe?' I said. 'What did you say to her?'

'Well,' said Suzie, blowing her nose loudly, -'she asked me all about what it was like being in prison and what it felt like to be treated like a common criminal…' She wiped away more tears. I feared the worst, but thought it better not to say anything at this juncture. After all, Trudy Stoker could decide on a different angle to the obvious one, possibly.

'Were any of the others given bail,' I asked.

'No, because the Judge said they would be likely to skip bail and leave the country to avoid the trial, so she refused. She told me I was very lucky, because it was a very serious case and most people would have to stay in prison until the trial and it could be months before it goes to court. Dora, I couldn't have coped with being in that place any longer – it was awful!' she dried some more tears.

'Look, Suzie, from what Andrew has told me, you are completely innocent so it's highly unlikely. Have you told Warren?'

'No.'

'Suzie! You must tell him.'

'I can't – I gave Cressida seventy thousand pounds to set up the business and it's all gone.' My eyes bulged involuntarily and I let out a small gasp of horror.

'I know,' said Suzie – 'Shocking isn't it! Warren will be furious. He was thinking about retiring next year. It doesn't end there either – I signed a 5-year lease on that shop….'

'So that's in your name then?' I asked, dreading the reply.

'Yes – Cressida said it would be better if it was just me because she said she had a slightly low credit rating – something to do with her ex-husband missing a mortgage payment…' I looked at Suzie incredulously, amazed that there was someone even more naïve than me at large in the world.

'So, are all the bills in your name as well?' I asked, somewhat needlessly.

'Yes,' she said, her lip trembling.

'I'm sure we can sort all this out,' I said, trying to cheer her up. 'There must be something we can do…' *What a bloody mess, I thought to myself.*

When Andrew came in from work, I tried to discuss Suzie's predicament with him but I got a non-committal response.

'I can't discuss my clients' cases,' he said bluntly.

'Not even slightly?' I asked.

'My lips are sealed,' he said. 'All I can tell you is that we are doing everything we can to help her. Now, get your glad rags on – we're going out at 7.30pm.'

'May I ask where we're going?'

'A party,' he said, beaming.

It turned out that the party was in honour of Shama's success in raising £6,500 for the new drug rehabilitation centre, which Sharp and Prentice have agreed to match pound for pound.

For the second time this evening I felt disappointment flatten my enthusiasm for a night out with my husband, but not wishing to throw a wet blanket on Andrew's obvious excitement at the prospect of a fun night out, I smiled dutifully and pretended I was as keen as he was. What I was actually thinking was, *Oh God! A night of Andrew's colleagues all fawning over the stick-thin beautifully turned out Shama, glowing with effervescent pride and smugness.* I chastised myself inwardly for being bitchy, but I wasn't able to modify my thoughts, and soon enough, my worst fears were realised. We arrived at The Priory Hotel, half an hour late due to my inability to decide what to wear before we left the house. Five changes later, we eventually got into the waiting taxi and sped off to Shillingsworth's most fashionable venue.

'Hello Dora,' Shama said, smiling charmingly, but looking beyond us into the far distance, as if searching for a lost dog. Andrew's smile was unnecessarily sycophantic, I thought.

The only person I could see who I knew was Melanie, so I made a bee-line for her, grabbing a glass of fizz on the way.

'Thank goodness you're here,' I said. 'I don't think I

know anyone else, apart from Andrew's colleagues.'

'Same,' she said. 'I don't know why I agreed to come, I mean look at them!' She pointed at the boys crowding round Shama like wasps by a wheelie bin. 'How can anyone be *that* thin and have boobs *that* big without toppling over? And did she *have* to wear a backless dress with an unfeasibly small amount of material at the front as well – I mean, how do they stay up? And,' said Melanie, getting into her stride, - 'more to the point, how do they stay inside that dress without bursting out? They must be false ones,' she concluded. 'Yes, definitely – they look like those things we used to bounce on with horns…'

'Space-hoppers,' I said.

'Yes!'

'But Melanie, those boys aren't bothered about the authenticity of them, as long as they look the business, they don't care do they?'

'It's so disappointing – I mean really! Why do we spend so much time trying to look elegant and tasteful – I might as well have come out in a boob-tube and a thong. Let's get another drink,' she said, making for the bar. 'So, Dora,' she continued when we'd replenished our glasses, - 'tell me how you and Andrew met.'

This question always raises a dilemma for me – do I tell it like it was in all its unattractive glory, or do I leave out the actual facts in favour of a more edifying version?

The night we met in the Student Union Bar, there was a cringingly awful band playing, and I was there with a girl in my year called Bev. Anyway, there he was with his friends getting totally smashed on Snakebites, and there we were, drinking pints of cheap lager and smoking Moor cigarettes (the height of sophistication – or so we thought) in the dingiest corner of the bar. It was a real dive – the sort of place where your feet stuck to what used to be a carpet, but had rapidly become unrecognisable as such. We sat on brown plastic school chairs round a chipboard and Formica table that wobbled no matter how many pieces of folded up bar mats you stuffed under the legs. The lighting was as unsubtle as a strip-lit supermarket and it reeked like the sweat-soaked, nicotine drenched, rarely-cleaned cave-dwelling that it was. Everything was sticky. Two of Andrew's friends came over and sat down next to us uninvited, to chat us up. They didn't get very far because we thought they were juvenile idiots.

After a bit, the puerile young version of Andrew shouted over to them – 'don't bother Giles, they're frigid.'

'What's frigid?' I asked.

Bev said, 'it's what you put the milk in, Dumbo.'

'They're probably todger dodgers,' said Andrew loudly, to howls of derision from his infantile chums.

The boys stood at the bar and laughed, occasionally pointing us out to their other friends.

'Right,' I said after a while. 'I've had enough of this.'

'What are you doing?' said Bev.

'You'll see,' I said, grabbing both our drinks.

'It's surprising how far two pints of lager can travel, especially when administered from a height of about two feet above the head of the intended victim. Andrew's reaction was to adopt the emergency brace position, therefore muffling his screams of protestation. His mates all contorted into fits of hilarity and Andrew became an instant anti-hero – the brunt of many a joke thereafter. Bev and I left the dripping Andrew and his drunken posse and went home. The next day, I bumped into him in the corridor on the way to a lecture. I tried to zip past him hoping that he was too drunk to remember and that he didn't recognise me, but he wasn't and he did. He actually apologised and then to my amazement asked me out.

I related all this to Melanie, who thought it was the funniest thing she'd ever heard – by now she was well-oiled and slightly staggering. When Andrew came over with Geoff, she asked him if he had any good chat-up lines she could borrow and then laughed hysterically.

'Oh, I get it,' said Andrew, - 'Dora's been relating historical events – I was only nineteen don't forget.' He gave me a faux scowl and ordered more drinks. We got home somehow, but I can't quite remember – after 11 o'clock, it all became a bit of a blur.

Saturday 23rd February

Mega hangover today: Andrew had to take the boys to play rugby this morning. He looked like one of those white cave salamanders with no eyes.

'I'll sleep in the car once I've dropped them off,' he said, in a small whispery voice.

'OK – see you later,' I said, shuffling across the kitchen to the fridge. It felt like an expedition across the desert. One foot in front of the other, slowly but surely I reached my destination and retrieved a box of ice-cold orange juice from the inside the door. I dropped two Alka Saltzers into a glass and poured the juice on top. I went back to bed feeling very annoyed with myself, but I blame Shama. If it wasn't for her, this wouldn't have happened. I only drank too much because my husband was definitely ogling at her cleavage for a disproportionate amount of party time, as were the other 99% of the people in the room, on reflection. Why didn't she just give a party for her breasts for God's sake! They were the centre of attention and very likely the real reason for her immensely successful fundraising. I mean, how many men are going to say 'no thanks' when presented with an eyeful of that and asked to support an outstandingly worthy cause? It's not that I'm jealous or anything, I just feel irritated by the shallowness of men and the fact that as humans we've evolved about as quickly as a giant tortoise – I mean the only new thing *they've* achieved in over 250 million years is a slightly longer neck, which as far as I can tell has the sole purpose of allowing them to see further into the distance, for shagging opportunities.

Flora informed me that she was going out with the dreaded Gaz for lunch and wouldn't be back till tea time. Billy came and asked if I'd like an ice-pack on my head, which I declined but it was very sweet of him to ask. At lunch time, I felt marginally better and made Billy some sandwiches and we watched *Batman Returns*, although I admit I did nod off quite a lot. Andrew came back about 2 o'clock having fed Luke and Tom on KFC. Andrew said he couldn't face it himself though and had to sit in the car to avoid breathing in the greasy chicken-air in case he threw up.

'I think we're getting too old for boozy parties,' I said to him.

'You're absolutely right,' he said, - 'until the next time.'

'No, I'm serious, Andrew – we should think about it – binge drinking is for teenagers and seasoned alcoholics.'

'Well, I'm certainly going to be abstaining for a few days – my skin feels alien – like a frog's, and the only thing I want for lunch is a glass of water and a dry biscuit – actually, no, forget the biscuit.' He went off upstairs to sleep until tea time.

Flora's entry into the house at 5 o'clock was obviously

meant to get everyone's attention, and it did.

'Aaahhh!' she screamed, banging the door, which bounced, so she banged it again. 'AAAHHH! That disgusting pervert! Look at this Mum – Dad! I found this in Gaz's room!' She threw down a tatty dog-eared paperback onto the kitchen table.

'So no Gaz then?' enquired Andrew, picking the book up and flicking through it.

'No! He's a repellent, vile pervert and I NEVER want to see him again, EVER!'

'OK,' I said, looking at the book and instantly recognising the source of her distress.

'And – guess where he got it? From Tom – that's where! How could he do this to me? I can't believe anyone could read that … that… PORNO FILTH!'

Andrew put the book down quickly.

'Boys are disgusting!' said Flora stomping off upstairs and slamming her bedroom door. Tom started to say something, but stopped himself.

'Never mind son,' said Andrew to Tom, – 'she'll get over it.'

'I'll go and talk to her in a bit,' I said.

'Oh well,' said Andrew, - 'at least Gaz's sexual orientation is no longer in dispute.'

Big Bertha's gargantuan assets filled the front cover and threatened to spill out onto the table. Tom moved to pick it up. I snatched it up first and shoved it in the cupboard.

'I'll take it back to the library on Monday,' I said. 'Go and tell Billy to wash his hands for tea,' I said to Tom.

'I didn't know libraries had stuff like that on their

shelves,' said Andrew.

'Well, neither did I – maybe this one was categorised as a memoire.'

'What will you say to Flora?' Andrew asked when Tom had gone.

'Well, I'll explain that most men can't help but revert to their base instincts where women are concerned – that they can't stop themselves from lusting after them in a primeval way, and are unable to restrain themselves enough to behave in an adult fashion, particularly when outlandishly over-inflated boobs are at large. How's that?'

'Well – that's about right – they're just normal teenage boys of course.'

'Well, you're no exception.'

'What's that supposed to mean?' said Andrew.

'Last night your eyes were on stalks – you can't tell me you weren't aiming them at every opportunity in the direction of Shama's very considerable bosom!'

'Well, OK, I was, a bit. But you can't blame me – it was unavoidable. She wasn't doing any restraining was she?'

This conversation could have gone on all night. I went and tried to comfort Flora and make her realise that Gaz wasn't evil or perverted – just a normal boy (*well, sort of*), and that she should go and make up with him because she wouldn't want him getting a complex would she?

'Boys are pathetic,' she said. 'I hate them.'

'They're just different,' I said, trying to be balanced and rational. 'They have a different agenda. They can't fight their genetics – it's pre-destined.'

'I'm *never* getting married,' said Flora defiantly.

Sunday 24ᵗʰ February

'We'll have to do something about that,' I said to Andrew, pointing at the brown muddy swamp which used to be the lawn - 'before the weather gets warmer and the boys want to play outside again.'

'I suppose so,' said Andrew, resentfully. To him, Sunday should be a day of slothful idleness. His reluctance to do anything other than the unavoidable and mandatory dog-walk, was self-evident.

'I think we should go and buy some turf,' I said, deciding for him. We had breakfast and went off down to S&M Garden and Building Suppliers, leaving the kids in the house together.

'I hope they'll be sensible while we're out,' I said to Andrew.

'What could go wrong?' he said.

I had looked in on them all before we left – Billy was busy constructing a mini assault course and twig garden for the few remaining stick insects salvaged from the airing cupboard last week. Luke was watching a football match, Tom was apparently revising for his exams but I suspected it was all a charade – the fact that his lap-top was open on some girl's Facebook page and balanced on top of his revision books told me otherwise. Flora, also in her room supposedly revising, was still fast asleep, with her favourite thrash metal band blasting in her ears through inadequate headphones.

'How can she sleep with that racket going on,' I said to Andrew as we drove down the road.

'I don't know – she must be trying to block out the nagging voice in her head telling her she should be revising.'

You'd think it would block out all intelligent thought completely,' Andrew said. 'By the way, did you tell them not to do any cooking, fire-lighting or chopping, and not to use any electric appliances unsupervised until we return?'

'Of course - and I told them not to answer the phone unless it's us.'

'Good – should be fine then,' Andrew said.

Turf, it turns out, is outrageously expensive. When we'd recovered from the shock and ordered the required amount, we left feeling utterly fleeced.

'Good grief,' said Andrew, - 'that's daylight robbery. No wonder people opt for concrete. How can grass cost that much? If I'd known, I could have driven up to the common in the night and hacked some off up there.'

'Well, apart from committing yet another criminal act, it's probably the wrong type of grass.'

'Humph,' said Andrew, looking at his credit card dismally.

'Never mind,' I said, - 'at least it'll be green all over, for a while anyway.'

We drove back home, feeling a lot poorer.

Nothing could have prepared us for the carnage which greeted us when we opened the front door and went into the house. Every drawer had been pulled out, the contents strewn across the floor, furniture had been knocked over, cushions were thrown around the lounge, the lamp which normally stood on the sideboard lay in a broken heap on the carpet.

'Don't touch anything,' said Andrew. 'I'm ringing the police.'

I ran upstairs to see where all the kids were, and breathed a sigh of relief to see Flora still asleep with her music blaring away, and Tom still in his room actually revising. I pulled his earphones out to get his attention.

'Mum!' Tom shouted, - 'you scared the pants off me!'

'Where are Luke and Billy?' I asked frantically.

'Dunno, what's all the fuss about?'

'Tom, didn't you hear anything? We've been burgled!'

He looked baffled, and followed me downstairs.

'Cripes!' he said, when he saw the mess.

'Out!' shouted Andrew, at the dogs, who were jumping all over the stuff on the floor. Fudge was trying to chew the staple-gun, while Cocoa was busy tearing an important looking document in half. Andrew ordered them outside. I shouted round the house for Billy and Luke. I was just starting to feel really panicky, when Andrew said he could see them coming down the road on their bikes.

'Where were you both?' I said to them crossly.

'At the Co-op,' said Billy.

'Getting sweets,' said Luke.

'We've been burgled,' said Tom, - 'in broad daylight!'

The police turned up quite quickly - they said Sundays were normally quiet, and of course they'd been here before, several times.

'Can you tell us if anything is missing,' said one of the officers.

'Oh, I don't know,' said Andrew, - 'we haven't checked.' The officers gave each other a look that said; *this guy's an idiot*. Andrew went off round the house to do a quick appraisal. 'I can't see anything missing at the moment,' said Andrew, looking a bit sheepish.

'Right then,' they said. 'How did they get in?'

'The doors were open,' I said.

The officers pursed their lips and mulled over the scene before them.

'I tell you what,' one of them said, -'try not to disturb anything at the moment. We'll send someone over to take pictures and forensics will come and dust for fingerprints. In the meantime, Mr Loveday, if you discover anything actually missing, please let us know.'

'OK, we will, thanks,' said Andrew, showing the policemen out.

'Now I feel robbed and humiliated twice in the space of an hour!'

'Thank goodness the kids had no idea what was going on – they could have been seriously hurt if they'd been here.'

'But why didn't they steal anything?' said Andrew, bemused.

'And why weren't they afraid of the dogs?' I said.

'You are kidding aren't you Dora?' said Andrew, laughing. 'Those two wouldn't scare the skin off a custard!'

'But a burglar wouldn't know that would he?' I looked outside at Fudge and Cocoa, lolloping round the mud garden with their tongues flopping about, looking about as scary as a bush baby's baby and thought what useless guard dogs they were. Nice but dim.

'Well, I was going to do some housework,' I said, 'but I'd better put it off in case I destroy any crucial evidence.'

'That's the best excuse I've heard yet,' said Andrew, - 'and I've heard most of them.'

We checked all the things we could think of that might be worth pinching, which didn't take long.

'Do you think Stan's got anything to do with this?' I said to Andrew.

'I don't think so – he's definitely in Spain – I got a postcard from Mum yesterday.'

'Well, I've never heard of a burglary where nothing was burgled – it's very strange,' I said, puzzling over it all. 'Maybe they took something that we didn't know was worth anything.'

'Like what?' said Andrew.

'I don't know – maybe that hideous vase that your aunt gave you – perhaps it's actually an invaluable antique from the Ming Dynasty or something…'

'Well, if it was, I smashed up our future security last month with a big hammer and tossed it in the bin, so it's definitely not worth anything now.'

I suddenly realised how late it was. 'Let's go out for a late lunch,' I suggested to Andrew. I feel depressed staying here.'

'Well, I suppose we've already spent a fortune today so a bit more won't make much difference.'

We gathered everyone together and left the devastation behind. Our local pub, the Press and Feather do a splendid Sunday Lunch – just what we needed to calm our nerves. Billy and Luke were unusually quiet during the meal and I wondered whether they'd been badly affected by the unpleasant experience of strangers coming into our house and disturbing everything. I mentioned it to Andrew when we got home and he said he thought that was unlikely.

'They're probably coming down from a sugar high after eating too many sweets this morning,' he said.

I went to bed tonight feeling a bit jittery. Andrew tried to comfort me by saying that lightening doesn't strike twice in one place. Then he remembered about that man who has been struck 9 times, so that didn't really help. I hardly slept a wink.

Monday 25th February

I was glad when the forensic people turned up – being on my own in the house suddenly felt unnerving. I almost wished that Billy or Luke had refused to go to school and that I'd given in to one of them for a change. Two unsmiling women turned up and very efficiently took pictures and looked for fingerprints.

'There are a lot of fresh prints on the stationary that's been pulled out of this drawer,' said one of them, 'and on the open cupboard doors.' They finally left an hour later, satisfied that they had enough material.

'You can put everything away now if you like,' they said. 'Don't worry, we've seen much worse than this – it doesn't look like a professional job though – we'll let you know as soon as we can if we have any news for you.'

I decided to go with the dogs and see Suzie when they'd gone, and tidy up later. I told Suzie about what had happened as we made our way across the common. She was sympathetic of course, but consumed with worry over her own terrible situation. She still hasn't told Warren about it, or her daughter Violet.

'Suzie, you must tell them – they'll find out soon anyway.'

'Oh, I know – but how can I explain how foolish I've been, and I'll have to tell them I might be going to prison ….'

Poor Suzie – she looked so forlorn, a shrunken, sad version of her former self.

'What if Warren wants a divorce?' she said, mournfully.

'Surely not,' I said, - 'he worships you.'

'I don't think he'll want a convicted criminal for a wife, and anyway he'll have an apoplectic fit when he sees how much money's gone – he could have a heart attack. Oh my God, I hadn't thought of that – he wouldn't be able to divorce me if he was dead would he!'

'Suzie, it won't come to that. How do you think Violet will react?'

'I really don't know. She's away working in London at the moment. She'll probably think her mother's having a menopausal melt-down, which is what I think myself, on reflection.'

'Try not to worry,' I said, - 'I'm sure Andrew will get you out of this mess – he's a very good lawyer Suzie.'

'Thank you Dora – I'm sure he'll do his best.'

I arrived home later, to discover another mountain outside our house. This time it was a massive pile of rolled turf, even bigger than the brick mountain.

'How much did you order?' I asked Andrew when he came in.

'I'm sure I told them 60 square metres,' he said, confidently.

'It looks as if there's enough to turf the entire street

Andrew; are you sure?'

'Yes of course I'm sure - I'll go and check.'

He came back out of the study looking decidedly glum.

'No wonder it cost nearly £2,000 – it appears we've accidentally ordered 600 square metres …'

'How did you manage to do that!' I said, exasperated.

'I don't know, but I don't think you're in a position to criticise,' he said. I remembered the ladle and bottle opener fiasco and decided to tone it down a bit.

'Do you think they'll take some of it back?'

'I'll have to phone them tomorrow and speak to the manager,' Andrew sighed.

I was vaguely aware of a rumpus going on upstairs between Luke and Billy so I went up to investigate. I found them in Billy's room. Luke had Billy in a headlock, who was by this time turning a worrying shade of purple.

'Let him go at once!' I shouted at Luke, - 'his lips are turning blue! What's all this about?'

Luke gave Billy an evil stare.

'Billy?' I said. Billy looked at the floor and refused to answer.

'Luke?' I said, - 'why are you trying to strangle your brother?' Luke refused to answer and looked at the floor.

'Right, the pair of you - get downstairs now!' I marched them into the kitchen and shouted for Andrew to assist me.

The doorbell rang before we could get any further. It was one of the forensic ladies.

'I've come to get everyone's fingerprints,' she said, - 'so we can eliminate family members.' Billy and Luke were a bit reluctant for some reason, as was Flora, who said that her human rights were being infringed and that she didn't want her DNA in the public domain. Andrew told her there wasn't much point in worrying about that when her Facebook page gives away all her personal information to the entire globe. It all took about half an hour and when she'd gone, we resumed our interrogation of Billy and Luke. Billy suddenly cracked and burst into tears.

'It's all his fault,' he said, pointing at the accused. Luke retaliated by saying no it wasn't, it was Billy's.

'I only wanted to get some sweets,' said Billy, hiccupping through his tears.

'It was your idea to look for money,' blurted out Luke.

'Luke says we could go to prison Mum,' said Billy, sniffling.

'What are you talking about?' I said, baffled.

Andrew cleared his throat to get everyone's attention. 'I think we may have found our felons, Dora.'

I was still in the dark. 'What do you mean?'

'We only took £2.20,' said Luke. 'Billy found a pound in the drawer and twenty pence behind the bookcase and I found a pound under the sofa cushions. Are we going to get arrested Dad?' Luke's worried face looked hot and blotchy with the pressure of a guilty conscience.

'Well,' said Andrew, milking it for all it was worth, - 'I think the police will want to take statements from you both – uncorroborated of course, so you'll have to be in separate cells. It'll probably take a couple of days so Mum had better go and pack you a bag each for overnight. Of course, there's no TV or anything, so you'll have to take a book and maybe some paper and a pen. That will be useful to correspond with us if you are kept for longer – maybe a month or so.'

'Andrew!' I said, - 'that's enough!'

'Well, look at all the trouble they've caused!

Just then the doorbell went again. This time it was a policewoman.

'Hi,' she said, 'I'm from victim support. Most people feel very vulnerable and often traumatised by an incident like this – a stranger violating your home and taking away your feeling of security. We understand what you're going through. I've come to see if you feel you might need some family counselling.' She smiled in a kindly way.

'Perfect,' said Andrew. 'Have a word with my two youngest would you?'

Tuesday 26th Feb

A very contrite Luke and Billy sat at the breakfast table this morning. After a long lecture from Andrew last night about wasting police time and resources, they felt thoroughly sorry for themselves. I thought Andrew had been a bit heavy handed to be honest.

'They've got to learn,' he said to me at bed time. 'Honesty is the best policy,' he'd said. I was tempted to remind him about the brick saga, but thought better of it. I made pancakes for them all to cheer things up.

'Let's try and forget about what's happened,' I said, doling out two pancakes each.

'If they had to go to prison,' said Tom, ignoring me, - 'I could've visited and sneaked in contraband.

'Yeah,' said Flora, -'like a penknife hidden in a cake so they could escape by carving a hole in the wall like in that film the *Shawshank Redemption*.'

'I'd want bubble-gum and comics and ice-cream,' said Luke.

'If I was in prison, I'd do loads of press-ups and stuff so that no one would dare to fight me,' said Tom. 'I'd be the one they were all scared of.'

'Gaz says prison isn't that bad,' said Flora.

'What!' I said. 'What on earth does he know about prison?'

'His uncle went there. He said it was OK.'

'Flora, don't you think you could find a different boyfriend. Aren't you concerned that there might be a bit of a cultural void between you two?'

'Uurgh, you're so middle class, Mother. Just because someone's been to prison doesn't make them a bad person!'

I raised my eyebrows but tried not to rise to the bait. 'I thought you'd gone off him anyway.'

'Oh, I'm over all that – Gaz and I have worked it out. We're cool.'

'I'd like a tattoo like his when I'm bigger,' said Billy, compounding my distress.

'Yeah,' said Luke. 'I'd get one that says 'Arsenal'.'

'I'm going to get one that says 'school sucks',' said Tom.

'Where?' asked Flora.

'That's enough,' I said, - 'it's time you all went to school and at least attempted to get an education.'

Honestly, I thought, when they'd all gone, what is the world coming to? How can I save my children from descending into the depths of depravity? Why can't their 'to

do' lists have things like: Must see Niagara Falls, climb
Machu Picchu, see the Egyptian Pyramids, read Plato,
Proust or Voltaire, and take up watercolour painting? But
no, it's; get a particularly vulgar tattoo, serve some time and
live off the proceeds of a criminal existence – great! Maybe
they've got a small point though - I mean, I had a good
education and look where it got me! And more to the point
- look where it got Suzie!

After breakfast, I went up to the co-op to get a few
things. The Citizen caught my eye and I picked one up.
There was a big picture of Suzie on the front page looking
sad with the headline:

'SMALL TO DO TIME', and then in smaller letters – (IF
FOUND GUILTY).

'That witch!' I said under my breath. I paid for my
shopping and went and sat on a bench nearby to read it
properly:

*'Local female entrepreneur, Suzie Small, could be
facing a long-term prison sentence if found guilty of
running an illicit brothel and employing a string of
illegal immigrants. I interviewed Ms Small shortly
after her release on bail, at her plush 5-bedroomed
mansion on the outskirts of Shillingsworth's most
prestigious residential area. She told me candidly how
she felt about her unfortunate situation. "I had no
idea," she said, - "what was going on at Pampers. I've
been taken for a ride and hung out to dry by the worst
sort of criminals. I'm being accused of the most terrible
things. None of it is true – you must believe me." Ms
Small said she met Ms Dasha Shadrova just a few
months ago, and had no idea she was an
internationally renowned money-laundering criminal
wanted in several countries for a variety of offences*

*which include GBH, theft, drug and people trafficking.
Ms Small said, - "she seemed like a nice person – she
even offered to house-sit for me when I went away – I
thought she was my friend." I asked Ms Small how she
felt about the devastating situation she now finds
herself in. "I can't begin to tell you how traumatic it
is," she said, - "my reputation is in tatters. I've lost a lot
of money and I'm facing the prospect of a long prison
sentence. I wish I'd never met that terrible woman."*

*So, it remains to be seen – was Suzie Small duped as
she claims, or was she a foolish woman motivated by
greed to enter into an ill-advised partnership and got
caught with her pants down? We'll be following this
case closely readers, so watch this space for further
news on Shillingsworth's biggest criminal case since the
hanging of Lucy Butterworth in 1953.'*

'Oh, for goodness sake!' I said out loud.

'Hello Dora!' said a voice. I looked up and saw it was
Melanie.

'It's terrible isn't it!' she said. 'Mind you, it's the most
exciting thing to happen here in years. Who would have
thought it!'

'I wish they wouldn't just focus on Suzie – why can't
they talk about the others as well - I mean Dasha's the main
protagonist.'

'People are fascinated about what their next-door
neighbours are up to – that's why - it's human nature isn't
it!' said Melanie. 'Fancy a coffee? We could go across the
road to Valentino's.'

On the way, we stopped outside the travel agency

window and looked longingly at photos of holiday destinations. 'I wouldn't mind going away for a few days, wouldn't you? There are some really good deals on at the moment.'

'I've been thinking about doing just that for a while now,' I said.

'We could go together,' she said, reading my mind.

By the time we'd had coffee, we'd planned the whole thing. I just need to check with Andrew and Mum, and then it'll be full steam ahead – I can't wait!

Today, of course, was my third pottery class with Pat. I looked at my ideas book and realised I'd got no further than the last time I'd looked at it. I grabbed some of Mum's knit and sew magazines and tried to find some things to cut out for inspiration. It was all a bit hurried really, as I didn't have a great deal of time. Anyway, I hastily cut a few pictures of flowers out and shoved them in loosely. I just made it in time for the beginning of the class.

Today Pat presented us with our slab pots, freshly fired from the kiln. Mine had sadly and rather disappointingly, collapsed. Everyone else's had come out fine.

'I think it's down to handling,' said Pat, 'you've suffered with warping. Never mind Dora,' he said, patting me, - 'we're moving on to throwing today – you can try your hand at that.'

My first attempt at it was an unmitigated disaster – a splodge of clay flapped around the wheel refusing to be moulded. I felt as if my hands had morphed into two bunches of bananas, so inept were they at shaping the rotating lump into anything recognizable. At the end of the class, Pat announced he wanted to look at our resource books.

'Sorry, I haven't stuck these in yet,' I said, as he opened the book in front of the class.

'Interesting,' he said, as my magazine cuttings spilled out onto the desk.

'Whoops,' I said, hastily turning them the right side up. I had managed to cut out two knitted egg cosies that looked like a pair of striped boobs, half a woman's bottom in appliqued underpants, and some big red letters which, rather embarrassingly, spelled *tit,* but had obviously come from a bigger word like 'stitch', before I'd chopped it out.

Pat smiled and said nothing. 'Next week,' he said, 'we'll be trying to improve our throwing skills. Now then Dora,' he said to me, - 'would you like some extra assistance at the wheel? I think I could show you a thing or two.'

'Ooh yes please,' I said, - 'I think that would be very helpful.'

'How about now?' he said, as the others filed out of the classroom.

Wednesday 27th February

I decided I needed a quiet day at home today. After yesterday's inexplicable turn of events, I don't know whether I'm coming or going at the moment. I must say, I've completely gone off Pat Handy after the unfortunate misunderstanding yesterday, at the end of class. I can't deny that I found him attractive and certainly, if I had been a free agent, there's no doubt that I might have agreed to a date of some description. But, he plainly doesn't believe in prevaricating where women are concerned. I genuinely thought that when he sat behind me at the potter's wheel and asked if he could guide my hands to raise it up, I thought he meant the pot. It was all very embarrassing. He even tried to infer that I'd deliberately given him the impression that I was 'up for it', as he so bluntly put it. I mean, really! Well, I don't think I can go back there again now. On the positive side, I'll get my money back, and one thing I've learned is that ceramics isn't really my thing – my creative urges obviously need to be channelled elsewhere.

Jess came for coffee and brought us some rock buns and a wonky flan. Things are going well for them at Paradise Bakery since they won the award so she seemed in good spirits.

'Have you seen Mum?' she asked.

'Not since last week,' I said.

'Well, I went round yesterday.'

'Was she OK,' I asked.

'Depends on how you look at it,' said Jess. 'I was rather surprised to see Reggie from next door ensconced in the sitting room, with his feet up reading the paper, and watching TV.'

'Yes, he seems to be round there a lot at the moment – what did Mum say?'

'She just said he can't get Monty Don on his telly. By the way, what is that huge mountain of grass doing outside your house?'

'Andrew got the measurement wrong – so now we've got heaps more grass than we need – you don't need any do you Jess?'

'No, Terry just started laying our new patio at the weekend – I'm a low maintenance girl when it comes to gardens.'

'Andrew's ringing the supplier up today to see if we can get them to take most of it back.'

'Good luck with that,' said Jess. 'Terry over-ordered the eggs last week. If I see one more omelette, I'll scream.'

'Jess, what do you think we should do about Reggie?'

'Nothing Dora – we can't stop her having a friend can we?'
'But she used to call him a 'grumpy old git' and now they seem to be best buddies – it's a bit odd don't you think?'

'Well, as long as she doesn't decide to marry the old bugger, we're safe.'

'God forbid! Dad would be turning in his grave.'

'I know,' I said, getting a flash of inspiration, - 'let's go and take her to visit Dad's grave – you know - to remind her of how irreplaceable he is.'

'Good thinking Dora – I'll suggest it pronto.'

Later on Andrew came in with a face like a wet weekend.

'Spill the beans,' I said.

'You know I rang S&M Building Suppliers today...'

'Yes...'

'Well, guess who the manager is?'

'No I can't.'

'The 'S' in S&M is Jim Scarman!'

'Never!'

'He delighted in telling me that they could come and take the extra amount away but as far as money was concerned, I could whistle for it. In fact, he said he would charge extra to take anything away.'

'What did you say?'

'I told him to piss off!'

'As diplomatic as ever then.'

Andrew continued to complain about Jim Scarman until he went to sleep. I don't know what we'll do now – try to sell it I suppose.

Thursday 28th February

I'm very excited about my planned trip away. Melanie and I have booked a week in an exotic location called Rabbit Island. Melanie says it's somewhere in Thailand so it'll be lovely and hot there in March. The travel agent got us a really good deal - honestly, if I'd known how much cheaper it is to go during term time, I'd have booked something ages ago. Melanie says she's amazed at what good value our hotel is – I mean you can't even pitch a tent for that price here. I suggested we went shopping for some swimwear and things we need for our trip so we went round town today like a couple of teenagers, trying on sunglasses and hats and things. We were having an absolute hoot in Primark, when I suddenly spotted my mother in the nightwear department perusing pyjamas. I was just about to shout over to her when I saw Reggie holding up a bright pink onesie for her approval.

'Look,' I said, to Melanie, ducking down. 'What's my mother doing out with Reggie buying night attire?'

'I hope she doesn't get that,' said Melanie, - 'Barbie pink isn't really her colour.'

'Is it anyone's?' I sneaked a bit closer round the racks of clothes but not so she could see me. I crouched down by the novelty slippers and tried to eavesdrop on their conversation.

I heard Reggie say – 'but Ruth, I don't see why we need to wear anything ...' I couldn't believe my ears!

Then my mother said, 'Well, I'd rather at least have a nightdress on – it's more in the spirit of the occasion Reggie. I mean, if you'd rather not wear anything, that's fine – I wouldn't want to impose...'

I crept back to where Melanie was and told her what I'd heard.

'Well, I suppose you can't expect your mother to be on her own forever Dora – there's no reason why she can't have a bit of romance in her life is there?'

'But she's 75!' I said.

'Well, there's hope for us all then,' said Melanie.

'But, Reggie! I mean, I thought she had better taste ...'

'Well, you can't be too picky at her age can you? Come on, let's go and look for some flip-flops.'

I must say, seeing my mother with Reggie out shopping put a bit of a dampener on my own shopping expedition. Melanie tried to tell me I was over-reacting, but it's all a bit worrying. I rang Jess when I got back.

'Good grief!' she said, - 'that was quick work! He hasn't finished forking over her raised beds yet. I thought he had an ulterior motive – offering to do all that gardening for Mum. Honestly, why can't he be content with a chicken pie and Sky TV? He has to expect something on the side as well!'

'We'll have to confront him,' I said. 'I can't let this go on – Mum's being taken advantage of. He's got more in mind than planting a few vegetables.'

'I don't think you should say anything,' said Andrew later. 'It's none of our business what she does in her private life is it?'

'Well, I think we should show an interest – what if she's going a bit doolally – then it's our business isn't it?'

'She's not though, she's just enjoying herself, and why shouldn't she?'

'Well, I can't be as blasé about it as you Andrew. If it was your mother, wouldn't you be worried?'

'No,' he said emphatically.

Flora appeared in the kitchen with Gaz and announced there was a party at the weekend she wanted to go to.

'Where is it?' I asked.

'Totness,' she said.

'That's miles away – how do you intend getting there?' asked Andrew.

'Gaz has a motorbike.'

'No,' I said flatly refusing to entertain the idea.

'For God's sake!' said Flora, folding her arms and striking an aggressive pose.

'Gaz, I'm sure you're a very safe rider of motorbikes, but Flora will not be accompanying you on this particular trip,' said Andrew firmly. Gaz looked at Andrew with an expression of disdain but said nothing. Flora flounced out of the kitchen saying we couldn't stop her and she'd do what she liked.

'Your Dad's an old fart,' we heard Gaz saying to Flora as they went out through the front door.

'God! They treat me like a baby – I hate them,' said Flora. 'Come on Gaz, let's go down to the swings in the park.'

'Don't be out for too long,' I shouted after them, - 'you've got school tomorrow Flora.' She stomped off with Gaz trailing behind.

'I suppose we can't actually stop her can we?' said Andrew.

'No, but we can show her lots of pictures of maimed corpses and really bad traffic accidents.'

MARCH

Friday 1st March

We got a postcard this morning from Bob and Barbara which was slightly concerning.

It said:

Dear all, things here not as good as we hoped. We may be returning to England sooner than expected – will update you shortly, B + B xx

'Oh no,' said Andrew when he saw it. 'I hoped they would last a bit longer than this – I wonder what's gone wrong.'

'I bet it's something to do with Stan – the whole thing smelt fishy to me. I mean, who has an empty villa just lying around? And why would you let someone stay in it for free?'

'That's very cynical Dora – what happened to good old fashioned generosity and kindness to friends?'

'You don't really think that do you Andrew?'

'No, I agree with you – something wasn't right about it.'

Andrew went off to work and I put it out of my mind – I've got enough to worry about – what with my mother's shenanigans and Flora's rebellious behaviour to contend with. Anyway, I had a huge pile of laundry to do today – it never goes away, just ebbs and flows like the tide. Today the washing heap is particularly mountainous. I don't know where it all comes from.

I got a phone call from Luke's teacher today telling me that he hasn't been handing in his homework regularly and that the school are concerned about his lack of engagement in lessons. Apparently he seems disinterested and doesn't concentrate properly.

'Well,' said Andrew when he came in from work, - 'that describes about 90% of the kids in school doesn't it?'

'We ought to take it seriously,' I said to him. 'Maybe he's got a problem that we haven't picked up on ...'

'Like what?' said Andrew. 'As far as I can tell, he just tries to get away with doing as little as possible.'

'What if he's got a syndrome?' I said.

Andrew laughed. 'The only syndrome he's got is avoidance syndrome otherwise known as lazy-itis. He's just like I was. Don't worry Dora – he'll pull his socks up eventually.'

I didn't feel very confident about that, but we'll have to see how this term goes. Perhaps we ought to give him some incentive to improve his efforts. It works quite well with Flora who is quite materialistic and can see the benefit of working harder, although we've drawn the line at her recent request for a pet python. Tom is more difficult to bribe, since all he wants are more games for his X-box which defeats the purpose as we want him to play less computer games and do more studying. We tried food instead which was quite successful. The only trouble with this though, is that I've noticed he's getting a bit chubby round the middle. Maybe we could persuade him to swap KFC for sushi.

I decided to go and see my mother this evening after tea. I told Jess to come too and meet me there so we can present a united front.

'Why didn't you tell me you were coming over?' said my mother when we arrived on her doorstep.

'We thought we'd surprise you,' said Jess.

Mum was wearing the pink onesie from Primark. 'That's very… umm … pink,' said Jess.

'Well, I'm glad you've come – you can tell me which outfit you prefer – this, or this?' She held up a black nightdress trimmed with black fur with a matching kimono.

'Definitely that,' said Jess, pointing at the fluorescent woolly, and highly unattractive onesie.

'I can't believe you're asking us about this,' I said, amazed at her coolness.

'Well, why not?' she said. 'I might as well, since you are here. Reggie will be here in a minute so I need to be ready.'

'Mum, you do know what you are doing don't you?' I said.

She looked a bit blank and said of course she did.

'I haven't got time to offer you a cup of tea I'm afraid,' she said, 'we've got to get on with things as soon as Reggie gets here – we're too old to hang about once we've decided to do something or we'll change our minds.'

'We're not very happy about this,' said Jess. 'I'm sorry Mum, but we're a bit worried about this relationship with Reggie.'

'Well there's really no need for you to be concerned,' she

said. The doorbell rang and she went to let Reggie in. He stood in the hallway dressed in plaid pyjamas, a Willy Winkie hat and some tartan slippers.

'You look marvellous!' said my mother.

'Has she gone completely mad?' said Jess, under her breath.

We heard Reggie say, 'Ahhrr, well I thought I'd better put som'at on to keep you happy,' said Reggie.

'Did you hear that?' said Jess. 'I can't believe it!'

'Evening,' said Reggie as he entered the lounge.

'Right Reggie, let's get to it,' said my mother – 'we've no time to lose. You two will have to push off I'm afraid.'

'Now just wait a minute,' said Jess, - 'I want to ask Reggie if his intentions are honourable … I mean it's all a bit sudden isn't it?'

'What are you talking about?' she said. 'We haven't got time for this – we're due at Sylvia Plunket's annual pyjama party down at the OAP's club – actually you could drive us down, then we could have a drink couldn't we Reggie? We can always get a taxi back if we feel like letting our hair down!'

Jess said she'd take them. I must say, we both felt a bit foolish, but even though we may have jumped the gun in this instance, we're not out of the woods yet.

Saturday 2nd March

'Rugby's cancelled,' said Tom this morning, but only after Andrew had got up, had his breakfast and was ready to leave.

'Why didn't you tell me earlier!' he said, crossly. 'I could have had a lie-in for once!'

Andrew came back to bed with coffee and toast for us both. Outside, the rain was pouring down in buckets against the window.

'At least it'll keep the grass watered,' he said, looking out onto the muddy mound. 'We should put an ad in the paper to sell the grass. I'll do it on Monday.' Andrew seemed to be in a reasonably good mood so I chose this moment to tell him about my holiday with Melanie.

'That's nice,' he said. 'I'm sure you'll have a lovely time.' I was a little bit surprised at how calm he was about this. Looking after all the children and having my mother to stay with him to help doesn't usually go down as well as this.

'Are you sure it's OK?' I asked.

'Yes, of course. We'll be fine.'

The thing is, last time I went away leaving the two of them in charge, it was a bit of a disaster. Even now, I'm still finding pieces of plaster in the lounge carpet – over a year later. It wasn't anyone's fault exactly, it's just that no one realised what Billy was doing in the bathroom, or thought to wonder why he was missing for such a long time. We'd bought him a remote-controlled boat for Christmas so he'd decided to play with it in the bath. Unfortunately, he left the tap running while he went off to a football match with Luke. Mum, was out at the shops buying something for tea, and Andrew said that he was outside doing some gardening. This I find slightly unbelievable. I think he was in fact having a kip on the sofa – I mean, how else can he explain the tidemarks on his trousers. I tried to get the black marks out, but beige rayon is an absolute pain if it gets a stain on it. Actually, I was quite pleased to have an excuse to chuck them out, since they were an unwanted cast-off from his father (in my opinion, beige slacks shouldn't be allowed out in public, along with old man cardigans and brown slip-on shoes).

Anyway, by the time I came back from my week away in Torremolinos with Jess, all the furniture was outside in the back garden, the lounge carpet was rolled up in the driveway and there was a hole in the ceiling the size of … well, the size of a bath actually.

'Oh my God!' I screeched when I saw it. Andrew's warning by text saying there'd been a bit of a 'flooding incident', didn't prepare me at all for the complete devastation that greeted me. Most of the lounge ceiling was completely missing. Light flooded in from the massive hole above, and every surface was covered in plaster dust.

'Don't worry Dora, we can get another one,' Andrew said, when he saw me looking at the blackened and soggy sofa. My eyes filled with tears – it was completely ruined. 'It's only a sofa,' he said, trying to cheer me up.

The thing is, I'd spent weeks looking for that very special Victorian Chesterfield sofa and I'd had it upholstered in beautiful green velvet. It was a beauty and Andrew had no idea how much I'd coveted it. I broke into floods of tears.

'Look Dora, no one's died for God's sake!' said Andrew.

If I'd had a weapon at my disposal at that particular moment, I'm sure I would have used it on him. Anyway, later on I put it all down to tiredness after a long and tedious journey, having been subjected to flight delays, Jess moaning about the flight delays all the way home, and the fact that the M42 was shut for road-works which meant further delays. So, when I finally got home and saw the wreckage and devastation, I admit I did behave a bit irrationally. Luckily, none of the children witnessed me throwing the bowl of fruit at Andrew's head, and anyway, it missed his head and smashed the front window instead. Afterwards, Andrew had to explain that Mummy needed another little holiday at Granny's house to get used to the idea that some of the furniture wasn't going to make it.

It's all water under the bridge now, and we can laugh about it – mostly. The bit about it that isn't funny though, is the home insurance premium which has gone up five-fold since then. Apparently we are a high-risk family due to the unprecedented number of incidents per year.

The weather today put a stop to all outdoor activities. Flora's expedition to Totness was cancelled much to her annoyance. Of course, we were delighted – the idea of Flora riding pillion with the gormless Gaz at the helm is terrifying enough, never mind in driving rain and gale-force winds. She went off to the cinema instead to see a 3D horror film called *Zombie Vampire Slayers* with Tom.

'I'm bored,' said Luke shortly after they'd gone.

'I'm bored too,' said Billy.

'How about playing a board game?' I suggested.

'I'm not *that* bored!' said Luke.

We ended up taking them out to the indoor bowling centre in town, where they spent a fortune on interactive games and snacks. Later, Andrew brought up the subject of my current employment status.

'Our bank account has taken a battering recently,' said Andrew, - 'we'll have to do something about it – we can't go on like this.'

'Mmmm,' I mumbled, avoiding the issue.

'Doesn't Jess need some help?'

'She might,' I said, non-committedly.

'Why don't you ask her?' said Andrew.

'Yes, possibly,' I said.

'I think it would be a really good idea,' said Andrew, persisting.

I tried to change the subject. 'When is your pay rise being implemented?'

'Not soon enough,' said Andrew, - 'which is why we need another source of income.'

I went to sleep with a niggling feeling of impending frustration and foreboding hanging over me. My days of pottering around unfettered and unregulated are obviously numbered.

Sunday 3rd March

It rained again, all day. I felt the dismal relentless certainty of it in my bones. I need to find a solution to our financially straightened circumstances soon. It's all very well though, Andrew complaining about our lack of money, but it's very difficult to find anything that fits around kids, dogs, and housework, not to mention the time spent supplying endless nutritionally satisfying meals and fresh clean clothes. Working with Jess would be an obvious solution and when she first set up Paradise Bakery with Terry, I did do quite a lot. The trouble is that it didn't go very well. Andrew says it was my fault and that I'm too impetuous – basically, if I'd read the instructions properly on how to operate the machinery, some of the accidents could have been avoided. Well, I don't think it was fair to blame me entirely – I mean, Jess and Terry shouldn't have left me on my own with mechanical things: Jess knows how hopeless I am with anything technical. They were insured of course, so they got the repairs covered, but as Jess so bluntly put it, 'we're not insured for loss of business due to incompetence.' She was looking at me with a particularly evil expression at the time. The mixer accident was really down to lack of experience. I was spooning flour out of a metal canister, when it just slipped out of my hands and the whole thing fell in. When the blades broke off, it made the most horrendous noise. As far as I'm concerned though, it shouldn't be that easy for something to fall into cake mix, should it? And then there was the oven disaster. I'd only gone outside for a short time to get some fresh air, but I must have missed the timer bell going off. Unfortunately, by the time I realised that I hadn't heard it, the whole place was full of billowing black smoke. It's a good job Terry came back just in time to turn the sprinklers off. Anyway, I got the blame of course, for 68 burnt bloomers, 50 charred cobs and 100 carbonised baps. Jess said it was my fault about the J-cloth as well, but she shouldn't have asked me to do cleaning in between making cakes – I'm not very good at multi-tasking despite what they say about women being better at it than men.

After that, Jess and Terry said they could manage without me, but I think they were definitely being a bit premature because no one can be expected to pick up new skills that quickly. I'm sure I'd have got the hang of it if they'd given me a chance.

Anyway, the long and short of it is – I don't really want to work for Jess because she's not very tolerant of people's short-comings. I need to be with people who appreciate me for myself. I'm not sure where that might be, but I'm sure something will come up.

Monday 4ᵗʰ March

As well as putting an advert in the paper about selling the grass, I decided to list some other items at the same time. We could do with the extra cash, so I advertised

Flora's old bike, Luke's football table, an old fridge, some lamps, a tatty leather brief case that's been hanging around unused for ages, and Billy's old high chair and playpen. All the children hated the playpen – they just stood at the bars wailing and refused to play with anything. It made quite a good dog cage though, when we had the puppies. If I needed to go out and didn't want them ruining shoes and things, I used to quickly lock them in there and it worked quite well. Anyway, it's just taking up valuable space now – like too many other things.

I decided to do some dusting after this, but really I was putting off the evil moment of having to think about job hunting. After spending quite a long time polishing the desk in the study, I sat down at the computer and looked at my CV. It needed updating of course, since I lost my job at JR's. The trouble is, whatever I do to try and improve the presentation of my employment history, it still amounts to very little. I've tried to be inventive and stand out from the crowd but it hasn't been very successful. For instance, describing my years of child-rearing as 'self-employed animal tamer' didn't seem to go down very well with the Job Centre. In fact, now I come to think of it, during the interview they asked me twice if I had my own social worker. Embellishing the truth didn't work too well either – describing one job I had as 'seafood technician' got me into trouble: -

'I saw you arranging the sprats on the ice, at Tesco,' said the stern-looking woman from behind her gold-rimmed spectacles.

My list of part-time and temporary jobs looks like a bizarre and wacky Pick & Mix. These jobs bear little relationship to each other – the only common thread is that they were jobs – a means to earning money. My most hated question in an interview is; 'why do you want this job?' *Why do you think? I always say to myself – I mean why does anyone want a job? Are these people even more dense than me?* Then there's the awful business of lying about how wonderful you think their business/organisation/one-man band is, and how much you are looking forward to joining them in their lovely shop/office/cabin or shed. I looked at my CV and decided it needed paring down a bit. For instance, I think I should probably remove all office based jobs, since I definitely don't want another of those. Then I decided to take off all the menial jobs like cleaning, looking after old ladies, and pet watching – after all, I've got enough of all that in my own house.

'Blimey,' said Andrew, when he looked at it after tea, - 'it's a bit thin isn't it?' He flipped it over to see if there was anything written on the other side.

'Well, I want a job I'll actually like,' I said, defending it.

'I understand that,' said Andrew, 'but you've only got three things on here…'

'I could pad them out a bit I suppose.'

'I think you'll have to,' said Andrew.

'But what more can I put about Venetian blinds and made-to-measure curtains?' I said, - 'or my egg-collecting job at the chicken farm?'

'I'm not sure,' said Andrew, 'but I think you could expand on the job where you were a tour guide at the old asylum perhaps…'

'The trouble is that I don't really have anyone I can ask for references.'

'What, none at all?' said Andrew.

'Well, you know I left under a bit of a cloud from some of these jobs,' I said, - 'so they're not going to give me good references are they? The curtain shop said there were too many measuring mistakes – they even tried to intimate that I'd lied about having a maths GCSE! The chicken farm people said I spent too much time talking – to the chickens that is, and that they weren't paying me to socialise, and the tour guide job only lasted three months – don't you remember? After my probation period, they said they didn't need me any more. I must say, I was pretty miffed at the time since I thought I was doing quite a good job.'

'Wasn't that the one where you added on an extra tour round to the village pub?'

'Yes, but the tourists loved it – they were really keen to see a traditional English pub as well.'

Unfortunately, my creative addition to their experience was not very popular with the organisers because they missed their afternoon visit to Shakespeare Country.

The trouble is, I find the world of work a bit disconcerting really. I don't think I was cut out for it.

Tuesday 5th March

Jess and I decided to go and take Mum to visit Dad's grave today. When Billy heard about it this morning, he wanted to come too. I thought his interest in death and burials had waned, but apparently not.

'My friend Sam says you can hear ghosts whispering in graveyards,' said Billy over breakfast.

'That's rubbish,' said Tom, - 'there's no such thing.'

'There is! Sam saw his Granny's ghost there last summer.'

'OK – what did she look like then?'

'All white and misty – like a ghost of course.'

'I don't believe it – you're talking rot,' said Tom.

'I want to come with you,' said Billy. 'Can't I stay off school?'

'No,' I said.

Jess turned up with Mum at about 10 o'clock so we had a cup of tea before we went. I must say, my mother is looking very well these days – she seems to have renewed vigour. I suppose it comes from having few responsibilities and the luxury of a comfortable retirement. I do feel slightly envious.

'I've brought a nice Hyacinth to put on your Dad's grave - he always liked them,' she said, wistfully.

We went off in Jess's car up to St Gregory's cemetery on the other side of town.

'Poor old Dad,' said Jess. 'He's missed out on so much since he died. I wonder what he'd be saying to us now if he was here.'

'Hello Mrs Jarvis,' said a voice behind us. We all nearly jumped out of our skin.

'Good grief vicar! You made us jump!' said Mum.

'Sorry,' he said.

'We thought you were a voice from beyond the grave,' said Mum. 'We're just visiting Gerald.'

'Yes. We all miss him don't we,' said the vicar. 'He was such a valued member of the community – always willing to help anyone in trouble. There'll never be another Gerald Jarvis, that's for sure.'

'No,' said Jess, 'did you hear that Mum – no one could replace Dad could they?' she said loudly. 'He was one-in-a-million, wasn't he Mum?'

'Gerald Jarvis certainly was a real gentleman,' said the vicar, – 'a man of great distinction in my book – everyone had huge respect for him – what a wonderful man he was…. I'm sure you must miss him a great deal.'

Later on after we dropped Mum off at home, we congratulated ourselves on a good job well done.

'That was a piece of luck, the vicar being there wasn't it!' said Jess. 'Hopefully it did the trick and reminded Mum that no one could hold a candle to our father – not in a million years!'

I hope Jess is right. Flora, on the other hand, thinks that it would be fantastic if Granny got married again. She's planned the whole ridiculous event in her head already – mainly because she's never been a bridesmaid and is desperate to find a way to be one. The thought of Flora trailing along behind my mother in some sort of Gothic eyesore doesn't bear thinking about. None of it does. I must put it out of my mind – after all, it's silly to dwell on something which couldn't possibly happen.

Wednesday 6th March

It looks as if we might have a buyer for the extra grass thank goodness. They're coming tomorrow evening. I've managed to sell Flora's bike and the football table today. I nearly sold the playpen and highchair, but the woman who came to look said she thought the numerous bite marks all over the playpen were a bit alarming, and the fact that there was an actual bite out of the edge of the tray on the highchair was a bit off-putting. I explained that I'd sprayed liberally with Detox, but she couldn't be persuaded. Anyway, she bought the brief case instead, so I'm now £60 better off in total – well, I was, until Luke said he needed new rugby boots. So, easy come, easy go!

We got another postcard from Andrew's parents this morning – even more brief than last time:

See you on Saturday – B+B xx'

'Oh no!' said Andrew when he saw it, - 'they've barely been away five minutes.'

'I hope they're not bringing Stan this time.'

'Well, we'll just have to see.'

'I suppose Dad can help me with the turf - make himself useful while he's here.'

'Don't take your eyes off him this time Andrew – in case he does something else.'

'Don't worry Dora, I'll be watching him like a hawk. By the way, have you seen my old briefcase anywhere? I put some documents in it from that big litigation case, but I can't find it anywhere. They've appealed the decision so I'm going to be really busy with it all again.'

The blood slightly drained from my face when he said this. I feigned ignorance and frantically tried to find the woman's number on the phone while Andrew went for a shower.

'Damn, damn, and double damn!' I said to myself when I discovered it was a 'withheld' number.

'You must be really tired,' I said to him when he came downstairs. 'Why don't you forget about the briefcase for now, and I'll look for it tomorrow.'

I tried to remember the conversation I'd had with her and whether there were any clues in it about where I might contact her. The only thing I could think of, was the fact that she'd said her toddler was at a nursery in town and that his name was Charlie.

I went to bed feeling quite off-colour and didn't sleep at all well. It's all Andrew's fault really – I mean, why did he have to put important documents in an old tatty briefcase? They should have been at the office along with all the other boring bits of paper, honestly! He did say that when he started at Sharp and Prentice, that he wouldn't be bringing work home, so if he hasn't stuck to his principles, it's hardly my fault is it?

Thursday 7th March

I spent all day trying to track down the elusive briefcase. What a nightmare! I had no idea there were so many nurseries. Who'd have thought that our small town would have forty eight of them! And some of those receptionists were very rude. I don't know why some people have to be so unhelpful. I mean, I know there are lots of boys called Charlie, but they haven't all got mothers who are short and round with fuzzy hair and a moustache. Most of the people I spoke to told me they wouldn't tell me even if they did have the right Charlie. One of them said they'd phone the police if I rang again – something to do with data protection control…. Honestly, all I wanted was a phone number! You'd think I was asking for the moon! I gave up after two hours of phoning to focus on applying for jobs. There isn't much on offer though. With a great deal of reluctance, I perused the part-time jobs section:

Lorry Driver – I'm not qualified and even if I was, I imagine disqualification would occur soon after I took a job like that, based on my lack of manoeuvring capabilities.

School Dinner Monitor - I don't think I really want to come into contact with children outside of family time – my sanity could suffer.

Doctor's Receptionist – This is more tempting – but I'm not sure I want to be near a lot of ill people every day – I mean, that could get quite depressing couldn't it? And I might catch lots of colds and flu and then give it to my family, and then have to put up with Andrew being ill which is worse than everyone being ill together, so 'no' to that I think.

Home-help – Definitely 'no' to that.

Shop Assistant for Newsagents – I don't think this would be a good idea – too many sweets everywhere. I'd probably spend half my wages on chocolate and lemon bonbons.

Supermarket Check-out Assistant – This would be OK, except that it involves mostly sitting, well – totally sitting actually, so I could end up looking like a dumpling after 6 months. I wouldn't be able to criticise Andrew for being overweight then, so it's probably 'no' to that as well.

Pooches Parlour Assistant – Now this one is a contender. I like dogs, and I've had plenty of practice washing them – definitely one to consider.

Telesales for Double-glazing firm – I don't think so, not after my last telesales job selling solar panels. That was a bit disastrous. How was I to know that Swansea is the wettest town in Britain. And being told to stand on a desk with a cone on my head for having the least amount of sales in a week was the last straw. I told that bloke he could stick his cone where the sun didn't shine.

Apart from the bar and waitressing jobs, that was about it, so I applied for the dog-grooming and the doctor's receptionist job even though I didn't want that one. It's really so that Andrew can see I'm making an effort. Of course, we wouldn't be worrying about lack of finances so much if Andrew hadn't bought all that extra turf. Anyway, the man came this evening and paid for two thirds of it in cash so that was a relief. The other thing that happened which was also a relief, was that Charlie's mother turned up at tea time. She'd brought the briefcase back and said she wanted her money back.

'I'm sorry,' she said, 'but I found a mouldy banana in the inside pocket.'

I very happily gave her the money back, but when I looked inside there were no papers.

'Did you by any chance find some letters inside it?' I asked her.

'Yes – I'm afraid I threw them away,' she said. 'They're in the dustbin outside our house.'

I really hope she didn't see me following her home in my car. I think I was fairly discreet, and I parked down the street and gave it at least fifteen minutes before I took the bin-bags out of her bin and shoved them in the back of my car.

'What are you doing that for?' asked Billy, when he saw me raking through piles of rubbish on our lawn in the dark.

'I've lost something important,' I told him.

'Yuk!' said Billy, looking at the discarded old food and smelly bits of cardboard and chip-wrappers.

'Eureka!' I said, on finding what I was looking for. Luckily, the papers were inside a plastic sleeve. I had a bit of a problem trying to cram the extra rubbish into our bin though.

Back inside the house, I wiped some old Ketchup off the front of the wallet and put it back in the briefcase. I left the blackened banana where it was. *How fortuitous, I thought - he'll never know the real reason those papers have such a rancid aroma.* I also couldn't help smiling at the obvious irony of his bag having a forgotten snack lurking within.

Friday 8ᵗʰ March

I decided to put the playpen and highchair out on the street with a note attached to say to any passers-by that these things are free to anyone who wants to take them away. Afterwards, I took the dogs out and went over to see Suzie since I hadn't heard from her for a while. She's lying low of course, after all the recent drama, and doesn't like to go out much. Suzie's daughter Violet didn't take what's happened very well. Apparently, she complained that there wouldn't be enough money for her impending wedding, which is planned for July. She also implied that it might be better if Suzie didn't go, to save all the embarrassment. When Suzie finally plucked up the courage to tell Warren, he was beside himself and didn't speak to her for a week. Anyway, I hope things have settled down a bit now. I noticed the Eros statue wasn't in evidence when I walked up the garden path. There were weeds and nettles sprouting up everywhere and the garden had an air of neglect about it which is not like Suzie at all. Inside the house, it was the same – there was a definite lack of housekeeping going on.

'I let my cleaner go,' said Suzie. 'I just don't want anyone in the house at the moment - or the garden. Brad and Jed have been deported anyway. I haven't replaced them – I can't be bothered.'

'I think you're depressed,' I said, stating the obvious. Suzie looked even more miserable than the last time I saw her. 'What's Warren doing at the moment?'

'He's coming back next week,' said Suzie flatly. 'He says he's taking another job in Dubai so he'll only be here for 10 days. He has calmed down now though.'

'Good,' I said. 'Let's go out with the dogs and blow some cobwebs away.' She agreed to come which pleased Ping-Pong. 'By the way, where is the statue?' I asked her as we left the house.

'I sold it, along with all the other stuff from the salon. It's gone up North to a nail bar in Newcastle. Good riddance to it too. Did you know, that glass counter was meant to be a You-Know-What? Cressida actually had it custom-made! And I can't believe I didn't notice how all the towels had embroidered copulating couples on them, or the enormous number of boxes of condoms - we were only supposed to be supplying them for fun instead of biscuits with your coffee – that's what Cressida told me anyway.'

'Suzie! That was pretty naïve, even for you!'

'That's what the police said. No one believes I didn't know all about it. If I go to prison, you will visit me won't you?'

'It won't come to that,' I said. 'Andrew will think of something – try not to worry.' I felt instantly guilty saying this – after all, I have no idea what will happen. I do have an unwavering trust in Andrew's ability to expose the opposition's weaknesses in an argument though, and so I hope I am right.

We walked down to the river and along the path beside it. Ping-Pong had clearly learned his lesson from the unfortunate near-drowning experience of a month ago, and steered well clear of the water. My dogs on the other hand leapt straight in to chase some poor unsuspecting ducks.

'My in-laws are about to descend,' I told her. 'I'm dreading it. They're a bit barmy to say the least.'

'How long for?' asked Suzie.

'That's just the thing, we don't know. They're homeless at the moment.'

'They could stay here,' said Suzie.

'What! Are you serious?' I said with surprise.

'Well, I'm going up to London to stay with Violet for a while – to try and smooth things over. My house will be empty. I'd rather someone was in it.'

'What about Warren?' I said, imagining the terrible combination of Andrew's wacky parents and a smart businessman like Warren attempting to co-habit. It was an unthinkable idea.

'He'll be in London too. It's fine, honestly,' said Suzie.

'But you don't know them,' I said.

She laughed. 'They can't be that bad!'

'Well, it would certainly help us a lot. When are you going?' I asked.

'Monday. They can come here Monday evening if you like.'

What a Godsend, I thought, planning for the long haul. Suzie usually stays at least two weeks if she goes to London.

'You are a star,' I said, feeling quite relieved.

I told Andrew as soon as he came in.

'Brilliant,' he said, - 'but did you warn her about them?'

'Sort of,' I said, 'but not in any great detail.'

'Right,' said Andrew, pursing his lips. 'Well, we'll just have to hope everything runs smoothly.'

'I found your briefcase,' I said, holding it up triumphantly.

'Even more brilliant!' he said. 'This calls for a Friday night celebration. Let's go into town for a curry.'

'What are we celebrating?' asked Tom, joining us in the

kitchen.

'That your mother is a genius,' said Andrew. And that I
have had a successful week at work. What about you Tom?'

'Umm, well … I got 70% in my maths test and beat
Mark Tanner at chess.'

'Well done son,' said Andrew. 'What about you Luke?'

'I got *no* homework detentions this week, and Mr Prosser
says I'm getting better at tackling in rugby without injuring
people.'

'Great!' said Andrew, - 'and Billy – what about you?'

Billy thought for a moment. 'Mrs Pincher had a spider in
her hair in assembly and it went down her jumper,' he said
with glee.

'Wonderful,' said Andrew. 'Where's Flora?'

'Out with her boyfriend,' said Tom.

'Gaz, you mean.'

'No – a different one – he's called Mathew.'

'Even more reason to celebrate!' said Andrew, digging
into his pocket for his car keys. 'Anyone coming?'

Saturday 9th March

At 8 o'clock in the evening, Bob and Barbara finally
turned up. I saw their battered old yellow campervan,
Mabel, hove into view from around the corner at the end of
our road, although we heard it before we saw it – it's a
noisy beast. They parked up and I was glad to see they were
unaccompanied this time. I made them a pot of tea and got
out some of Jess's cake.

'Oh, we've had a terrible journey,' said Barbara, flopping

down on the sofa. 'They stopped us at Dover when we came off the ferry and did a spot search of Mabel – we've been stuck there for hours. It was a very frightening experience I can tell you – we were treated like criminals. The sniffer dogs kept barking at poor Mabel and so they took everything out and searched absolutely everywhere.'

'Bloody Fascists!' said Bob. 'They didn't find anything. Picking on innocent people like us – they should be concentrating on the real criminals.'

'We'd had a terrible day already – I am utterly shattered – I don't suppose you've got any brandy or whiskey for this tea have you Dora?' Barbara held her cup out hopefully.

'Well, I'm not surprised the dogs were interested in you,' said Andrew. 'They can sniff a spliff from a mile away Dad.'

'Well, for your information son, I didn't have any with me – I'm not as daft as that.'

'So what else happened?' I asked.

'Well,' said Barbara, launching into a tale of woe, - 'Stan asked us to bring back something for a friend of his – one of those Spanish leather pouffes. We stopped for a picnic in the French Alps – oh it was lovely - the scenery was just magnificent. Anyway, I got it out to sit on – my arthritis is playing up terribly at the moment. After we got back in the van and drove off, it was about an hour later that we remembered the pouffe – we'd left it behind. Well, we had no choice but to go back for it – Stan expressly told us how important it was to get it to his friend. It was one of the few possessions this friend's mother had owned you see. Stan told us she'd died and left it to him in her will. We drove all the way back, but the trouble is, all those mountain streams look the same, and the roads are like a spider's web. It was hopeless. We searched for two hours and had to give up. I feel terrible about it,' said Barbara. 'How are we going to tell

Stan's friend that we've lost his poor, dead mother's only heirloom!'

Andrew couldn't help himself, and burst out laughing, much to his mother's disgust.

'I don't know why you think it's so funny,' she said. 'You're being very insensitive.'

'Mum – you won't like what I'm going to say to you, but you've both been taken for a ride by your so-called friend Stan.'

'What do you mean?' said Bob.

'Come on Dad! The only reason you're not sitting in the police custody facility in Dover is because you lost Stan's dodgy beanbag!'

'What's he talking about?' said Barbara, - 'I'm confused.'

'Stan used you both as drug-runners Mum. That thing you were sitting on was probably stuffed with massive amounts of an incredibly illegal substance – it's a good job you left it behind.'

'Well, I can't believe Stan would do such a thing,' said Barbara with a tear in her eye.

'It would account for that sniffer dog's obsession with your trousers,' said Bob.

'Oh Andy, it was awful – I had to have one of those special investigations ….' said Barbara, blowing her nose.

'Well it seems to me, you've had a very lucky escape,' said Andrew. 'I think it's time you parted company with Stan, don't you?'

'But what if it's genuinely just a pouffe?' said Barbara.

'Trust me,' said Andrew, - 'it wasn't.'

They were so exhausted by their experience, they decided to go straight to bed and tell us the rest in the morning.

'Didn't they like their holiday?' asked Billy.

'I don't think it was as good as they hoped it would be,' said Andrew.

'Can we train Fudge and Cocoa to be police dogs?' asked Billy. 'They could catch criminals and bite them – that would be awesome.'

'They're probably not of the right calibre,' said Andrew.

'You mean they're too brainless,' said Tom. 'They can't even work out which pocket the dog treat is in - they'd be rubbish.'

Billy looked downcast.

'Not all dogs make good sniffer dogs Billy,' said Andrew. 'Some dogs are much better at being pets. Fudge and Cocoa are that sort.'

'OK,' he said, seemingly mollified.

'Do you think my parents are becoming senile Dora?' said Andrew when we went to bed.

'No, they're just too trusting of other people's motives,' I said. 'It's just that *you* find that difficult to understand – you are trained to be suspicious – that's part of your job, isn't it?'

'I suppose so, but they do seem to get themselves into a lot of trouble don't they? I wish they'd just settle down somewhere and lead a boring but predictable life. I've got enough to worry about. I hadn't planned on becoming my parents' keeper – not yet anyway.'

'I'm sure they'll sort themselves out in a bit,' I said, not believing a word of it.

Sunday 10th March (Mother's Day)

Billy was the only one of my children who brought me anything for Mother's Day, and that's only because Mrs Pincher makes the children produce a card every year – hand-made of course. He very carefully gave it to me along with a cup of tea he'd made with Flora's help. The card had a picture of a mad-looking woman on the front with a green face.

'That's you,' he said. 'I didn't know how to make skin colour so it went a bit wrong.'

'It's lovely,' I said, pleased to be getting anything at all. He'd written a sweet little poem inside:

<u>My Mummy</u>

My Mum is like the sunshine

She always makes me glad

She gives me lots of yummy treats

And hugs me when I'm sad

'I can hug you when you're not sad too,' I said, giving him a squeeze. He wriggled free and ran off.

'Look what Billy gave me,' I said, showing Andrew.

'Do you think he had help?' said Andrew.

'You're so cynical,' I said. 'Even if he did, I'm putting it in my treasure box.'

There was a lot of sniggering at the breakfast table this morning. Billy had asked quite innocently what a pouffe was and why Granny was sitting on it. Tom and Luke thought it was the funniest thing they'd heard for weeks.

'Pouffes were very popular in the seventies,' said Andrew, - 'we had several in the house.' This made them even more hysterical.

'Can I have one in my room?' asked Billy, while his two juvenile brothers nearly choked on their toast.

'What's so funny?' asked Billy, getting annoyed.

'They're just being silly,' I told him. 'Just ignore them.'

'I think someone should explain it to him,' said Andrew.

'Well, don't let it be either of those two,' I said, eyeballing Luke and Tom.

Bob and Barbara made an appearance shortly after the boys had left the table, which was a mercy.

'It's nice to hear them laughing,' said Barbara, - 'after everything that we've been through in the last couple of weeks.'

'So,' said Andrew, 'tell us all about your trip.'

'Well, to be honest, we didn't enjoy it very much, did we Bob?'

'How was the villa?' asked Andrew.

'Well, it wasn't exactly a villa – more of a sort of cave…' said Barbara.

'It *was* a cave,' said Bob.

'In the side of the cliff – a house in a cliff,' said Barbara.

'That sounds interesting,' said Andrew.

'Well, it wasn't – it was dark and very damp – much worse than being in the tepee. My knees were as stiff as boards.'

'Oh dear,' said Andrew.

'And there were rats,' said Bob. 'And no proper toilet – we had to go down the road to the public loo and it cost us two euros every time.'

'I thought you liked living rough,' said Andrew, provocatively.

'Not like that Andy,' said Barbara. 'There was no community spirit. We had no garden and it was miles away from the nearest town.'

'Where was Stan while you were stuck there then?' I asked.

'He said he had to go to Madrid to see someone.'

'Why didn't you stay in the campervan and travel around – you would have had a much better time.'

Bob looked slightly sheepish. 'We lent it to Stan, so he could get to Madrid – he said he'd only be a couple of days…'

'I see,' said Andrew, trying not to roll his eyes in despair.

'Well, you're back now and all's well that ends well!' I said, cheerily.

Flora emerged from her bedroom to come downstairs for something to eat, wearing what could only be described as an outfit made of string which left little to the imagination of what was underneath.

'Do you think it might be wise to put something warmer on Flora – it's quite cold today,' I said.

She shrugged. Andrew was more forthright – 'Flora, for God's sake cover yourself up – you look like a harlot!'

Flora looked at Andrew with total disdain. 'Nobody says 'harlot' Dad – you're so Neolithic!'

'Really,' said Andrew, colour rising in his cheeks. 'I'll tell you what Flora, if I'm so 'Neolithic' as you call it, then your allowance can be paid in rocks instead of your usual £20 this week – OK?'

She flounced out of the kitchen and went back upstairs to put something more acceptable on.

'You know she'll change back when she goes out don't you?' I said to Andrew.

'Well, at least I don't have to see it,' he said. 'What do these girls think they're doing going out half-dressed!'

'I'm glad I only had boys,' said Barbara.

The afternoon was spent getting the grass laid at last, although with everyone suddenly being an expert in turf-laying, it wasn't without its tribulations. Anyway, I feel a great burden has lifted – in fact, it literally has, and is now beautifully settled, flat and lush. My view from the kitchen window is vastly improved, and the boys will once again be able to play outside and mash it all up with their football games.

Monday 11th March

'For Pete's sake!' said Andrew this morning, when he looked in the briefcase. He retrieved the papers and discarded the bag. 'Who the bloody hell left rotten food in there?' he yelled.

'You did,' I said.

'I don't remember having anything with Ketchup on it – I don't even like Ketchup,' he said, flapping the papers in the air to get rid of the pong. He went out looking very disgruntled.

'Just spray them with Pledge or something,' I suggested as he got into his car. Honestly, men are so fussy sometimes – they don't know how to make the best of a situation.

Just to compound things, Billy gave me a letter from school before he left this morning which I should have had a week ago, saying that he needs a jellyfish costume by tomorrow for his class assembly.

'Mrs Pincher says, if it's a problem, she will ask the other mothers if they've got something,' said Billy.

'No, that's fine,' I said through gritted teeth. 'Don't worry Billy, I will sort it out.' There's no way, I thought, that Mrs Pincher is going to get one over on me – absolutely not - *'ask the other mothers'* indeed! How humiliating! I'm a creative person after all – I should be able to cobble something together. I bet she gave Billy the most difficult costume deliberately.

'A jellyfish!' said Barbara. 'That's quite hard isn't it?'

'Yes, I suppose it is, but I'm sure I can think of something.'

'Can't he be a fish or a rock or something?'

'No, I'm afraid not – his teacher has asked him to be a jellyfish, and Mrs Pincher is not to be trifled with.'

'I'll help you,' said Barbara.

I was actually quite grateful – Andrew's mother is nothing if not resourceful. I mean, she's had several years of fashioning found objects and other people's rubbish into useful things, so between us we should be able to think of something.

'Where's Bob?' I said, suddenly wondering where he was.

'He said he was taking the playpen and highchair somewhere for you,' said Barbara. 'Apparently, someone saw them and asked him if he could deliver to their house.'

'Oh, good,' I said, - 'it's nice that someone has found a use for them.'

'There's something very satisfying about recycling,' said Barbara. 'I just love it!'

It's amazing what you can do with some coat-hangers and a net curtain. Those Blue Peter programmes weren't wasted on me. Barbara made a wire hat to fit on Billy's head to attach to the jellyfish – like a giant umbrella over his head.

'That's brilliant!' I said to Barbara. 'He'll be really pleased. 'It just needs a bit of colour don't you think?'

'What about these?' said Barbara, holding up some old purple tights with holes in. 'We could cut them into strips - for tentacles.'

'OK – yes I'm sure Flora won't want them in that condition.'

How wrong could I be…

'Mum, I can't believe you did that!' she shrieked when she came in from school and saw the remnants lying on the floor. 'They're my favourite tights!'

'I'll get you some more,' I said.

'They cost £40,' said Flora.

'What!' I said, reeling with shock.

'They're special ones,' she shouted, stomping off upstairs.

'How can a pair of tights cost £40?' Andrew said with astonishment at tea time.

'I've no idea,' I said, - 'but they are now adorning Billy's costume, which is for tomorrow morning by the way, and we are supposed to go – it's his class assembly.'

'Why has Billy got a giant lampshade on his head?' asked Luke when he sat down to tea.

'It's so he can't bite people,' said Tom, - 'like when Fudge had one on his head to stop him biting his stitches.'

'It's his costume,' I said. 'He's meant to be a jellyfish. Billy, please take it off at the table – it needs to stay intact until tomorrow.' He reluctantly removed it.

'Some jellyfish can kill people,' he said. 'They've got poisonous tentacles.'

'You can eat some jellyfish too,' said Bob.

'Yuk,' said Flora.

'When we were in Spain, we had some in a stew with bird's eyes.'

There was a minutes silence until we all realised their Grandad was joking. You can never be quite sure with Bob though.

After tea, they followed us down to Suzie's house in their van. They couldn't believe their luck when they saw Suzie's virtual palace.

'This'll do nicely,' said Bob.

'Oooh, a proper kitchen,' said Barbara. 'I do miss having a kitchen.'

'The garden could do with some work though,' said Bob.

'As long as you don't do anything too radical Dad,' said Andrew. 'No re-arranging things.'

'Don't worry Andy,' were Bob's parting words as we left them to settle in.

'Well, they've got a couple of weeks to think about where they'll go now. At least they're not staying with us,' said Andrew happily.

Tuesday 12th March

The school hall was overflowing with other dutiful parents and grandparents when we got there, but they'd all been more organised than us and got better seats. Andrew and I sat with Bob and Barbara at the back with the pregnant mothers and other people who might need a quick exit to the nearest loo, or just a quick exit.

'How long is it?' asked Andrew, - 'only I've got a meeting at 10 o'clock.'

'Shush,' hissed someone behind us.

Mrs Pincher led her class onto the stage with a loud and out of tune rendition of *Octopus's Garden*, quickly followed by some fish dancing to *Rock Around the Croc*. Billy the jellyfish, I realised, dominated all the available space with his voluminous costume, and had to be accommodated in the wings where he couldn't be seen very well. The other thing I hadn't considered was the fact that he couldn't see properly through the net curtain and had to be guided up the steps at the side of the stage by a sea-slug and a lobster. Most of the music was murdered and Andrew whispered that he wished he'd brought his earplugs, but there were some enchanting cameo performances by the chosen few of course, which saved the day: Felicity Beaumont (angel fish) sang a song about how useful friends are, and Ben Findlay (dressed as a barnacle), did a lively and impressive tap dance. When it was all over, Mrs Pincher beamed with pride and of course, everyone applauded enthusiastically.

'It reminded me of your school concerts Andy,' said Barbara. 'You used to sing so loudly – it was really funny.'

'Oh yes, that's right,' said Bob, - 'they had to ban him eventually didn't they!'

'Rubbish!' said Andrew.

'No it isn't – your music teacher said you didn't have a volume control.'

'So, no change there then,' I said, laughing.

'Yes, all right – thanks parents, for the vote of confidence.'

'Look Andrew, Billy's waving at us,' I said, giving him a wave and blowing a kiss in his direction.

'Well, I'm glad that's over,' said Andrew, - 'they ought to provide cushions – these chairs are torture.'

Just as we got up to leave, there was an almighty crashing noise from behind the curtain, followed by an even louder shriek. We knew straight away it was Billy.

'I'm afraid,' said the nurse at the hospital, - 'he's probably broken it. We'll have to wait for an x-ray to confirm it.'

Billy clutched his arm in pain and was as white as a sheet.

'How did it happen?' she asked.

'I was waving at my Mum, and my costume fell off and the lobster tripped over it, and then a walrus fell over on top of me,' said Billy.'

'I see,' she said.

'School assembly,' I explained.

'Well, Billy, I'm afraid you won't be doing any more waving with that arm for a while.'

'Poor Mrs Pincher,' I said. 'Everything had gone so well until the end.'

'Will I still have to go to school?' asked Billy.

'Yes,' said Andrew.

'But I can't write or anything.'

'You can still listen though, and you could try and write with your left hand – like Grandad. He's ambidextrous.'

'Wow,' said Billy. 'That's so cool!'

Andrew went into work five hours late, and I spent the afternoon showing Billy how to do things one-handed.

'Well, I suppose all three of you boys have now broken at least one arm each, so hopefully that's it,' I said.

Billy contemplated his new orange plaster cast. 'I can't wait to show it to Dan Herbert – mine's much bigger than his was.'

When the others came back from school, Billy had his moment of glory. Luke and Tom wrote some rude things on his plaster which had to be scrubbed off later and Flora drew a picture of Scratch on it with a pretend paw-print. Of course, the novelty will wear off very quickly and then I'll have to listen to weeks of grumbling. What joy!

Wednesday 13th March

This morning I got a letter addressed to me that wasn't a bill or junk mail, so that in itself was quite exciting. It turned out to be an invitation to an interview on Friday at the dog-grooming place: Pooches Parlour.

'Great,' said Andrew, - 'that's really quick. They must be desperate – you'll be in with a chance.'

'Thanks a bunch,' I said.

'I didn't mean it quite like that,' said Andrew, although he did, in actual fact.

The usual morning routine was more of a trial than usual, with Billy's arm out of action. He tried to pour milk onto a bowl of cornflakes and it went everywhere but in the bowl. The dogs rushed to lap it up off the floor and nearly knocked Billy over onto his other arm.

'Billy, you have to sit down and let the boys help you,' I said. 'Boys, help Billy please.'

'But I'll be late for school,' said Luke, making for the door.

'And I need to look for my chemistry book,' said Tom.

'Typical,' I said. 'Never mind Billy, I'll do it.'

I decided to walk Billy to school this morning as it's his first one-armed outing in public. On the way down the drive, I saw a big luminous notice stuck to our bin.

'What's that?' asked Billy.

'It's a notice from the Council,' I said, trying to pick it off. 'It says our bin has too much rubbish in it. They won't take it because the lid is sticking up.'

'That's stupid,' said Billy.

'You're telling me,' I said, - 'it's 'Health and Safety' gone mad.'

'What's that?' asked Billy.

'You'll learn all about it when you're older,' I said. 'Suffice to say, common sense is a thing of the past and it's been replaced with lots of boxes you can tick.'

'Dan Herbert says where he lives people just throw their rubbish on the ground,' said Billy.

'Really! That's not very nice is it?'

'No - but people come with spikes and take it away, why don't we throw ours on the street too?'

'That is an interesting solution Billy,' I said, - 'and although it's tempting, I couldn't possibly do such a thing – anyway I could be fined if someone saw me.'

'What will you do with it then?'

'I'll have to go to the tip.'

What a bore – the tip is three miles away on the other side of town. Of course, I could put some of it back where it came from – I mean it's not all my rubbish is it? This seemed like a much better plan.

After I'd walked the dogs, I went to meet Melanie at Valentino's for coffee. We needed to firm up our holiday plans since it's a week on Saturday that we go.

'I'm so excited!' said Melanie. 'I've been looking on-line at all the lovely beaches. There are hammocks everywhere, and coconuts cut fresh from the trees, and cocktails served to you by the dozen. It looks amazing.'

'I've been dreaming about it for the last two weeks,' I said. 'The thought of someone else cooking is the best bit.'

'Can't Andrew cook?' said Melanie.

'Only basic things – he's not adventurous. That's partly why my mother will have to come and stay with him. Anyway, I'm not going to worry about them – they'll be fine.'

'It'll be good for them to do without you for a while – they'll find out how much you do won't they! By the way, Geoff has offered to take us to the airport the morning of our flight.'

'Oh, that's good of him.'

'He says he doesn't mind getting up at 5 o'clock in the morning.'

'Is it *that* early?!' I said.

'I'm afraid so – our flights are at 7.30am. Here, look – I'll show you. Here are the tickets.'

I looked at them for a minute or two. 'Why does it say 'Hiroshima' there, Melanie?'

'I don't know,' she said, frowning.

'I thought we were going to Thailand.'

'I expect it's a stopover or something ....' She folded the tickets up again and put them away.

'That's two thousand miles in the wrong direction!' said Andrew, when I told him. Japan is nowhere near Thailand.

'Well, I thought it seemed a bit strange,' I said.

'If I were you, I'd go back to the travel agents and check it out.'

After tea, I went outside and opened the overflowing bin. By now, the rubbish was pretty whiffy. I held my nose, and took out three bin bags. I shoved them into the boot of my car and opened all the windows. At night, it doesn't take too long to get around town so I was at Charlie's mother's house in no time. Luckily, all was quiet, and their bins were easily accessible on the other side of a low fence. I drove right up next to them and quickly transferred the stinking bags back into their bin. Unfortunately, the last bag split as I was heaving it over the fence, and out spewed a pile of tins and mouldy Spaghetti Bolognese.

'Bugger!' I said loudly. Then I heard someone open the back door, so I had no choice but to leave the mess on the pavement, jump in the car and drive off before anyone saw me.

'Where have you been?' asked Andrew when I got back into the house.

'Oh, just to post a letter,' I fibbed.

'What's that smell?' he said, sniffing the air.

'Must be one of the dogs,' I said. I ran upstairs to have a shower and change my clothes before he could interrogate me further.

Thursday 14th March

I suddenly realised that Tom has grown in the last few weeks because his trousers are an inch too short, and he's towering over me. This is quite disconcerting. It's bad enough that Flora is taller than me now. It's very difficult trying to wield power and influence when you have to look up to your insubordinate children. I think I might have to purchase some shoes with a bigger heel.

I rang Bob and Barbara to see how they were getting on in their holiday home, and if they needed anything.

'We're fine thanks,' said Barbara. 'Bob's been very busy

tidying up your friend's garden, and I've been doing some sewing – Suzie's got a lovely sewing machine – it doesn't look as if it's ever been used.'

'That sounds nice,' I said, hoping that it would give them the incentive they needed to consider living like normal people again. Andrew has put their names down on the council house waiting list - unbeknown to them.

Jess turned up this morning with some broken biscuits and left-over flapjack and stayed for a cup of tea.

'How's the bakery?' I asked, - 'and Terry?'
'Oh, Terry is fine – as long as I keep him in line that is. He wanders off-course if I don't keep a sharp eye on him.' I bit my tongue.

'Anyway, I've got some exciting news,' she said. 'We've been asked to make a cake for a celebrity – for their birthday celebration. We haven't been told who it's for, but the party is at The Savoy in London at the end of March.'

'That's wonderful!' I said, - 'but if you don't know who it's for, how do you know how to decorate it?'

'We've been given strict instructions,' said Jess. 'It's all very hush-hush!'

'Maybe it's for royalty,' I said excitedly.

'They haven't given us any clues I'm afraid – it could be anybody.'

'So what have they asked for then?'

'Well, it's a bit strange, but they want it to be green all over – we can decorate it how we like as long as everything is green.'

'Maybe it's for a famous sports personality.'

'Or it could be for a pop star or an actor.'

'Or a celebrity gardener like Alan Titchmarsh maybe,' I suggested.

'We won't know until the day – but if Terry and I do a good job of it, the agency will ask us for more so it's great for business. Talking of which, I've brought you a copy of the Citizen to show you our latest editorial. She showed me the page where she and Terry were proudly presenting a large basket of rolls, with the caption '*Award Winning Bakers Bring in the Dough*'.

After Jess had gone, I idly flicked through the pages of the paper. An article on the pros and cons of buying second-hand items for children caught my eye – another of Trudy Stoker's sensational pieces, I thought as I perused the article. Scanning the page, my eyes were drawn to a photograph of something familiar: It was Billy's old play pen and highchair. The accompanying text went something like this:

These seemingly harmless items were recently acquired by an unsuspecting parent who was horrified to discover they were covered in thousands of bite-marks and scratches. "Heaven knows how long a poor child had been cooped up in that pen – it doesn't bear thinking about. And even worse – the highchair had an actual bite out of it – the poor child must have been literally starving!" said Mrs Cross of 32, Primrose Gardens. "I'm very upset that someone had the nerve to give these things to anyone, in that condition," she said. "I'll be contacting social services, and the police - I have their address and this note which was attached to it." In the photograph, a small pinched looking woman was holding up the note I'd written, and was pointing at the highchair, which had been mauled by Fudge one rainy afternoon, four years ago.

'That bloody woman again!' exclaimed Andrew when he saw Trudy Stoker's article. 'Look Dora, you haven't broken the law, so there's nothing they can do,' he said, seeing how upset I was.

'But this is awful - it makes us look like terrible parents.'

'There's a perfectly plausible explanation for the damage to those things. That woman just fancied her moment of fame, and Trudy Stoker is always happy to oblige where there's a story. Anyway, that woman can conjure up a story out of thin air.'

'But what if the police come? She's got our address.'

'Dora, stop worrying. It's just a few dog bites – they'll soon realise there's nothing sinister going on.'

My holiday away can't come soon enough, I feel quite drained at the moment.

Friday 15th March

I think the interview at the dog grooming place went quite well today. A nice, matronly woman called Jack interviewed me. She showed me round and introduced me to another woman called Bertie, who looked remarkably like a Spaniel, I thought. Come to think of it, Jack looked a bit like a Bull Mastiff. It started me thinking about dogs and their owners. I asked the kids this evening if they thought we looked like our dogs at all. Fudge and Coco are large, brown, short-haired mongrels with waggy tails and floppy ears – probably a mixture of Labrador, Terrier, Spaniel and who knows what! Certainly the mongrel bit could be likened to our family, and the running around chaotically is something we all do a lot of. Anyway, I could imagine myself working at Pooches Parlour, if Jack thinks I would fit in. She did ask me if I would be put off by being nipped or bitten by a customer, which was slightly worrying, but I didn't want to spoil my chances, so I said no, I didn't think so. At first I would be doing washing and shampooing using their new Hydrobath because I would have to be trained in clipping and stripping (whatever that is), although I must say I'm not sure I want to become an expert in canine ear-cleaning. I tried to give her the impression I was willing to learn though, and when I left, Jack said she'd let me know by Wednesday evening.

Flora brought her new boyfriend Mathew round for tea this evening. Andrew couldn't help himself and gave the poor lad the usual grilling. Fortunately, he didn't seem to mind too much. This one is a marked improvement on Gaz anyway, since he actually speaks and can raise a decent smile. Flora of course, looks most put out that Andrew's jokes get a favourable response from Mathew, since she'd rather we behaved like mute house-slaves and merged with the furniture. I can relate to Flora's pain though – I remember quite clearly an old boyfriend of mine attempting to ingratiate himself with my father. Unthinkable!

I tried to explain this to Andrew, but he said I was talking nonsense and there's nothing wrong with having a laugh and a joke with your children's friends.

'I don't see what the problem is,' he said, looking at me, perplexed.

'Teenagers are very sensitive about these things,' I said. 'They are basically very insecure and you are providing too much competition.'

'I'm just trying to be friendly,' Andrew said, defending himself.

'Well, try being a bit less obtrusive,' I said.

'Then I'm not being myself am I?'

I gave up at this point – honestly, it's like trying to run up a sand dune. Why does he have to be so uncompromising?

Saturday 16th March

Bob and Barbara invited us over to Suzie's house today for lunch. Flora and Tom tried to get out of going by saying they had schoolwork to do, which was perfectly true of course, but you can guarantee that if the outing had involved a quantity of money to spend as they wished, the homework would suddenly have evaporated into the ether.

'I don't care what your excuses are,' said Andrew sternly, - 'you're going.'

'I'm only going if I can bring Mathew,' said Flora.

'And I'm only going if I can take my X-box,' said Tom.

'Yeah,' said Luke.

'For Goodness sake!' said Andrew. 'It's only for a couple of hours – you'd think we were asking you to fly to the moon.'

'That would be easier,' I said.

Mathew turned up at 11 o'clock and very politely thanked us for inviting him along. I must say, I feel slightly suspicious of this alien behaviour from a teenager – it's thrown me completely. I noticed Flora looking a bit puzzled herself as it was quite a contrast to Gaz, who could barely manage even the most monosyllabic utterances. Anyway, we'll see how long his charm offensive lasts at Bob and Barbara's luncheon. I dreaded to think what culinary surprise awaited us. (I packed some sandwiches and a selection of fruit in case of an emergency).

'Can Fudge and Cocoa come with us?' asked Billy. Against my better judgement, I agreed, although Suzie's garden has fallen below its usual high standards so anything untoward the dogs might do, will hopefully not be noticed anyway.

When we arrived, we had to park on the road because Bob had already been up to his usual tricks and acquired an old rusty caravan. They'd hung a For Sale sign on it in big red scruffy writing which you could see from half a mile away. Next to it was a rickety table with a crate of green potatoes on it and an honesty box. Barbara had been very busy sewing hundreds of purses and cushions which she'd also put out for sale.

'Oh dear,' said Andrew, - 'there they go again, bringing down the tone of the neighbourhood. It didn't take them long did it?'

In the kitchen Barbara was stirring something green which smelt of damp woodland and tom cats.

'You've been very busy haven't you?' I said.

'I found some old curtain-lining lying around,' said Barbara, 'so I made some things to sell. And Bob saw that caravan abandoned in a lay-by so we decided to try and sell it as well.'

'That's very entrepreneurial of you,' I said.

'Well, we need to earn some cash. Bob got those potatoes from the market – they were throwing them out onto the road.'

'Is that what we're having then?' asked Andrew, slightly worried.

'No, we're having nettle soup and Bob's special meat pie,' she said. It didn't sound too bad, but I didn't think the children would like the soup and of course, I was right.

'It's very healthy – full of iron and vitamins,' said Bob,

slurping from his spoon.

Actually it was quite nice but the children have an automatically negative reaction to anything unusual or untried and wasted most of their first course. Bob's pie went down better – a delicious meat pie with carrots and spinach.

'Well,' said Andrew afterwards, 'I must say, Dad, that was really good – you'll have to give us the recipe.'

Matthew offered to help with the washing up which made Flora look a little peeved as she followed him reluctantly into the kitchen.

'That's a first!' said Andrew.

'Ssshh!' I said. 'We don't want to start a war.'

'You should get your kids to help more,' said Bob. 'You're both too soft if you ask me.'

'We didn't ask you Dad,' said Andrew, rising to the bait.

'Let's go out into the garden and check on the dogs,' I said, trying to change the subject. Outside, Fudge and Cocoa were busy digging up the rock garden and chewing the potatoes they'd stolen from Bob's crate.

'Those dogs are a bloody menace!' said Bob crossly. 'That's money down the drain,' he said gathering up the mauled potatoes.

'Sorry Bob,' I said. 'They're just having fun.' Then I saw that Cocoa had something furry hanging out of his mouth that looked like a tail. On closer inspection, I realised it belonged to a squirrel.

'Leave!' I shouted at him, to no avail. Then everyone was chasing him round trying to get him to drop it. He eventually did, but it was only the tail.

'Yuk!' said Luke. 'Cocoa's eaten a whole squirrel!' Then Billy was shouting that Fudge was running round with a squirrel's head between his teeth.

'You should have buried them deeper,' said Barbara to Bob. 'I told you one foot down wouldn't be enough!'

'Can you believe it!' said Andrew, when we were going up to bed. – 'that he actually thought it would be OK to give us squirrel pie for lunch!'

'Well, I thought it tasted quite good,' I said.

'If the kids had found out there would have been a riot!' said Andrew. 'Imagine if Flora knew!'

'Don't EVER tell her!' I said. 'My ears couldn't cope with the noise!'

Sunday 17th March

I realised that I hadn't seen my mother for quite a while and so I rang her up this morning to invite her over for lunch and then I thought we could go to town and meet up with Jess.

'Yes, I think I can fit that in,' she said, 'but I have to be back by five o'clock.'

It seemed that she and Reggie had planned a trip to the cinema to see *Brief Encounter* as it was 'Golden Oldie' night at the Odeon.

'I loved that film,' said my mother, – 'it was *so* romantic.'

'Good Grief!' said Jess, when we met up with her in town, – 'why do you want to see an ancient film out of the ark like that when there are so many great new films to watch?'

'I don't like all that noise and all those flashing lights, and you can't hear what anybody's saying. Anyway it's lovely to watch a film like *Brief Encounter* – it brings back old memories and reminds me of my youth,' said Mum wistfully.

'Do you go to the pictures a lot with Reggie?' I asked.

'No – they don't always have ones I want to see. Last week it was *What Ever Happened to Baby Jane?* – it's got a mad woman in it who keeps trying to kill her sister. It reminds me too much of your Aunt Alice.'

'I'm surprised Reggie wants to see *Brief Encounter*,' said Jess.

'Well, he's got a soft side to him has Reggie,' said Mum. 'He's not what he seems.'

'I see,' I said. In truth, I fail to see what she finds appealing about him. To me, he seems gruff and illiterate – I hope she comes to her senses soon.

When I grumbled to Andrew about her evening excursion, he said I was over-reacting.

'It'll probably blow itself out,' he said, - 'you know, like one of those rocket balloons that whizzes round madly for two minutes and then plops onto the ground when it runs out of air.'

'Mmm,' I said, - 'interesting analogy – I'm not convinced though. I'm thinking more of a wrinkly party balloon hanging round in the corner of the room refusing to shrivel up completely and quite tough to pop.'

'You're being very negative about him Dora,' said Andrew. 'You might like him if you made an effort to get to know him.'

I can't help thinking sometimes Andrew is on another

planet to me – things seem so much simpler to him.

Monday 18th March

We had the usual Monday morning mayhem today with all the children leaving late for school. Billy seems to be managing to cope during the day with one good arm, although I gather from his Head Mistress, that he tried to set himself up as a charity on Friday and collect money and sweets for 'people who've been injured at work' (namely himself). He has obviously been watching those lawyer adverts on the TV. I'll have to get Andrew to explain to him about the moral impropriety of eliciting money for doubtful causes.

At 10 o'clock, just as I was trying to make some headway with the ironing pile, there was a knock at the door. When I opened it, it was one of the policemen we'd seen before, when we thought we'd been burgled but hadn't.

'PC Harding,' he said, sternly. 'I just wanted to ask you a few questions – may I come in?' He marched into the lounge and we sat down. 'We've received a complaint about a child's playpen and highchair that you apparently left out on the pavement – which by the way you should have acquired a licence for, from the local council.'

I must say, I thought he was being a bit heavy-handed. I mean, the pavement is pretty wide outside out house – you could park a car on it and still have plenty of room to walk past, so saying that these things posed a dangerous obstacle for pedestrians to have to negotiate, seemed a bit over-the-top. Unfortunately, he didn't see my point of view, and said he hoped I hadn't tried to park my car on the pavement, because driving on the pavement would be contrary to Section 72 of the Highways Act and I would definitely get an FPN. He then went on to ask about the play-pen and highchair. I called the main offenders into the lounge to meet PC Harding. Cocoa and Fudge greeted him in a friendly way, and luckily didn't embarrass me by jumping up, licking his face or sniffing inappropriately. I showed him other evidence of their indiscriminate chewing antics. He peered closely at a variety of items such as the TV remote, various chair legs, the kitchen cupboards, the cat litter tray, and a selection of shoes and handbags. He seemed satisfied with my explanation at this point, but warned me to be extra vigilant about obstructing public walkways with household rubbish in future, and suggested the local tip would be a better place to dispose of dilapidated play equipment. I breathed a sigh of relief when he finally left.

I rang Suzie afterwards, to see how she was getting on in London.

'Violet has calmed down a bit,' she said. 'She's agreed to cut down on some of the costs. We'll send back the silk georgette ordered from France to make her dress for instance – that'll save £800 straight away.'

I suddenly had an awful sinking feeling in my stomach. 'What did it look like?' I asked her.

'Ivory with pale gold flowers embroidered all over it – very pretty, but Violet has changed her mind anyway and wants something more trendy.' I pictured Barbara beavering away at the sewing machine and swallowed hard.

'How are your parents getting on?' she asked.

'Fine,' I said. 'They're keeping themselves busy.'

'Oh good,' said Suzie, oblivious to my sudden painful realization that Violet's ridiculously expensive fabric from some exclusive design house in Paris, has now been chopped into a zillion patchwork pieces, in order to make some uninspiring pin-cushions and lavender bags for a street trader's market stall.

I told Andrew about PC Harding's visit when he came in from work.

'Oh well,' said Andrew, - 'he was just doing his job I suppose.'

'But it was humiliating,' I protested. 'PC Harding seems to have no sense of humour at all.'

'Well, it's *hard* in his profession,' said Andrew. 'He has to be *hard-nosed* – he's probably become *hardened* to his job,' said Andrew, smiling at his own pathetic jokes.

I couldn't bring myself to tell him about Barbara's hatchet job on the fated fabric. I'll save it for another day when I'm feeling stronger.

Tuesday 19th March

I had to take Scratch to the vet's today – he seems to have developed a fear of going outside. I've never heard of an agoraphobic cat before, but apparently it can happen, although it's usually cats that live in flats, not ones with their own reasonably-sized garden. The vet thinks he might be suffering with 'separation anxiety' brought on by his brief but traumatic week at my mother's empty house with no one to pet him. That's all I need, a psychotic cat with a phobia as well. I don't really believe it though, mainly because Scratch is not very family-friendly. I think Flora is right when she says she thinks he might be scared of another cat from down the road called Clinton – a big white Persian cat even more vicious than Scratch. The vet reckons that certain animals should be issued with an ASBO, just like humans. He told me this last year after treating Scratch for an eye infection and receiving a nasty bite on his arm for his trouble. Since then, the poor man always looks nervous when I bring Scratch in to see him. Anyway, he said he couldn't do anything about the agoraphobia, except that we could perhaps try to entice him outside with a couple of sardines or some catnip. I must say, I feel slightly fleeced having to pay £30 for that consultation. The children have already been trying things like that anyway. Billy found a dead pigeon on the road outside our house yesterday and put it on a shovel on the back lawn, but Scratch wasn't interested.

'Maybe he's depressed,' said Luke. 'Animals can be depressed just like humans – I saw it on *Animal Park.*'

'Yes, that's a possibility,' I said, - 'but what's he got to be depressed about?'

'Maybe he's clinically depressed,' said Tom. 'He might need some drugs.'

'I don't think you can get anti-depressants for cats can you?' I said.

'We could get him some alternative therapy – like acupuncture maybe,' said Luke.

'And which brave sole would be prepared to perform that on him Luke? We can't even get him to take a pill without being shredded by his claws.'

'We could try some aromatherapy on him and soothing music,' said Flora – it works for women in labour.'

'I think you're right about that white cat from number 64 Flora,' I said. 'We'll have to think of something to scare it off. Clinton doesn't seem to be scared of dogs though, so Cocoa and Fudge are no good. Any ideas?'

'We could tie a dead cat to the fence,' said Luke, - 'like farmers do with crows – you know, to get rid of other crows.'

'Where would we get a dead cat from?' said Tom.

'Dunno – maybe we could get a stuffed one.'

'No,' I said, - 'that's horrible - we can't have dead things dangling from the fence - apart from the fact that it's macabre and the neighbours will complain about the smell.'

'We could spray water on Clinton when he comes in our garden,' said Billy.

'That's very good Billy, but someone has to see him to do that.'

'I could borrow Dan Herbert's air rifle,' said Luke.

'Certainly not!' I said. 'That cat is someone's pet! Imagine how you'd feel if someone shot Scratch!'

After a while we gave up trying to think of anything since no one could come up with a good plan. Perhaps we just have to accept we have an indoor cat. He'll pick up fewer fleas I suppose, and can't get into any fights or come home covered in creosote or ant powder, or go missing again.

Wednesday 20th March

'Why haven't I got any socks or pants?' grumbled Andrew this morning.

'I don't know Andrew,' I said, - 'possibly because they're all in a pile on the floor *next* to the laundry basket.'

'But why weren't they washed?' he griped.

'Because they can't climb into the laundry basket by themselves,' I said.

This is a fairly common exchange in our house – usually ending in some shouting and a bit of door slamming. It's not that I want to pick a fight, but if Andrew can't even manage to follow a few simple domestic rules, what hope have I got with the others.

'You'll have to borrow some of Tom's,' I said.

'Oh for God's sake!' said Andrew.

The trouble with Tom's underpants is that they're a bit neat on Andrew – he'd probably have to spend the whole day mincing around like Mr Humphries from *Are You Being Served.*

'You could go commando,' I said, -'or wear your cycling shorts.'

He opted for the latter, and went off to work in a bad mood muttering about poor service and low standards.

Anyway, I've got more important things to think about than whether Andrew has enough undergarments or not. Not long after everyone left for the day, I got a phone call from Jack at Pooches Parlour. She said I'd impressed them with my willingness to learn and since no one else had applied for it, would I like the job? Of course, I said 'yes'. So, I'll be starting on Tuesday 3rd April straight after I come back from my holiday with Melanie. Which reminds me, I must find out why we are flying to Hiroshima – something isn't right about that.

When Billy came in from school today, he told me they'd had a talk on being responsible citizens.

'That's great,' I said, only half listening as I was trying to untie a knot in a shoelace.

'A policeman called PC Harding came to speak to us and show us some films.'
'Mmm …' I said, - 'good.'

'Mummy, you were in a film we saw about litter.'

'Oh, yes … I mean, what? What do you mean 'a film'? What film?'

'He called it … CCV… I think.'

'CCTV,' I said. 'Why was I on CCTV?'

'Well, the policeman said that bad people throw litter on the street and that they can get caught and fined lots of money and then he showed some people being bad and then I saw you putting rubbish in a bin but it wasn't our bin and then lots of rubbish went on the ground….. and then you ran away.'

He had my full attention now. 'How did you know it was me?' I asked him. 'Wasn't it too dark to see?'

'I recognized your voice Mummy – you swore!'

'Did you tell PC Harding any of this?' I asked him.

'No,' he said, emphatically.

'Why not?'

'Because he said that really bad people get arrested and put in prison.' I looked at Billy's innocent little face and felt terrible. Then I thought of something else – the car was right by the bins.

'Could you see my car Billy?'

'Oh yes – but PC Harding said it was very frustrating because the person drove off with the boot open so they couldn't see the registration plate.' I breathed a huge inward sigh of relief.

Trying to explain to a six year-old that PC Harding's version of events might look damning, but the truth was that I was just returning something that didn't belong to me, just seemed to make it worse. Billy looked very confused.

'The main thing you need to know, Billy, is that your mother hasn't done anything wrong, but it would be best not to mention any of this to anyone.'

'OK Mum,' said Billy. 'Can I have a biscuit?'

Luckily for me, a six year-old's memory-span is pretty short and Billy's penchant for chocolate wafers comes in very handy.

Thursday 21st March

Andrew was pleased this morning to find his underwear drawer miraculously replenished.

'Thank God for that,' he said, 'those cycling shorts were chaffing me all day – look!' He showed me two big glowing red stripes on his thighs.

'Well, it's because you had to wear your trousers on top of them,' I said. 'You've probably over-heated your you-know-whats as well.'

'Isn't that dangerous?' said Andrew, looking worried.

'Not really – you don't want any more children anyway do you?'

'No, but I'd like to think I can decide for myself - not because I'm medically inhibited…'

'Oh don't worry Andrew – look at the McCarthy's down the road – they've got fifteen children and Jim Mc McCarthy's never out of his boiler suit so it didn't stop him did it? They even had a letter from the Vatican congratulating them on their 'bounteous productivity'.'

After everyone had gone, I rang up the travel agent to check on the flights. The girl on the other end of the phone had a look and said that the nearest airport to Rabbit Island was Hiroshima and that we would be getting a boat from the mainland. When I said that I thought that would take several days to get to where we were going, she said it was only 12 minutes. When I said that I thought we were going to Thailand, there was a bit of a silence.

'The Rabbit Island you're going to is just off the Japanese coast,' she said. 'It's an interesting destination – I'm sure you'll enjoy it. It's famous for its wild-life ...'

'How could they have made that mistake!' said Melanie when I rang her up. 'It's a disaster,' she said, - 'we'll have to get it changed.'

'We can't,' I said. 'I've already asked.

'What a calamity,' said Melanie, - 'it's not at all what I had in mind. Why would anyone choose to go on holiday to an island where chemical weapons were tested on hundreds of rabbits during the 2nd World War? The island's probably still contaminated!'

'Oh dear!' said Andrew later. 'Well, at least it will be sunny there.' He peered at the computer screen. 'What amazes me is that anyone would choose to go there on holiday – I mean one day would be enough.'

'Most people do go for one day Andrew, that's the point.'

'Just look at all those rabbits – there must be thousands of them,' said Andrew. 'No wonder there's no grass anywhere.'

We looked at a photo of the hotel. It looked like an office block.

'Well, maybe you could find a better one,' said Andrew.

'That's the only one,' I said.

'There should at least be some things to do – maybe a health spa or some old buildings to see…'

'There's a Poison Gas Museum, a ruined chemical factory and the remains of a secret war-time laboratory.'

'Well, the beaches look OK don't they?' said Andrew, getting desperate.

I went to bed feeling quite despondent. My dream of a luxury holiday lounging in hammocks, being served a myriad of exotic cocktails by a handsome waiter, has turned into something more than disappointing. It certainly brings a whole new meaning to slurping Jäger Bombs on the beach. And, if I'd wanted to go on an animal-watching holiday, I'd have chosen camel racing or swimming with dolphins or something – not a week surrounded by thousands of radioactive bunnies. I mean – do I need to pack surgical gloves and face masks now? And factor 500 sunscreen? Maybe a bag on my head would be better. Shouldn't I be worried about exposure to dangerous chemicals?

'Don't worry Dora,' said Andrew. 'I've checked on the internet. It's fine – you're not in any danger – none that anyone knows about yet anyway. You might see a few mutant rabbits hobbling about, but apart from that you're OK to go!'

Friday 22nd March

Today I stacked up on holiday necessities including extra packets of anti-bacterial wipes, super-dark sunglasses and sandals with heavy-duty soles to protect my feet from possible sand-contamination. Melanie did much the same thing.

'We'll just have to make the best of it,' she said on the phone. I've made a tick list – shall I read it out?'

'Oh, OK,' I said. Of course, I'd done no such thing. Melanie is obviously one of those really organised mothers. I hope she doesn't try to organise me too much or this holiday could end up being an even worse idea than it already is.

Later, when Andrew watched me pack my suitcase, he remarked on the very large carrier bag from the local chemist.

'Are you allowed to take all that medical stuff?'

'I don't care,' I said. 'I'm just being extra cautious.'

'Do you really need all those steroid creams? They'll have to re-stock the shelves in Boots now!'

Well, I'd rather be safe than sorry,' I said, cramming it all into my over-packed and bulging suitcase.

'Tom says you're going to an island of poisoned bunnies,' said Billy at the tea table, just as we were about to eat.

'Don't listen to your brother,' I said, scowling at Tom.

'I wish I was going on a nice holiday,' said Flora. 'Why can't we come?'

'Because,' said Andrew, 'Mum needs a relaxing break away where she doesn't have to think about looking after anyone else for a bit.'

'But who's going to look after us?' asked Billy.

'Me of course!' said Andrew. A worried look came over Billy's face. 'Oh, and your Nan's coming to help.' Andrew added.

Billy cheered up. 'That's OK then,' he said.

'Yes,' chimed in the other three, - 'that's much better.'

'Thanks for the votes of confidence!' said Andrew, looking a bit put out.

Saturday 23rd March

Well, the big day arrived and I woke up feeling a peculiarly heady mixture of excitement and foreboding.

Melanie arrived in the taxi and Andrew wrestled my case into the boot. 'You'll have a great time,' he said. 'Just forget about everything and relax.'

That's easier said than done, I thought, as I spied Luke balancing an egg on Billy's head through the open door. Upstairs, the curtains of Tom and Flora's rooms were shut tight.

'I'll tell them you said goodbye,' said Andrew, blowing me a kiss. The taxi sped off down the road and as I watched Andrew getting smaller and smaller, I couldn't help remembering how my last trip away ended. I've never liked that replacement bath – it squeaks when you move.

'Dora, they will be fine,' said Melanie, 'What's the worst that can happen?'

I decided not to recount past history on this occasion. After all, this was meant to be an enjoyable trip and some things are best forgotten.

I must say, going through security was a bit of a palaver. These people can be so officious. Honestly, I don't know why they have to make such a fuss about things – I mean how do they think you could possibly attack someone with some miniature nail scissors and a sewing kit! Melanie said that if I hadn't joked about it being a weapon of mass destruction, they wouldn't have put us in that interview room for so long – honestly, we nearly missed our flight! Melanie was a bit frosty with me for a while after that, but after a couple of gin and tonics, she forgave me. After all, twelve hours is a long time to be next to someone you're cross with. The man sitting on my right (called Ken), could certainly have done with a drink or two – 'I hate flying,' he confessed, as we left the runway. When he gripped the arm rests his knuckles went white and I could hear him hyperventilating behind his trembling beard. We tried to persuade him to have a drink to calm his nerves, but he refused saying that flying always made him want to throw up and the smell of alcohol would only make it worse – particularly gin. 'Even the smell of it makes me want to heave,' he said, as I took possession of my favourite tipple.

'If you drink it through this straw, he won't notice,' said Melanie.

'I'm not sure I want to risk it…' I said, looking at his pale face and staring eyes. What Melanie had neglected to say, having suggested this solution, was that you get drunk quite fast on two double gin and tonics imbibed through a straw in quick succession – something to do with vacuums and membranes… Anyway, I thought I'd chat to Ken to take his mind off things. After an hour, he asked if I wouldn't mind being quiet as he thought he could probably nod off for a bit. I felt quite pleased I'd helped him. Melanie said later that my incessant babbling probably acted more as a verbal tranquilizer, because she managed to go to sleep for four hours straight. I didn't sleep at all – a mixture of being too excited about going away, and wanting to remain vigilant in case Ken suddenly took a turn for the worse.

Sunday 24th March

I am feeling quite jaded today, which isn't helped by

Melanie being so jolly and full of beans.

We arrived on the island at about 11am. Our rooms were actually very nice with a wonderful view of the sea, so I was feeling a bit more optimistic about the whole thing – that was, until I went to unpack my case.

Melanie heard my shriek of horror from her room and rushed in to see what the matter was.

'It's not *my* case,' I wailed.

'Oh no! We'd better phone the airport and report it. Someone might have handed yours in – you never know.'

'What am I going to do now? I was hoping to have a shower and change my clothes.'

'Well,' said Melanie, 'you can borrow something of mine for now.'

I looked at the case. It was exactly the same as mine. Unbelievable! I mean, what are the chances of two people having the same twenty-five year-old orange and pink spotty suitcase on the same flight! Just my luck! And, taking a quick look at the contents, there's no way I could wear any of these clothes. They plainly belonged to a woman twice my size, who must only be about four feet tall.

'With any luck,' said Melanie, bringing me a little pile of clothes, 'they've got it at the airport and will send it today.'

I hoped she was right. Melanie's taste in clothes is quite different from my own, and although it's very sweet of her to share them, twin-sets and slacks are not really my thing.

Later, we had a delicious lunch in the hotel restaurant

followed by a walk round the island in the afternoon sunshine. We took lots of photos, mostly of rabbits, and by 5pm we'd been round the whole island twice. When we returned to the hotel, there was still no message from the airport about my case which was disappointing. But, on the bright side, Melanie it seems was thinking like me, and also packed copious amounts of medical supplies just in case of any emergencies, which is comforting. However, I don't know how I'm going to survive without my books - one called *Pet Grooming for the Uninitiated*, and *Watership Down* – a last-minute travel gift from Andrew. Melanie offered me one of her books to read, but her reading preferences are so different from mine. I don't think I can seriously get into books about scaling the heights of Mount Fuji with only a couple of packets of freeze dried vegi-mix and a Kendal Mint Cake, or sailing round the world in a laundry basket without a compass. I want my own books back. I am not a happy bunny.

Monday 25th March

There's still no word from the airport, so I'm wearing Melanie's things again. She is slightly thinner than me, well more than slightly actually, so I don't feel at all flattered by these garments. I caught sight of myself in the long mirror in the hotel foyer, and not recognising the clothes, I found myself thinking *'that woman needs some serious advice from Trinny and Susannah'*. Then I realised it was me. It's a good job there's no one here who knows me.

Three hours later, whilst we were wandering around Downtown Hiroshima, who should I spy but my old college friend Bev (well, ex-friend really). I couldn't believe my eyes! There she was, that treacherous little round witch, looking in the same shop window as Melanie. Beverly (snatchit) Hatchet and I had parted company fairly acrimoniously at the end of our final year at college due to her 'borrowing some lecture notes' (her words), or 'misappropriating my friend Jane's final dissertation' (my words).

Unfortunately she saw me before I could escape.

'Fancy you being here!' she crowed.

'Yes,' I said, 'fancy ...'

'You haven't changed a bit - are you on holiday then?' she asked.

'Yes, with my *good* friend Melanie,' I said, as I suddenly noticed she was wearing the exact same scarf I had brought with me on holiday. It was then that I suddenly remembered we'd bought the same suitcases when we were students all those years ago. How fortuitous, I thought, that we should have bumped into each other like this out of the blue!

'Did you by any chance pick up the wrong suitcase at the airport Bev?' I asked her.

'Yes! How did you know?'

'Because you haven't changed much either,' I said, looking pointedly at my green polka dot scarf.

'Oh,' she said, suddenly realising her very obvious faux pas.

'Well, isn't this lucky,' said Melanie. 'You can swap your bags and get your things back Dora!'

There was an awkward silence.

'Bev, you *have* got my case haven't you?'

'Sure,' she said, with a thin and less than convincing smile.

It transpired that Bev was staying at a hotel outside the city attending a Scottish knitwear conference.

'It's all the rage in Japan,' she said. 'They just love our Harris Tweed and Shetland jumpers.'

We arranged to meet the next day at the same place, same time to swap bags.

'Did I detect a slight frost in the air?' said Melanie.

We went into a noodle bar and I filled her in over lunch.

'The worst thing, was that she tried to implicate me in all of it!' I said, finishing off the story. 'That pilfering plagiarist hasn't changed her spots either – she was wearing my scarf!'

'No!' said Melanie, aghast. 'I hope she gives it back to you!'

Tuesday 26th March

'I'm sorry about all this,' I said to Melanie this morning as we headed back to the city again.

'Oh, don't worry,' she said graciously, 'It's fine. Let's just hope things go to plan.'

We waited around at the shopping precinct until Bev's large shape came into view from across the street.

'She hasn't got your case!' said Melanie, stating the obvious.

Bev appeared, smiling strangely. 'I'm sorry Dora, but your case accidentally got taken to a charity shop.' She tried to take hers from me but I held on.

'What do you mean 'accidentally'?' I said.

'Well, I put it in lost property at the hotel yesterday and now it's gone.'

'Where?'

'To the Homeless Charity on the east side of the city – here's a phone number. Can I have my bag back now?' asked Bev, wrenching it from my grasp. She marched off into the distance as quickly as her little legs could carry her.

'She hasn't changed a bit,' I said bitterly. 'We'll try this number – maybe we can track it down.'

Of course, the person who answered only spoke Japanese.

'Let's go and find someone who speaks English,' said Melanie. After a lot of messing around, we found our way to the shop in amongst a myriad of little winding streets and went in. The shop was full to brimming with piles of jumble and household things.

'How will we find it here – it's like an Aladdin's Cave!' I said.

'Draw a picture,' commanded Melanie - 'of your case.'

'Aaahhh!' said the Japanese lady, encouragingly, and she disappeared into the back for what seemed like an eon. Finally she re- appeared with my case.

'Oh that's wonderful!' I said, pleased as punch.

'Hold your horses, said Melanie, 'look - there's nothing in it!'

I admit, I did have a little cry at this point. It was all too much, what with the mix-up over the holiday, the awful re-appearance of the atrocious Bev, and now the loss of the only decent clothes I own, my pretty toiletry bag (a rare present from Flora), my silver jewellery (probably purloined by the aforementioned evil witch), Andrew's book, and a funny drawing of a green rabbit with no eyes that Billy had given me to take on the trip.

The lady in the shop had no idea what was going on. Melanie tried to explain, but it was impossible. After raking through some piles of clothes, I found a pair of trousers, two shirts, my SpongeBob pyjamas (Luke last Christmas), and my pink cardigan. I also found my books.

'Well it's better than nothing,' said Melanie trying to be cheerful.

Since I'd just forked out 8,000 Yen to get my own stuff back, it was hard to feel up-beat about it. As we left the shop, I noticed the lady had stuck Billy's green rabbit up on the window – for good luck I suppose. I hope it brings her more good fortune than I've had.

Wednesday 27th March

I had quite a nasty hangover this morning. Last night I felt it necessary to drown my sorrows after such a traumatic day. Melanie had not needed much persuasion to join in, so she's not feeling tip-top either.

'I hope I never see that appalling woman ever again,' I'd pronounced as I downed my third gin and tonic before the sun went down.

'She's probably a sad old cow with no friends,' said Melanie.

'Yeah - a sad, fat, ugly, old cow with dandruff and halitosis ….'

This bitch-fest went on for a bit until we got bored and moved on to a much more erudite discussion about whether George Clooney is better looking than Denzel Washington, and whether it's better to have great legs or big breasts when it comes to attracting the opposite sex. We went to bed at midnight, having sunk enough gin and tonic to float the Armada. So, this morning actually didn't happen. At lunchtime we surfaced, ate a very light lunch and retired to the terrace with a book. I tried to read, but the words kept mingling together and anyway, I wasn't in the mood for *Born Survivor* – Bear Grylls might be Melanie's choice of bedfellow but I've had enough excitement for quite a while thank you very much. I decided to go for a walk on my own down by the sea. I'd recovered enough by tea time to eat some soft rice and vegetables, but an early night was called for and Melanie agreed she felt the same inclination. Well – every holiday has to contain one lost day to a hangover doesn't it? It's not a proper holiday otherwise.

Thursday 28th March

'What shall we do today?' said Melanie, now recovered and full of enthusiasm.

'Well, it's a choice between the Poison Gas Museum, the Chemical Weapons Facility and the Toxic Gas Reactor, or the Golf Course.'

'It's a 'no-brainer' then,' said Melanie.' Are you any good?'

'Well I can do Crazy Golf.'

'Great! I'm sure if Geoff can manage a round of golf, I can!'

By 12 o'clock, we were bored with golf – it was only a six-hole course, so after three times round we'd perfected our putting, nearly eliminated half a dozen rabbits with our death-defying long-shots, and we were beginning to suffer from repetitive strain injury.

'How about a swim after lunch?' suggested Melanie.

'But it's freezing!' I said, exaggerating, but it wasn't particularly warm.

'It'll be bracing – good for our complexions,' she said.

'I haven't got a swimsuit any more,' I said (*thankfully, I thought*).

'I've brought a spare one!' said Melanie.

'Oh, how lucky,' I said, not at all enthused by the prospect of plunging into the murky, possibly toxic, and certainly very cold island waters.

After we'd eaten, we set off to find a nice, secluded part of the beach.

'This will do,' said Melanie when we found a stretch of sand to lay our towels on.

'What do you think that is?' I said, pointing at a signpost with a picture of a fish with a big red cross over it.

'Probably means 'no fishing',' said Melanie, matter-of-factly.

She wasted no time getting changed and ran full pelt into the sea. I, on the other hand, hung around at the edge putting off the evil moment until it was too embarrassing to delay much longer.

'Come on Dora, it's fine when you're in.'

I didn't believe her, but I finally got in after a bit more coercing.

We swam along, keeping the beach in sight until we reached the hotel where we decided to turn round.

'Look Dora, the waiter's waving at us!' said Melanie.

'They're very welcoming here aren't they!' We waved back and carried on swimming.

'He's coming across the lawn,' I said. 'His waving is very animated Melanie, and he seems to be shouting something.'

Suddenly I felt a sharp sting on my foot, like a burning hot needle.

'Ouch!' I yelled, 'I think something's bitten me!'

Melanie looked at my foot when we got out of the sea and said she thought we should get back to the hotel ASAP.

'It looks a bit puffy and well, sort of black.'

'Well, pull it out then,' I said.

'No, I meant your foot,' she said.

By the time we got back to the hotel foyer, my foot was twice its normal size and burning like a flambéed chilli pepper. I don't remember much after this except a doctor was called and I was put in my room with a bag of ice round my foot.

'Nice Dr Noro is going to give you an injection now,' said Melanie's decapitated head, floating like a blurry cloud before my eyes. In broken English, the doctor said that the sign we saw was to warn people about the Japanese Lionfish.

'It is mating season,' he said. 'Lionfish very active in sea – will stab you with poisonous spine - you very lucky!'

'Really!'

'Yes – you only got one spine in foot.'

'What happens if you get more?' I asked.

He drew two fingers across his throat indicating instant death.

'Bloody Hell!' said Melanie.

'You rest now. Tomorrow you OK,' said Dr Noro.

Friday 29th March

Well, I don't know where all the time went but I woke up at 10 o'clock this morning feeling as if I had another colossal hangover. Melanie came in to see me with some tea.

'God, you look a bit rough,' she said, - 'but the main thing is that you're alive. I would have felt terrible if I had to go home and tell your family you'd been killed by a fish.'

'Well, I don't feel great,' I said, - 'look at my foot!'

Melanie recoiled at the sight of my giant purple foot.

'How am I going to get a shoe on that?' I said, mournfully.

'Mmmm...' Melanie pondered for a moment. 'We'll have to improvise.' She went out and came back after 15 minutes with an interesting solution. 'It's two hotel slippers stuck together to make one big one – I've used the receptionist's stapler,' she said, proudly holding up her DIY prototype.

'Thank you,' I said weakly. Well, I suppose I'm already going around in ill-fitting, borrowed clothes, so a gargantuan make-shift shoe will hardly make things any worse.

'I suppose you're going to be a bit out of action today,' said Melanie. 'I'm really sorry – it was my idea to go swimming.'

'Well, it could happen to anyone...' I said. *I'm beginning to think that a certain Romani fortune teller did more than read our palms and stroke her crystal ball all those years ago. I'm sure she put a curse on us! Andrew shouldn't have scoffed at her when she read his tea-leaves, predicting a life-changing windfall around the summer of 2009. What actually happened was quite the opposite – we'll never know how those people got hold of our credit cards, or how they managed to spend £10,000 in one day without the bank noticing! I mean, the most we've ever spent at once was when Andrew bought two washing machines by accident on the internet. I told him he already had one in his basket – it was about that time that he finally admitted he needed glasses. Anyway, it all got sorted out in the end, but it was all very stressful.*

'I thought I'd go into the city and get a few souvenirs today,' said Melanie. 'Would you like me to get you anything?'

'No thanks,' I said, suddenly feeling a bit tearful.' I'll just stay here and rest,' I said, pathetically.

In the afternoon, I hobbled about for a while outside and read some of my pet-grooming book in preparation for my new job. I must say, since coming here, I've gone off rabbits a bit. Maybe I should have waited till I got home to read *Watership Down* – the rabbits here do seem almost human, following you around and staring at you with their impenetrable shiny black eyes – it's a bit spooky to tell you the truth. I will be quite glad to get home tomorrow – life there seems so normal compared to this place.

Saturday 30th March

It was with some relief that I packed my few remaining possessions and left the hotel with Melanie this morning for the last time.

'I'm a bit sad to be leaving,' said Melanie as we climbed onto the ferry.

'Really?' I said with obvious surprise.

'Well, I know it's been an odd sort of holiday, but it's been fun,' she said.

Well, Melanie's idea of fun is obviously very different from mine, I thought as I hobbled off the ferry at the other end. Of course, she's not the one with a foot the size of a small planet to contend with. Maybe if I hadn't been attacked by a sword-wielding stickleback, I would be feeling less disenchanted with the whole experience. Oh well, there's no point in crying over spilt milk – I'll just have to put my best foot forward… Anyway, I like Melanie so I suppose I ought to try and be positive about it. After all, it was quite good to be away from all the domestic chores at home, and much as I love my family, it was extremely gratifying to escape from them for a while.

I had lots of time to ponder on things during the long flight home. There are quite a few unresolved issues going on – Bob and Barbara for instance: Where will they end up living? The thought of them coming to us for longer than a day or two is quite worrying. Then there's the situation with my mother and her bizarre choice of man-friend – where will it lead? I mean, there's no way I'm ever calling Reggie 'Dad'! And then there's poor old Suzie - I hope Andrew has found a good defence barrister for her – I really don't think she would last two minutes in prison – in fact I'm pretty sure she would go quite loopy and have to be transferred to a mental health unit pronto, and then Warren might decide to disown her and poor Violet's wedding will be a total fiasco!

I wondered how Billy was getting on with his arm in

plaster – I'm feeling quite guilty about that because if I hadn't been so obsessed with what Mrs Pincher thought, the whole thing probably wouldn't have happened …. And Flora – is she going to get any A levels at all whilst being completely distracted by boyfriends and Thrash Metal? And Luke – well Luke may or may not surprise us (currently I'm leaning towards the latter) – still, he has other talents, bless him. Tom at least seems to be buckling down and studying more but he's a bit of a dark horse and we never know what's really going on in his head.

Then I started thinking about my new job. How am I going to manage like this? I hope the swelling goes down in time – the last thing I need is to be starting a new job on the wrong foot…

Sunday 31ˢᵗ March (Easter Sunday)

The children were all in bed when I arrived home last night which was a good thing because I was exhausted. Andrew waited up for me. He was a bit taken aback when he saw my deformity.

'It's OK,' I told him, 'it's half the size it was.'

Apparently, while I was away there were only a couple of small breakages – a Sharp & Prentice mug (*thank God for that – it was hideous*), and Scratch's water bowl (the result of Luke and Billy playing one-armed catch).

'So, a quiet week then?' I said to Andrew this morning, whilst sipping a cup of proper tea and enjoying being back in my own bed.

'Yes, actually!' he said. 'I know it's hard to believe, but no one sustained any life-threatening injuries, no one died of food-poisoning and the house is still standing. Oh, and nothing was lost or stolen,' he said, smiling smugly.

The irony was not lost on me, but I chose to ignore it. 'Well, I'm glad you managed so well with everything here Andrew – I could go away again without worrying now.'

Jess and Terry came in the afternoon and brought Easter eggs for the kids and an Easter cake for us. They wanted to know all about my holiday – well, for the first five minutes anyway, but they were obviously dying to tell us about the previous night at The Savoy, and we were all ears.

'So, spill the beans!' said Andrew.

'Well,' said Jess, 'it wasn't quite what we'd imagined…'

'The cake looked amazing,' said Terry, - 'the best we've ever made!'

'And…!' I said, - 'come on, who was it for? We're all dying to know!'

There was a pause.

'Well,' said Jess, 'it wasn't exactly for a person…'

'No,' said Terry, 'but he *is* an international TV personality and film star…' He opened an envelope and held up a glossy photo.

'It's Kermit!' shouted Billy, 'Kermit the Frog!'

Poor Jess,' I said to Andrew later, when they'd gone. 'It wasn't quite what they were hoping for was it!'

'Well, I think celebrating Kermit the Frog's 50th birthday will give them some great publicity – even Trudy Stoker couldn't put a negative spin on that.'

Mum stayed on and made a lovely roast dinner for all of us, despite the fact that she'd been cooking all week for them.

'Dad didn't do anything,' said Tom, snitching on him.

'Well, I did have to go to work,' said Andrew, 'and Nan's cooking is so much better than mine.'

My mother smiled benevolently at my devious husband – 'I could see he needed feeding up a bit,' she said.

'So, what have you all been up to while I've been away?' I asked them.

'Flora's been with Matthew the whole time,' said Tom.

'Shut-up slime ball,' said Flora, flicking a pea off her plate at his head. Tom ducked and the pea landed in Billy's squash. Billy tried to remove it with his spoon and knocked the glass over, sending a river of sticky juice across the table and onto the floor.

'Oh, it's great to be home', I said.

ABOUT THE AUTHOR

Nicola Kelsall is an artist and writer, living in a little village in the Cotswolds with her own chaotic and noisy family, plus their latest addition, Chester the dog. She has loved being an artist and writer from childhood. She trained at Edinburgh College of Art, later becoming an artist and illustrator. Over the years, she supported her life as an artist by working in a wide variety of other professions.

Her eclectic assortment of jobs have included; Chambermaid, Barmaid, Driver, Shop Girl, Secretary, House and Pet Sitter, Child Minder, Dresser for the Royal Scottish Ballet, Printer, PA, Designer, Illustrator, Singer in a Medieval Banquet, Event Organiser, Teacher, PTA Queen, and most importantly – wife and mother extraordinaire.

"I used to worry that some of the dead-end jobs I did, represented huge amounts of wasted time and often felt trapped and frustrated. Now of course, I am grateful for all the interesting experiences and funny characters I've met along the way. Having a family has given me another very different perspective on life, and luckily inspired this – (Bedlam), the first book in the series Diary of a Stressed Out Mother. I've enjoyed every minute of writing this book and I hope my readers love it too!"

For more about Nicola Kelsall:
www.facebook.com/stressedoutmother
@StressOutMother

Printed in Great Britain
by Amazon